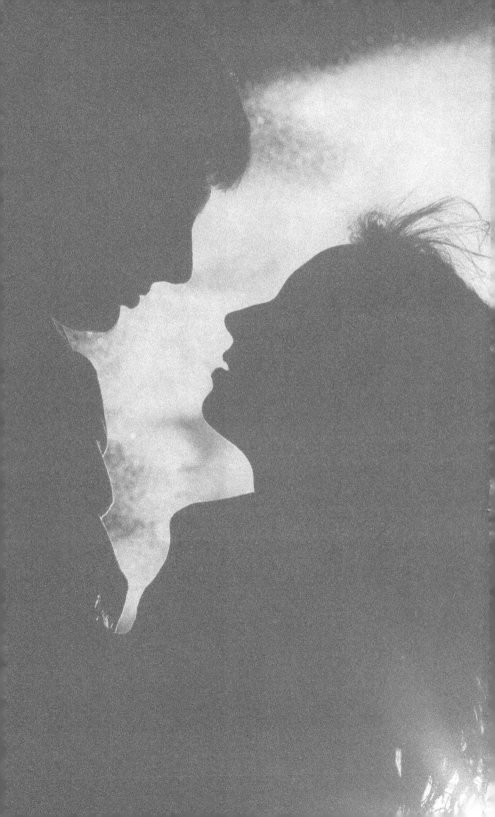

Destiny Fulfilled

Laire McKinney

Windswept

Livonia, Michigan

Edited by S.M. Ray

DESTINY FULFILLED
Copyright © 2018 Laire McKinney
All rights reserved. Except as permitted under the U.S. Copyright Act of 1976, no part of this publication may be reproduced, distributed, or transmitted in any form or by any means, or stored in a database or retrieval system, without prior written permission of the publisher.

This book is a work of fiction. The characters, incidents, and dialogue are drawn from the author's imagination and are not to be construed as real. Any resemblance to actual events or persons, living or dead, is entirely coincidental.

Published by Windswept
an imprint of BHC Press

Library of Congress Control Number:
2017964656

ISBN: 978-1-947727-22-9

Visit the publisher:
www.bhcpress.com

Also available in
hardcover (ISBN: 978-1-947727-63-2)
& ebook   (ISBN: 978-1-947727-64-9)

To the small yet mighty group of Panera writers.
Rock on, ladies.

Dear Jerry —
Happy reading!!
Laini McKinney

ACKNOWLEDGMENTS

I am eternally grateful to BHC Press for their hard work and enthusiasm; to my husband and children for cheering me on and thinking I'm more famous than I am; and to my mom who says, "Don't you dare give up," anytime I have a bad writing day. I am also grateful to my author friends who get why I just can't stop writing, no matter how rocky the road.

"It is never too late to be who you might have been."

~ George Eliot ~

DESTINY FULFILLED

1

Wren O'Hara slammed the door to her truck and crossed the parking lot. Through the glass door of HELP, a nonprofit agency where she worked, she could see the young receptionist, Tiffany, filing her nails.

Wren pulled open the door. "Hey, Tif. Like the hair."

"Why, Wren O'Hara," Tiffany cooed, fingering a strand of her neon pink hair. "Just the case manager I, or rather *he*, was expecting." Tiffany slid her heavily charcoaled eyes toward the man snoring in the waiting room chair, his long legs thrust midway out into the floor, hands dangling by his sides. His mouth hung open wide as evidence of his slumber reverberated through the otherwise quiet reception area.

"He's been here since seven thirty." Tiffany leaned forward behind the desk, pinching her nose. "And he needs a bath in a bad way."

Wren gathered her resolve, digging deep into her shallow reserves. "I'll talk to him about it. Just don't wake him yet. I need coffee like the desert needs rain."

She hurried down the hall but stumbled to a stop when a booming voice shook the walls around her. "Is she here yet? Ain't Ms. O'Hara here yet? I been waitin' all day."

Jerry Smith, dressed in paint-stained jeans and layers of flannel, clomped over to her with surprising speed considering the heavy, too-small-for-his-feet boots. "Ms. O'Hara." He said her name like a punctuation. "They won't let me in the food bank if I don't get new clothes." He shoved his hands into his pockets, forcing his pants to dip so low he could be arrested for indecent exposure. "And I'm tired of living by that creek. Them bears is gonna eat me up one day."

Tiffany rolled her eyes as she continued shaping her orange nails. Wren scowled at her before turning back to Jerry.

"Mr. Smith, please, not so loud. There's no need to yell." She took his elbow and led him back to his seat, ignoring the scent of unwashed body and bad breath. "I'm glad you came in today, though. I have clothes, soap, and shampoo for you. We'll get you cleaned up and you'll be good to go."

"But Ms. O'Hara. They won't let me EAT." Jerry yelled into Wren's face, displaying evidence of another rotten tooth that would need to be pulled. She'd have to make him a dental appointment when she got to her office.

Jerry jiggled his collection of random keys as his eyes darted around the room.

"Mr. Smith, when is the last time you took your medication?" Jerry, a paranoid schizophrenic Vietnam veteran, was often told by the voices in his head that he didn't need medication and would stop taking it. She suspected now was one of those times.

"Mr. Smith?"

"Huh?"

"Did you take your medication today? The ones you got the last time you were in the hospital?"

"No. Someone stole my bag."

"Someone stole your bag? When?"

"They's another man who sleeps under the bridge. The Upton Bridge. I bet he stole it."

"Do you know his name?"

Ignoring her question, he studied his key ring like the answers to his problems rested along the metal wire. "Had my meds in it."

"When was your bag stolen?"

"I dunno."

"Okay. You need to shower and change your clothes."

The keys stopped jingling, and she continued. "Mr. Smith, please sit down. I need to go into my office and get some things together before we meet." She waved at the chair he had vacated.

He said nothing, as if he hadn't heard her. How many voices was she competing with today?

"Mr. Smith?"

No response.

"Mr. Smith?"

He turned his head toward her though she didn't think he recognized her face. Was he having visual hallucinations, too? He suffered auditory hallucinations even while heavily medicated but hadn't had visions since he thought the president was hiding inside a port-a-potty at the local park. That was last year.

She tilted her head back to study him and being only five four to his six two, the stretch made her muscles ache. It was only eight o'clock in the morning, and the day already seemed interminable.

With a *pfft*, he shuffled back to his chair. "Well, the president told me he was gonna visit today."

Wren leaned over Tiffany's desk. "Is that new doctor coming in today?"

Tiffany smirked then looked down at the paper calendar on her desk. Spilled nail polish and soda stains covered most of the appointment listings. "Yeah, he's coming in at ten. He's scheduled to come in several times this month. Wonder why that is? We go from no psychiatrist to one we can't get to leave."

"Who knows? I'll catch him when he gets here." As Wren headed down the long corridor to the staff's kitchen, she tried to stretch the stone of tightness out of her neck.

Please let there be coffee. Please let there be coffee.

She was greeted by a cold, empty pot, and an encroaching irritability that instinct told her wasn't going to go away after one meager cup of joe.

She grabbed the handle, filled it with water, then dumped coffee grounds into the filter. Pulling a chipped mug out of the cabinet, she thought about her own mentally ill mother.

Diagnosed with schizophrenia like Mr. Smith, Annie O'Hara's health had been a constant concern to Wren for as long as she could remember. Her father left during one of her mom's many hospitalizations and never came back, leaving Wren as her caretaker ever since.

"Wren." Tiffany's voice made Wren's shoulders rise. "Your sister's on the phone."

"I'm coming."

Thank goodness the nurse was visiting her mom today. That was one less thing to worry about.

With steaming cup in hand, she walked down the hall, past her colleagues' empty offices and into her own small, windowless box.

A dull throb was making its way from the back of her head to the painful spot in front, directly behind her left eye. It was too early for a headache, usually taking until noon for life's stressors to overwhelm her, but today seemed to be an exception. She rubbed her temples, then massaged her scalp, pulling her black curls through her fingers.

It didn't help.

Before picking up the receiver, she searched her desk for the migraine medicine the doctor prescribed last year. She'd suffered headaches since childhood, but the pain had turned into migraine caliber when she returned home after college to care for her mother full time. What caused them, the doctors didn't know, though they said it was likely stress. It didn't take a medical degree to figure that one out.

She popped the lid off the bottle and threw two tiny white pills into her mouth, taking a long pull of water. Steeling herself, she lifted the phone.

"Wren," yelled her sister, Erika. "Where the hell are you? That so-called nurse just called here asking about Mom's medication. I thought you were supposed to take care of her." Wren ignored the permanent accusation and irritation in her older sister's voice.

"She was sleeping when I left this morning and was fine last night, but I'll give Kelly a call and see what's going on."

"Well, hurry up. I don't like her calling here. The twins are asleep and I can't leave. And try to get her a real nurse next time." The line went dead.

Wren replaced the receiver and picked at her cuticle until it bled. She fished a Band-Aid out of the desk drawer and wrapped it around her finger before searching for the clothing vouchers Jerry needed.

RIAGAN TENMAN LED the young maid through the Grove, careful not to alert the druids guarding the Cauldron. He doubted he would be missed, and besides, he had needs to take care of.

He wove through the enormous trees, their trunks rotund, their canopies interwoven, and into the thick overgrowth that covered the ground near the river. This place always worked as a haven for his liaisons. It was dark, hidden, and quiet. Never had he been interrupted whilst pursing his endeavors.

He turned, yanked the young woman to him, and tickled her sides, silencing her giggles with a kiss. Riagan didn't know her name, nor did he care. She was one of the new girls brought on to do the weaving for the warrior druid sect called Brotherhood of the Sacred Grove, of which he was a member. He was one of twelve immortal men born and sworn to protect the ancient Murias Cauldron, a magical object brought forth and placed in the druid realm by their ancestors.

The artifact, as old as time itself, held within its iron bowl the ability to heal as well as grant immortality to all who drank from its waters. No attempt had been made to steal it in all the years of Riagan's life, so he freely, and liberally, left his post to satiate his insatiable needs.

He traced a finger over the waist of her skirts, but she was impatient and with one swift pull, she had them hiked up around her waist, exposing all she had to offer.

And he liked what he saw. Nakedness. Bare, beautiful, feminine nakedness.

"You waste no time, do you, lass?" he whispered, and giggles erupted from her thin lips.

He preferred women who made him work for the sweet reward, but there was little time to waste today. He had to get back since the Arch Druid, Caswallen, had been agitated as of late, barking at the Brotherhood like a feral, famished dog. Though he was not one of the twelve who made up the Brotherhood, he was charged with order in this realm, and in charge of the order of the Brotherhood.

First things first.

Riagan slid out of his clothing, a long cloak made of light wool and dyed a rich green, then he pushed the maid to the ground. Judging by the swiftness with which she spread herself for him, she was as eager as he was.

No maiden was she.

As he stared at her, his manhood pulsed. He'd not had a woman in three days' time and his body ached. Without a moment's delay, he fell on top of her, teasing and tickling until she squealed with delight. Just as he was ready to mount her, a flash of black caught his eye.

He whipped around, scouring the land with his laser-sharp vision for any sign of an intruder. His hearing was as precise as a hawk's but he heard nothing amiss, though the air smelled acrid, putrid. Was it an animal?

Then the flash again, followed by the sound of pounding footsteps, many footsteps. He yanked the cloak about him and unsheathed his dagger before motioning for the girl to stay on the ground. Several bodies ran past, then he heard the sounds of a struggle in the distance that ended almost as quickly as it began.

By the gods, the Cauldron.

He crouched, ready to sprint to his post. Before he could move, though, Caswallen appeared in the distance, clad in ceremonial crimson robes saved for only the most extraordinary of circumstances. With purposeful steps, he moved forward.

Riagan jerked up straight and bowed his head. "Arch Druid."

"Riagan, son of Ragda." Caswallen's voice was high pitched and suddenly, unexpectedly painful to Riagan's ears. "Why are you not at your post?"

Sweat erupted on his back. He'd gotten caught. But what was there to say?

He willed his breath to slow as his mind launched into race mode. Had there been an attempt to steal the Cauldron after all this time?

Caswallen's gray eyes locked on his. He'd known this Arch Druid for years. Though he was not an immortal like Riagan, they'd shared many years of teachings, purpose, and friendship. He'd have mercy—it was just a simple lover's tryst. Besides, Caswallen wouldn't be standing there if the Cauldron had been taken.

But then the Arch Druid continued, obliterating his hopefulness. "Riagan, there was an attempt to steal the Cauldron on this night."

Dread washed over him like rain. Ice cold. Frigid. Glacial.

"How many times have you left your post these past moons?"

Riagan examined the moss by his feet as he struggled to form an answer. "I did leave my post," was the best he could do. This was a serious offense but he knew not what to say in his defense; for indeed, he had none.

The girl whimpered behind him. She had nothing to fear, though. This druid sect did not kill their help, except under the gravest of circumstances, and there was no way this qualified as a grave circumstance. Did it?

"Girl, leave us and return to your hut," commanded Caswallen. "Your work awaits you there. You are new to our sect and our ways. You will not be punished for this offense. But remember, child, one offense is all you are allowed."

The girl covered her mouth, grabbed her skirts, and fled toward the huts like a raging fire was burning at her heels.

In an instant, the rest of the Brotherhood appeared in that ancient and mysterious way of the druids—out of the mists. Like fog, or ghosts, or phantoms of the underworld.

Each had changed from their daily green robes to their ceremonial red cloaks, of the same crimson hue as the Arch Druid's. Around their waists hung the woven hemp belt, and from that fell the symbol of their Brotherhood—the sickle of their ancestors. The weapon was small, barely three inches long, but lethal and forged from the silver iron of the mountains of Ural, woven with the magic of their ancestors. Each druid's blade shined with the light of the moon.

Riagan tensed, forcing his body to remain tall, powerful. He was a warrior druid of the Sacred Grove, after all. Whatever this sudden Council was about, he would handle it with the strength known to his kind. But he couldn't ignore the perspiration pooling at his lower back, moistening the cloak. Nor could he ignore the look in his twin brother, Drake's, eyes as he stared at him. Was it fear he saw there?

"Riagan, you are a born and sworn Protector of the Murias Cauldron. You were taken as a babe, pulled from your mother's warm breast, and cast into the household of warrior druids to train for this post. You took the oath, Riagan, to lay down your life for the protection of this treasure. You have risked not only the Cauldron's safety within this realm but also the fate of the worlds.

"The capture of this artifact by one of evil intent would put all realms at risk. Our ancient history and knowledge would be lost, gained by a new immortal that could use that power to control the worlds and enslave its peoples."

Riagan knew all of this. What was the point of this Council?

Caswallen moved within inches of Riagan's face. His eyes glowed by the moon's light and held a coldness Riagan had never seen. "And on this night, Riagan, son of Ragda, when there was an attempt to steal this Cauldron by the one known as Master, you were not at your post."

Panic knocked on the steely wall of Riagan's mind. He'd heard of this Master, one as fluid as a ghost and as evil as a demon. The Brotherhood had been warned of his presence within the realms but never expected he would be able to penetrate the Brotherhood.

"You are hereby banished to the realm of man."

A gasp burst from his brother's lips.

"There you will remain until you can find love and have love given to you in return, for it was your need for the physical act of love that has put us at this grave risk."

Something foul and tepid oozed off Caswallen like a stench.

"When you do find this *elusive love*, you must return to this Council where you and she will proclaim said love for all to bear witness."

Riagan's fingers curled inward until his nails punctured the skin on his palms. Banished to the realm of man? Until he found *love*? Wasn't love the one thing they were taught to live without?

"You have made unfortunate choices for one of your standing. Now you will have one more choice to make, and this time it will be for your life or your death. Riagan, because your offense is so grave, you will either remain in the realm of man, in that prison of your own making, or you will learn to love truly and deeply. If you do not find love, you will die a mortal's death."

Riagan stiffened. Shocked. Confused. Devastated.

A single, silvery tear escaped Drake's eye.

Caswallen raised his hand and forked his fingers. "Let it be."

And Riagan was gone.

2

Early the next morning, Wren awoke to find her mother missing. This was not unusual, but the hour of the day was. Her mother always stayed in bed until exactly ten o'clock in the morning. But when Wren peeked into her mother's room at six forty-five, the bed was empty, neatly made like she'd never slept in it.

"Mama?" Wren walked down the narrow hall of their trailer. This old home was tucked against a steep mountainside, way up an isolated holler, where her mother, her mother's mother, and generations before them, had been born.

It was in this holler that, as a child, her mother had captured and kept dozens of wrens, the bird she'd been named after. Now, though, the little brown birds and their melodious songs were gone.

But there were pictures of these birds all over the house, along with shiny ceramic or wooden figurines, especially in the kitchen, where Wren stood now. The world lay gray and somber outside the windows, indicating another cloudy autumn day in October.

Wren turned on the dim light over the stove. There were no dishes in the sink or food on the counter.

"Mama?"

Outside the window, the trees were bare, the ground covered in decaying brown leaves that smelled of mold and earth, even inside the house. Walking out the creaky front door, Wren was hit with a blast of cold and her breath escaped in white wisps. Duke, her beloved bloodhound, followed her out.

"Mama?"

She continued into the front yard, past her old red pickup truck, and scanned the lawn. Seeing nothing, she veered around back where the mountain soared skyward like an impenetrable wall. The grass, brittle and dead, crunched under her feet.

"Mom!"

Sometimes caring for her mother was like caring for a child.

"Here I am, Destiny." Her mom only called her Destiny—Wren's first name—when she was off her medication. It was one of the many quirks Annie possessed.

Her mom's voice sounded alert, but shaky, like her teeth were chattering. Pulling her own sweater tight, Wren hastened toward the edge of the forest.

"Mom, are you in here?"

"Yes, honey. I'm right here."

Wren found her mother several yards in with nothing on but an opened robe. Pieces of dried brown leaves and purple berries peppered her graying red hair, and dirt was smudged on her cheek. She was dancing to a rhythm only she could hear, right in the middle of a perfect circle of gray stones.

Duke sniffed, then peed on a nearby tree, grunting in satisfaction. Wren cracked a smile. She loved that dog and his simple manly delights.

"Destiny." Annie's graceful hands were floating, waving, and twisting through the air like a ballerina's, her hips swaying side to side. "Did you know that it's almost the autumnal equinox?"

"No, I didn't."

"Oh, but dear." A serene smile pulled Annie's lips upward. "It is. Such a beautiful time of year." She grabbed handfuls of leaves and threw them in the air, then twirled beneath them as they cascaded around her.

"Mama, I have to get to work." Wren motioned for Annie to leave the circle of stones.

Relenting, Annie tiptoed out of the forest as if something would bite her heels should she flatten her feet.

"They said they were going to visit today. Or did they say at the equinox?" Annie stopped at the bottom porch step and turned to Wren, their noses inches apart. "You know, Destiny, that's only a few days away."

"Wren, Mom. Call me Wren."

"But Destiny is your name."

"Yes, but I go by my middle name, Wren. I always have."

Annie pivoted back toward the house and scrambled up the stairs unassisted, passing through the weathered door without another word.

"Mama, who was going to visit?" She hoped her mom meant the nurse.

"The little people."

Nope. That wouldn't be Kelly who was nearly six feet tall. "Oh, okay. Well, maybe they were busy. Did you take your medicine before you went outside?"

When her mother didn't respond, Wren led her to the recliner and wrapped an old quilt around her that Annie's great-grandmother had woven. The colors were faded, the thread unraveling, but it was soft and always brought solace to her mother, like a child with a blankie.

Wren searched for the pillbox that Annie had moved from its resting place by the kitchen sink, and found it in the breadbox. A quick rattle of the plastic confirmed she hadn't taken her meds today. In fact, it was likely she'd been spitting out the pills for the past several days. Sometimes when Wren dropped her guard, this kind of thing happened.

"Mama, I know it's early, but I have to leave for work. I'll call a little bit later so make sure you answer the phone."

Annie stared at the muted television and said nothing.

"Answer the phone when it rings, okay?" She handed her a glass of water and the medicine.

"Okay."

"Kelly will be here later. Okay?"

"Kelly who?"

"Kelly is your nurse. You know, she visits you every week? Twice a week?"

"Okay. Destiny?"

"Yes?" Wren swallowed a sigh the size of a walnut.

"Is Kelly a real nurse?"

Wren bit back a surge of anger. She knew these were Erika's spiteful words.

"Yes, and take your medicine before I go."

Annie popped the pills into her mouth.

"Show me."

Annie opened her mouth and moved her tongue around to prove she'd swallowed the pills.

Wren kissed her cheek and stroked Duke's big head. "Watch over her, boy." She locked the door behind her.

Her mother's behavior had become such the norm that she rarely noticed it anymore. What she was beginning to notice, though, was her own mental health. Now *that* was becoming a cause for concern. Annie had been twenty-two when she'd had the first breakdown that landed her in the psychiatric ward for a week and led her to being branded with a diagnosis she would never recover from.

Wren was twenty-one and just starting to hear strange sounds, like little voices chattering over her shoulder. She'd whip around to find who was talking, but no one was ever there. Ever.

She'd mentioned it to her therapist but didn't want to divulge too much information lest she be forced into a hospital and unable to take care of her mom. There couldn't be two crazy women in one household, could there?

Thankfully, the chatter was subdued today. At least for now.

She suppressed the weighted sigh hovering in the back of her throat and slid into her old truck. To say she had a busy morning was an understatement, with finding Jerry shelter at the top of her list. He was going to hurt someone if he had to keep sleeping under the bridge, or he would die from the bitter cold like he almost had last winter.

She maneuvered the one-lane road as it twisted around a mountain that soared to the side. On the other side was a plummeting drop into a dark ravine. The only protection from falling over the edge was her focus on the road, and a metal guardrail that didn't elicit the confidence it was meant to instill.

The foggy morning hid the distant peaks behind a white, hazy blanket, and Wren drove with both hands clutching the wheel. Her office was ten miles away, nestled in a row of abandoned buildings that represented the sparsely populated area perfectly. Twenty minutes later, she turned into the empty parking lot, slid out of the truck, and started toward the office.

She inhaled, letting the air, fresh and crisp, cleanse her lungs. The moistness of the fog filled her nostrils like cool steam.

"Miss O'Hara?" The question was simple. The sharp burst of syllables behind it was not. She whipped around as Jerry stumbled out from behind the corner of the building.

He moved forward, his gait heavy and unsteady and jerky like he'd spent the night sitting on a metal chair. His slurred speech suggested he'd been on the bottle last night, or this morning, or just a minute ago. He looked impatient, angry, psychotic.

"Jerry." A gentle voice usually placated him.

"You no-good bitch. You ain't done shit for me."

Maybe that tone wouldn't work today.

The hair on her neck bristled and rose to salute. A quick look around the lot told her not another soul was around.

"Jerry, look at me."

His eyes were darting yet unfocused. He stood several feet from her, his tall frame skeletal in the layers of ill-fitting clothes. With hands outstretched, she backed toward the office.

His brown eyes followed her, but he didn't seem to register her words. Did he even see her? And if he didn't, what was he seeing?

She took another step back. Though the mountain air was cool, perspiration peppered her hairline, and a bead of sweat traveled down her spine. The sound of the silence surrounding them was deafening, stifling. Terrifying.

He tilted his head and stared out of the corner of his eye, listening to voices she could not hear.

She stole a glance at the door to the agency, confirming Tiffany wasn't at her desk on the other side of the glass doors. Confirming there was no one to call 911.

It was so quiet she could hear Jerry's labored breathing.

"Look at me." Jerry bared his teeth like a feral animal.

"Jerry."

"What?"

The stench of his unwashed body made her eyes water.

"Have you taken your meds today?"

"No, I ain't taken my medicine. Did you forget that asshole stole my bag?" With each word, he bobbed his head closer and closer to hers. "I told you that yesterday."

Right. "I thought you were given new meds from Dr. Martin."

"That asshole stole 'em."

"The new meds?"

Jerry mumbled a clipped string of words she didn't understand.

"Dr. Martin will be in again today and we can get you more meds." She fought to keep her voice calm, but the thunderous pounding of her heart—*ba bomp, ba bomp, ba bomp*—told her she was on the verge of panic.

She was just a case manager, for goodness' sake. Not a therapist or psychiatrist. Or a black belt in Tae Kwon Do.

"Do you want to go to the hospital? Remember how much that helped last time?"

His shoulders, thin as reeds, tightened.

He glanced toward the office door.

She took another step back. Even if she got to the office door, her keys were in the bottom of her large bag. If he didn't calm down, there was little she could do.

But he would calm down. He always did. Though, if she was honest, he'd never been *this* agitated.

"Do you remember the last time you were in the hospital? How well you ate? And didn't you stay up all night watching television?" Her lips shook against her teeth as she forced a smile.

He'll calm down. He has to.

She watched his lips move, speaking words she could not hear, like a television on mute.

Then a shot of laughter burst out of his mouth, loud like a foghorn, quick like a bullet. Just as suddenly, his face fell to stone, and his gaze landed on her once again.

"I ain't goin' to no hospital. You just wanna send me back there so you don't have to help."

"We've worked hard to get you off the streets. As you know, there's not that much housing." What she wanted to say was, *It is so hard for an alcoholic, schizophrenic veteran to find a job that will pay for an apartment*, but she decided now was not the time.

"You're worthless."

"Please don't say that." Her voice cracked with the plea, like a walnut shell at the wrong end of a hammer.

He laughed again, the sound hysterical and unhinged. "I'm gonna kill you."

Someone help, her mind screamed as every cell in her body coiled with blood-red terror.

"Look." He pirouetted, slowly, slowly, in a circle. "You're all alone."

"Help me." Her voice was nothing but a whisper—swallowed as soon as it was released. Her knees knocked together, and she tried to force them to statues of marble.

A Mustang's tires squealed down Main Street but the driver did not pull in. Likely didn't even look over.

"Jerry, I'm sorry you're angry with me. Let's try to work this out."

He lunged for her.

She cried out as he shoved her to the ground. She slammed into the concrete, her head cracking into the solid surface. Flashes of light burst in front of her eyes like fireworks.

"You BITCH. You ain't gonna help me."

He grabbed her arm, his fingers an unyielding clamp.

"You ain't done nothin' to help me." He jerked her to her feet like a rag doll.

She screamed, the force of her own sound surely splitting her skull into tiny bone fragments. Her head hurt so badly; bile shot up from her stomach and pooled in the back of her throat.

He reared back with his free hand, then smacked her across the face. The hard, angular surface of his ring, the only valuable he owned, cut across her cheekbone like a sharp knife's slice. He dropped her to the concrete, and she hovered on the edge of a black abyss.

She tried to sit up, but her mind and body no longer seemed connected. Her head. Her head hurt so badly she couldn't see. She couldn't think. Vomit threatened but remained settled—for the moment.

She tried to roll over, but her body wouldn't respond to her wishes. It felt broken. Disconnected.

Blinking, she tried to force her eyes to focus. When she did, she saw his booted foot coming straight for her head.

She screamed.

RIAGAN STRUGGLED TO breathe, suffocating in this new, foreign realm. Sure, he'd visited most of the varying realms, including that of man, but he'd never done so in a human body. A mortal body.

As soon as he materialized on Earth, he found an isolated and remote forest where he could remain hidden, and he gave up. He let hopelessness and resignation settle into his soul like a fatal disease.

It was the height of irony that to become a druid of the Brotherhood, he had to forgo any and all emotion. He was not even allowed to love his own mother, having been taken from her when he was just two, never to see her again other than during fleeting moments over her life span. And now he was supposed to find love, as if he'd recognize it, and fall into its intricate web of ways?

Insane.

Now, he lay on a bed of soft moss, his druid senses dull as his body settled into the mortal life. First his sight dimmed and everything turned blue, then gray, then black when he closed his lids, unable to bear the blurring of his formerly razor-sharp vision. Then his sense of smell shut off like a switch and the metallic scent of the universe was gone.

Then feeling. The nerves in his body shut off one by one, like he was hibernating. Suddenly he couldn't feel his toes. The tips of his fingers went numb. His mind told his hand to clench, but there was no way of telling if it responded.

He was falling into a stupor, a fog, a coma of his own making. Maybe it was a way of protecting himself against the inevitable—he wouldn't know he was dying a mortal death if he was already unconscious. Brilliant logic, he decided and allowed his breath to become shallow as he slipped further into the trance-like state.

His mind numbed, and soon he could no longer feel a heartbeat, could no longer move his muscles, could no longer form a thought.

But then, in the farthest point of darkness, he heard a voice. He did not want to hear a voice.

Somehow it pierced the void.

Then the dimmest of lights appeared, bright behind his closed lids. He did not want to see a light.

His eyes struggled to focus when they opened.

It was a woman's voice. He certainly did not want to come across a woman. Wasn't a lass the root of all his ills?

The voice grew louder. The light became brighter.

Life began to pump back through his body, despite his desire to stay in a subconscious state.

The voice carried across the wind.

She was upset.

It became louder, more frantic, more upset. The fire pumped through him now, with the regular rhythm of a human heart.

Why?

Because of the voice.

He opened his eyes, and the brilliant sun nearly blinded him.

She was screaming. Frightened, terrified.

His body burst with a thousand beating rhythms and jerked him upright until he was standing in the middle of the forest.

The voice was deafening. "Help me," it cried.

He took off in a sprint, toward where instinct told him the voice would be. He did not question how his mortal hearing picked up the distressed call from seemingly so far away.

Thrashing through trees, bolting down roads, flying past abandoned buildings, he chased that voice until he found from whom it sprang.

3

"Lass, are you ok?"

The question came through a tunnel, a long, narrow tunnel — somewhere to the right or the left, or to the top or the bottom. It was a man's voice, only Wren didn't know whose. She knew she should open her eyes but couldn't remember how to work the muscles.

Did he ask if I'm okay? No, I'm not okay. I have a headache. That's why I can't open my eyes. My head, it hurts.

A cool hand, so large her entire face fit in it, cupped her cheek. She felt its warmth and struggled to blink. When she managed to focus, she saw an angel kneeling before her, a heavenly man with a halo of straight blond hair so fair it was white. The sunlight glistened through the long strands that fell well over his shoulders. His eyes, glassy as marbles, were vibrantly green against his pale, translucent skin. His lips were dusty pink and full.

If I'm dreaming, do not wake me up.

"Lass?"

"Quit calling me that." The angel should not talk like a Scotsman.

His hand moved from her face to her arm, and he helped her sit up. The light, though dim, hurt her eyes, and she squinted as she tried to focus on his beauty. Yes, beauty. He was the most beautiful man she had ever seen.

Was this the angel of death? If so, where were his clothes? She kept her eyes glued to his face, not his unexpectedly nude body, though somehow she'd managed to notice a torso so toned, she could count the muscles.

"Be careful, la—I mean, miss." The deep baritone caressed her eardrums.

"Be careful?" Her mind could not merge words with meaning. The knot on the back of her head was huge and sensitive, even to her light touch.

"You must move slowly. You are hurt." When he spoke, his lips parted to reveal perfectly shaped white teeth. And she knew his breath would be fresh and warm, like a cup of honey-sweet tea. But that should be irrelevant, shouldn't it?

"Who are you?" She touched her cheek and flinched at the tender skin.

The blond angel said nothing as he watched her, his sandy-colored brows pursed. He reached out to caress her cheek, but she yanked away, fearful the touch would be painful. After a moment's hesitation, he leaned down and locked eyes with her, muttering an incomprehensible tumble of words. In an instant, she calmed, like his words were an accelerated sedative her body was all too willing to absorb. She allowed him to examine her face.

"You're bruised and cut."

She had no good response, so she stared at him.

"Nothing is broken." He paused, scanned the lot, then said, "I must go."

"Go? Where's…where's…?" Before she could speak the word *Jerry*, she saw her client, lying nearby in a pool of blood.

"Oh my—Jerry." She tried to stand up, but the man with the halo held her back.

"He's gone, lass. Gone."

"What do you mean, *he's gone*? What happened? Who did this?" Her voice shrilled higher with each word like notes on a keyboard, and her body shook like a dryer. Jerry, her client, was motionless, and blood seeped out from behind his head.

"Call 911. Now."

She was vaguely aware of a car pulling into the lot, and then another, and of the blond angel darting away.

Noise erupted as doors slammed.

Thank God, help is coming.

She struggled to all fours and crawled toward Jerry. She sobbed. "Jerry?"

Footsteps pounded and voices carried, but she couldn't understand what they said. Jerry's skin was turning gray.

She fought for breath as several hands grabbed her, pulling her back.

"Wren, are you okay?" It was Tiffany, finally showing up to work. Wren curled into the secretary's slender arms.

"Call 911," barked Dr. Rick Martin before leaning down into Wren's face. "Ms. O'Hara, what happened here?" His voice was curt and impatient, the same voice he used with the clients.

Someone wrapped a blanket around her shoulders and folded the sides together under her neck. The only things she was really conscious of, though, were her throbbing cheek and head. Sirens blared their approach and she cringed.

Tiffany rocked her back and forth. "I think she's in shock, Dr. Martin."

A new voice appeared, one she vaguely recognized. "What happened?"

"No one saw anything?" came another new voice.

"There's no way she could do this to a man his size. Maybe someone else attacked them both."

She glanced at Jerry just as a haze of white gaseous air lifted from his still body and floated away.

Good-bye, Jerry.

"Ms. O'Hara?" Dr. Martin fought for balance with his cane then leaned down into her face. "Who did this?"

Sirens screeched to a halt. More voices erupted like a volcano, but all Wren wanted was quiet, quiet, quiet. And for someone to explain the last ten minutes of her life because they were a blur and a whir of hazy-white confusion.

"What happened?" someone asked.

"Who did this?" someone else asked.

"Are you hurt, miss?" a third person asked.

She could hear the questions but couldn't remember how to respond. Her throat felt swollen, locked.

Dr. Martin leaned into her face again, his breath a mix of cigarette smoke and mint gum. He was so close she could count the white hairs in his dark beard.

"Ms. O'Hara."

She cringed at the loud crack of his voice, like a whip snapping against her skull. No wonder Jerry and her other clients didn't seem to like him as their psychiatrist.

"I'm fine," she managed.

"Well, what happened then?" he demanded as a police officer hunched nearby.

"I'm Officer Buford. Who is in charge here?" He glanced at the EMTs as they tried to resuscitate Jerry.

Couldn't they tell that was useless?

Dr. Martin stood, leaning on his cane, the paunch of his belly pushing against his button-up shirt. "I am Dr. Rick Martin. I am the psychiatrist at this agency. You can address any questions to me."

Officer Buford wiped his forehead with a handkerchief. "With all due respect, sir, it appears I need to speak with the young woman. If you don't mind." He stepped in front of the doctor and bent down.

Dr. Martin snorted, indignant, and shuffled to Wren's other side.

"What happened?" asked the officer as sweat pooled above his thin lip.

Someone handed Wren a paper cup filled with water. After a sip, she forced her mind to piece together what she knew.

"I'm not sure. Jerry was here in the parking lot when I pulled in. He was mad, and it was clear he hadn't taken his meds." Her voice sounded foreign, as if it belonged to someone else. "He started shouting at me. Then he—" She remembered slamming into the concrete. "He pushed me, and I fell, and I guess I blacked out. I don't know." She suddenly remembered the angel. Where was he? Had she imagined him? And if she did, who had saved her?

The EMTs covered Jerry's body with a sheet, then talked quietly to each other, stealing glances her way.

The angel. He had been here, hadn't he? He must have stopped Jerry from kicking her in the head. She shivered as the memory of his booted foot hurtling toward her head played like a slo-mo short film. The angel was the only person who could've stopped him.

Was he the one who killed Jerry?

It hurt to blink.

Then hands were on her head, feeling over her skull. Other hands were at her face, putting something cold against her cheek. The pressure stung and tears sprang to her eyes.

Dr. Martin was in her face again. "Who did this to Jerry?"

She didn't know how to answer that question, couldn't risk them thinking she was crazy like her mom. Telling them an angel had done it seemed nothing short of insane.

There had been someone else here, but then, where was he now?

Officer Buford tried again. "Who hit you?" He pulled out a little pocket notebook, licked his finger, and then flipped to a clean page. Dr. Martin threw his free hand on his hip and stared at the officer.

"Jerry. I told you that already."

"Jerry hit you?"

"Yes. Jerry attacked me."

"Who did this to Jerry?"

She glanced at Jerry's blood, drying into the cracks of the concrete.

"Did you attack Jerry, Ms. O'Hara?" Dr. Martin loomed over her. "Did you do this?"

"I…I don't know who did it. I must have lost consciousness. I didn't see anyone else." She met Dr. Martin's accusing eyes. "I did not do this to him."

"BY THE GODS, what have I done?"

Riagan held his hands in front of his face, his mortal hands with small splatters of blood on them.

"What have I done?" He wailed to the trees as if they could provide him the answers he sought. He stood at the edge of the woods, right beyond the parking lot where he'd just killed a man.

He fell upon his knees. The pulse pounding in his temples made him cry out. Where had this aggression come from? He was a Protector of the Cauldron, *not* a protector of this woman. Why had he committed murder over someone he didn't even know, didn't want to know, and never cared to see again?

He raised his head at the shrill ring of a siren and watched a speeding car with flashing lights race away from the lot.

I can't be seen. By the heavens, no. Mortal and imprisoned is not an option.

Naked and exposed, he darted, crouched like an animal, into the forest where the thick growth of the trees would provide the safety and security he needed.

The cool, crisp mountain breeze carried a small sliver of solace to his skin. Going deeper and deeper into the forest, he was soon surrounded by aged trees, tall and thick. Protruding roots, fallen limbs, and dead leaves covered the ground. He stubbed his toe several times but suppressed a cry of pain. Nothing could compare to the inner despair consuming him.

Eventually, he stood upright and walked, certain there was no one around. He spotted a black bear and two of her cubs. When she bared her teeth at him, he eased in the other direction but paid her little attention otherwise. Owls peppered the branches of this forest, and several times he spotted deer in the distance, staring at him with gentle brown eyes.

His mind felt choppier than the Earth's ocean waves during a hurricane.

He would need to leave this area, that much was certain. But the fact that he landed here after his banishment from the Sacred Grove meant a portal to the otherworlds must be nearby. He knew not where others rested on this realm of man and hesitated to veer too far.

Even though he suffered almost no hope for a return to his realm.

But yet, if he moved away from this area where he'd landed, it took that *almost no* hope and made it *zero* hope. Null and void hope. Forget about it, don't think about it, don't even play with the idea *hope*. That was a big risk to take.

Being a member of the Brotherhood was all he knew—protecting that ancient artifact the meaning of his existence.

No, he couldn't leave. Not yet at least.

He continued forth until his human heart pounded. Lost in thought, he failed to notice the change in the forest. He did not think he'd walked into the night but the sunlight was dim now, so dim there was hardly any light at all. The trees had become taller and taller, rounder and rounder.

He slowed and studied his surroundings. The trees were so closely grown together he could reach out and touch several of them. The limbs, high above his head, were naked but thickly intertwined, obscuring the sunlight. The ceiling of this forest was as dark as the ground.

Then he noticed that every single tree was an oak, and not just any oak—the white oak—the only trees known to survive centuries and across realms. He scanned the forest. Indeed, there were no maples, poplars, or spruce trees any longer. Not a one.

Strange that an earthly forest would harbor such a vast grove of the sacred tree.

To the right, his ears picked up a faint droning vibration that carried through the wind like a lover's breathy sigh. He maneuvered in that direction, slowly and with deliberate steps, touching the trees' rough surfaces as he went, feeling the coolness absorb into his fingers. His mind was alert now, searching.

Light appeared ahead. As he stalked toward it, he had to turn sideways to fit through the growth it had become so thick. The light became brighter, the droning louder. His human heart lurched.

A portal lay nearby.

By the gods, he'd found the portal.

He was closer than he could've ever prayed to be.

He pushed ahead on silent feet, tentative and cautious, for he knew not what creatures rested near a portal to the otherworlds.

Coarse bark scratched the bare skin of his body but he did not notice. He came to a small clearing, a perfect three-yard radius of a circle made by the trees at the periphery. Inside the ring of trees, the clearing flattened, free from leaves, overgrowth, or any type of forest debris.

He sucked in his breath and maneuvered between the trees that formed the last line of defense, a wall of protection, and he knew his instinct was correct. Only magical trees of a portal forest held the ability to obscure, protect, and defend.

He may be mortal now, but he would always be druid-born.

Dark green moss covered the ground. Riagan ran his hand over the surface, so like the soft floor of his realm.

Pain and longing tugged at his heart.

The trees started moving, swaying together in timeless rhythm, from their trunks that fed into the earth all the way up through their limbs. They moved, not from a mountain breeze, but from simply being *alive*.

The portal.

Yes, the trees murmured.

Riagan bowed his head and lifted his hands in supplication.

Why have you come? Their ancient song filled the air.

"Tree-friends, is there a portal between the worlds here?"

Yes, the otherworlds are close, and the veil is thin here. What ask you of this sacred land?

"If I may be so bold yet humble, I ask for protection and permission to pass through the portal; to reunite with the Brotherhood of the Sacred Grove; to reestablish myself as a Guardian of the Murias Cauldron and live my life as a druid among my own kind." The words tumbled out of his mouth, unscripted, uncensored, and he flushed at his lack of control.

He did not know if the trees knew of his betrayal or punishment, and did not ask.

You may reside here, near the portal, until the full moon looms at the autumnal equinox. Then the veil between the worlds dissipates and you may attempt contact.

"Have you any news of my Brotherhood? How fares the druid realm?"

But the trees hardened en masse and said no more.

He clenched his teeth. All because of a woman and her haunting voice. Wasn't it a woman who had gotten him banished to the realm of man in the first place?

Fisting his hands, he started pacing, first around the clearing, then around a wider arc. He created a well-worn path before he started allowing his feet to carry him where they would.

He walked until the trees shrunk in height and grew apart enough for him to pass through easily. After a while, the variation of trees he expected appeared—mostly maple and spruce trees, some poplars and a flowering dogwood here and there. The yellow rays of the Earth's sun replaced the portal's luminous light. The beams did nothing to warm the air, though, and he shivered from cold.

He knew not if he walked in the same direction from which he came—he'd been far too preoccupied to pay attention—but soon he arrived upon a clearing where an old, rectangular house sat, white but rusty. It looked like it had been pushed into the side of the mountain, from where it protruded like an ugly sore. The shutters hung off their hinges and part of the roof threatened to sink in with the next big snow. Grassy patches mixed with dirt patches, and the whole place appeared abandoned.

He eased forward, hoping to find clothes there. He had days until the equinox. He couldn't very well roam the earth nude. Now that he was human, he would need to eat and find water.

So inconvenient it is to be mortal.

He crept to a window and peeked in. The home was dark; an older woman reclined in a chair, sleeping. Her red hair, generously mixed with gray, was pulled back from her face in a long braid. The pink housecoat had fallen open revealing heavily freckled skin.

He listened for other sounds and heard nothing. Convinced she was alone, he stole through the front door, careful not to wake her. The house, in contrast to the outside of it, was clean, pristine almost.

He came to a room at the end of a short hallway. The bed was neatly made and the room was immaculate. Not even a thread of dust wafted through the air. There was a large, clear window that gazed upon the forest. On the nightstand sat a small lamp and a book. There was no other furniture so he went to the closet.

Only a handful of clothes, replicas of the same housecoat the woman had on now, filled the space. At the far corner was a battered footlocker where he found men's clothing.

Perfect.

He yanked out jeans, a T-shirt, and boots. They fit, except for the shirt, which was too tight through the shoulders and chest, but it would have to do. He grabbed several more items from the box and stuffed them into a bag he found under the bed.

A tarnished full-length mirror leaned against the wall, and he had to take several steps back to fit his entire body into its reflection.

The clothes were tight, but fortunate was he that the first place he looked had clothes he could wear. He scrutinized himself in the mirror, appreciative of his powerful body, typical of a warrior druid of his kind. Though he had to admit, his physique was blessed, even among his fellow warriors.

"More like a Greek statue, if I say so myself. Too bad I must cover up with clothing."

A growly snort erupted behind him, and he pivoted to see a dog lying on the floor.

Riagan resisted the urge to pet the animal's head, unsure if it would nip him. Giving it a wide berth, he tiptoed down the hallway then slipped out of the house, the woman's snores growing quiet as he headed toward the forest.

4

"Master." Gwyon bowed, the undyed woolen robe falling forward. "I have but just returned from the realm of man and am here to report that Riagan has killed a man. It will be impossible now to fulfill the requirements to ease his banishment. Jail is an unlikely place to find love."

Gwyon willed his knees to stop shaking. Leaning his weight on the boulder behind him, he tried to breathe as he awaited Master's response. His clubbed feet were pained, and it took all the strength in his being not to show weakness.

The moon loomed to the right, mere days from achieving its fullness. The energy from the enormous orb reverberated through the air, sending small shockwaves across Gwyon's skin. Or it could be the excitement over this latest development.

Finally, the statuesque figure in front of him swiveled, as if on a pivot. The hood of the black cloak hid the Master's face, and the only part of his body Gwyon could see were the ashen gray hands, with long fingers protruding from the sleeves like fallen sticks. Thin. Dead. Master stood as still as the ancient oaks surrounding him.

Master pushed back the hood, allowing Gwyon a view of his entire face. Even though he'd known that face for as long as he held memory within his mind, the features still frightened him, with cheeks sunken so deep Gwyon could see the skeleton underneath the paper-thin skin.

"I have seen it." Master's soft voice, more like a prepubescent boy's than a man's, was just loud enough for Gwyon to hear.

Had the time come? Would Riagan and Drake suffer now as Gwyon had suffered?

Gwyon and the other subordinates failed during their first attempt to take the Cauldron but had succeeded in getting Riagan banished to the realm of man. With one of the Brotherhood gone, the line of fortitude was weakened and there was little to stand in their way of capturing the revered artifact during the next attempt.

Nothing thrilled Gwyon more, and even Master's stormy stare could not deter the surge of excitement.

"The wheels are in motion, are they not, Gwyon?"

"Yes, Master. Riagan was the strongest link among the Brotherhood, as you know. Now that he is banished, their line is weakened. We await only your word and we will strike to take the Cauldron. This time we will succeed."

Master clasped his hands behind his back. "Yes. Riagan's training has all but guaranteed he will be unable to find love. Ever. And certainly not before the equinox. He is as good as dead."

Gwyon straightened his shoulders and steeled his jaw. Straight. Proud. Ready.

Master continued. "The time has come."

A smile stretched across Gwyon's face as he allowed himself to return to rest upon the boulder.

WREN SAT IN her office's guest chair, trying not to hyperventilate. This room was, on a good day, no bigger than an empty shoebox. Today, though, it felt like a matchbox, with Dr. Martin taking up residence in her desk chair and Officer Buford standing in the corner, shifting between his feet.

"No one else was around?" Buford held a tiny pen ready to take down every word she said, every word she'd already said, over and over and over.

"No, I didn't see anyone else. I must've blacked out. I hit my head pretty hard."

"I see. And you say Jerry Smith attacked you?"

"Yes. I came to work and he was waiting in the parking lot. He seemed to be experiencing auditory hallucinations so I think he has been off his medication for a while."

"*Had* been off his medication," said Dr. Martin, interrupting.

"Excuse me?" What was he talking about now?

"He's dead." The doctor's air of superiority and authority was as thick as molasses. "He *had* been off his medication, Wren. Using the word *has* insinuates he is still alive, but alas, he is dead."

Wren gathered her proverbial daggers and shot them at Dr. Martin. "I think he *had* been off his medication for a while."

Officer Buford flipped the notebook shut. "Dr. Martin, do you have any other questions?"

The doctor gazed at her from unblinking eyes, his index fingers joined and resting under his chin. "No. I have nothing at this time."

Officer Buford made his way to the door. Dr. Martin followed but turned before passing the threshold. "Take the rest of the day off."

"Thank you." Her tone was neutral as she said the words, though she couldn't help but feel Dr. Martin was dismissing her rather than offering her a sign of goodwill. Did he really think she killed Jerry?

The men walked down the hall, and she resisted the urge to slam the door. Tears threatened to spill.

The bastard.

Glad to have the men out of her office, she fell into her chair, which smelled like Dr. Martin, and nausea rolled through her empty stomach. She sprang to her feet and returned to the guest chair.

The last person who had sat in that chair was Jerry.

No longer able to stop the tears, she let them slide over her cheeks, muffling her sobs behind her fisted hand.

There was no window to stare out of so she closed her eyes, shutting down each painful memory of the day one by one. She was good at channeling her thoughts away from the unpleasant. She had been doing it for years.

Settling into their wake was an image of the blond angel crouched over her, the dim light filtering through his long hair. She knew the strands would feel like satin if she were to touch them.

If he was real.

Had Michelangelo sketched a picture of the perfect man, it would be this blond angel. His face was so flawlessly chiseled he was almost too beautiful. Surely, he was a hallucination.

Raw, masculine power oozed off his skin, and she could feel the effects all these hours later. He was a large man, the width of his shoulders alone massive. Powerful.

And he was naked, wasn't he? Where were his clothes? This little detail didn't bode too well in the sanity department. If he were real, wouldn't he be dressed?

Yes, he must've been an angel—of death, mercy, or heaven. She didn't know which, and she didn't care.

Unable to sit in the cavernous office a minute longer, she grabbed her things and hurried to her truck without a word to anyone. In the parking lot, she avoided the spot where Jerry had died, catching flashes of the yellow police tape in her peripheral vision.

She peeled away, and within minutes was headed down her backcountry road. Soon, but not soon enough, she turned onto the dusty, pothole-filled driveway. Shoving the truck into four-wheel drive, she maneuvered her way over the dips and craters that made her head pound and protest.

As the truck lurched up the mountainside, the sun's rays burst through the windshield, and she reached down to get her sunglasses. When she looked up again, she slammed on the brakes, blinking, blinking, blinking. The truck skidded in the dirt, blowing puffs of brown dust into the air.

The blond angel.

Tall, beautiful, insanely muscular.

Thankfully, or not, he was clothed, his long hair blowing in the mountain breeze. Now wearing a T-shirt that was too tight, and a pair of jeans, his clothing could pass for any man's for miles around. But the body that filled those clothes…well, she'd never seen anything like it. Certainly not on her boyfriend, Brian. But that was irrelevant, wasn't it?

Tension squeezed in her lower abdomen, tightening like the balling fist of a linebacker. She gulped, then bit the inside of her cheek as an unfamiliar burning flame shot through her body.

Why was he in her mother's driveway? Wearing clothes that looked like something her father used to wear?

She reached for the door handle just as he disappeared into the forest.

Vanished.

OCH, BUT THAT *is the lass. The voice.*

He'd recognize that curly head of raven hair and that pouty red mouth anywhere. She held the voice that had gotten him into this new mess. What was she doing all the way out here?

Her mouth opened in a perfect 'O' as she stared out the window. Did she recognize him? He knew she'd seen him, had even talked to him. But she had been hurt, and he hoped didn't remember.

When she shook her head as if to clear her mind, clear her vision maybe, curls flew around her face, brushing against alabaster skin. A faint pink flush burst over her cheeks.

When she threw open the door and started to get out, he crouched, preparing to flee. There was much to clarify in his mind before they met again. He couldn't just say he was an ancient druid, could he? Nay. That wouldn't do at all.

So he ran.

He risked one glance behind him as he maneuvered through the trees. Standing beside her truck, she didn't call after him but remained as still as a pillar, a mask of perplexed aggravation settling over her face.

He reached the small clearing of the portal and fell to his knees, gasping for breath. As he heaved, the sudden tinkling of bells burst alive in the air—mingling, magical, melodial. A faery was signaling its arrival.

Well, they waste but no time, do they? I have been man merely a day.

He stared to the right of the circle of stone. Out of his peripheral vision, he saw movement and struggled to keep his eyes averted. He had enough troubles without becoming a slave to the wee folk, and everyone knew that watching a faery materialize was the surest way to become just that.

The bells, more beautiful than those that rang in medieval churches, stopped as suddenly as they'd started.

In the clearing, lighted upon a small stone, was a miniature faery, so tiny she was no longer than his thumb, and colorful beyond the myriad of the rainbow. Riagan struggled to focus on her teeny form.

She perched with one leg crossed over the other. Her wings flapped iridescent and shimmering behind her slender back. Her hands crossed about her knee, and she stared at Riagan.

He nodded in greeting.

She flashed him a smile that burst with light. He looked away.

I must remember my old teachings. These wee faeries are fickle things. They draw you in with their beauty, then hypnotize and kidnap you. I must remain alert.

"Riagan?" Her crystallized voice filled the air, voluminous for such a small creature.

"Yes?"

The trees swayed.

"Why are you here?"

He remained silent. She would likely know why he was here. The otherworlds were more gossipy than an old woman's parlor at tea time.

"Riagan, you have traveled far to come to this place. And I see that you are mortal."

He shuddered. *Mortal.*

The faery lifted off the stone and fluttered forward. Her eyes were oval, large, and luminous, bursting forth with beams of yellow like the sun. "Have you word from your Brotherhood?"

Tension filled his mortal veins. "Nay. Have you word to give me?"

She tilted her head and her sunshine eyes turned liquid, undulating in rich yellow. He knew not whether to trust the wee faery. The miniature folk of the fae realm were great tricksters and often reveled in the fun of toying with the lives of others.

"Riagan, what I am to tell you is truth."

It was as if she could read his thoughts. "Okay, then. What?"

"There is great trouble on the druid realm."

The trees droned around him, their vibration creeping beneath his skin until he felt he was vibrating too.

"What trouble? Pray, faery, tell me. What of my Brotherhood? Of my brother?"

She watched him as if trying to decide whether to tell him the whole story or tease him with snippets. "There will be an attempt to take the Murias Cauldron."

"An attempt? Mean you another attempt? There was an attempt the night I was banished." He fought to slow his tumble of words.

"Aye, druid. There will be another attempt, and this time they will succeed."

"Pray that you are lying." He tried to unclench his clenched fists but could not.

"Nay, druid, I lie not. The one they call Master is determined to gain possession of this most sacred treasure. Its powers are very desirable."

"You need not tell me what I already know, faery. I know well that the Cauldron promises immortality. Why think you there is a need for the Brotherhood to protect it?"

The warrior blood that ran deep within him smoldered, simmered, seared. The need to protect the Cauldron shook him so completely, he wondered if the innermost part of the Earth could feel it. "Who is this one they call Master? Know you of him?"

"Nay. We of the fae realm know only his name and that he is determined to gain possession of the treasure. He is not an immortal but likely wants to be thus. He uses magic to dwell outside the veil and cannot be seen."

Riagan rubbed his jaw, oblivious to the newly grown hair that had appeared. Whoever this Master was had been able to gain entry to the druid realm and enter the Sacred Grove. To gain access to the Cauldron, one had to have the warrior gene in his blood, like one of the Brotherhood. Was there a traitor among their midst? The possibility was too alarming to consider.

Did Caswallen know of this?

"Tree-friends, does the faery speak the truth?"

We know not, druid, but the otherworlds are unsettled.

He stared hard at the creature hovering before him. "Tell me the truth, faery, or you will regret crossing the portal on this night."

"Druid, do not challenge me. I speak only the truth. Loss of this treasure affects the fae realm as well. We rely upon the druids to keep the artifact safe so when the worlds are in need of its powers, it will be there. Know you not that we are in this together? If the one they call Master obtains the Cauldron, he will gain immortality and the worlds' ancient secrets will be his to use as he will."

She put her hands to either side of his mouth. The air from her wings cooled his skin. "I speak the truth, Riagan."

Growling like a famished bear, he stalked around the stones. "What can I do? I am a human now. A mortal. I cannot cross to the druid realm as a human. I have to fulfill my terms of punishment, or I will face certain death if I try to cross the portal."

"Riagan, something you seek is near."

He leaned against one of the trees and its bark gave way to cradle his long body. "How much time do I have?"

"We believe Master has given permission to take the Cauldron at the full moon in three days' time."

"At the equinox?"

"Aye. When light equals dark, when day and night are balanced, the moon looms full."

He couldn't cross the portal as a human. He would die and then be of no use to anyone. His punishment stated that he must find love, true love, for the banishment to be lifted.

Impossible.

Any ability to feel love had been squashed when he was a babe. A Guardian of the Cauldron could feel nothing but the need to protect the Cauldron—everything else was considered a distraction. Then why had the Arch Druid given him such a punishment?

He repeated the faery's words in his mind. *Something I seek is near.* Stepping away from the tree, he walked toward the faery. "The raven-haired woman?"

"Mayhaps."

"What is your name, wee one?"

The faery flew into the circle of stones and hovered, wings flapping rainbow colors. "Oephille."

She disappeared.

Riagan turned to the trees. "What say you, tree-friends? What is it Oephille speaks of?"

A low murmur carried through the wind and the trees swayed. *We know not, druid. Seek you more than just the portal?*

Riagan thought about the dark-haired woman, whose lips resembled plump cherries kissed by the morning dew.

A rustling of leaves jerked him from his thoughts.

Standing in front of him was the woman. "Who *are* you?"

5

Wren collapsed against a nearby tree, unable to hold her weight a minute longer.

He was standing there before her. In the flesh.

Or was he?

A white hazy light swirled around him, making him appear almost translucent. His skin was pale, flawless, and as smooth as marble. His green eyes flared, almost iridescent and almost glowing.

The chatter in her head erupted into a hundred small voices, and she wanted to scream. Digging her nails into the bark of the tree, she started to cry. She couldn't tell if he was real.

Was this what her mom felt when she had her first breakdown? Unable to tell what was real and what wasn't?

Wren's worst nightmare was unfolding, page by page, right in front of her, like a novel whose pages were being flipped by a ghost.

"Why are you crying?" the deep voice asked.

She jerked her chin up. *He spoke, didn't he? He just spoke. Does that mean he's real?*

Hope bloomed in her like a flower. If he spoke, that meant there was a man standing before her. But she had heard him speak before when he'd called her *lass*. And her mother often thought her delusions were real, going so far as to try and bring Wren into the conversations.

The fleeting hope became muted by a pain that bubbled up from deep within her heart, from the darkest place where she laid all her fears. It spilled out into her bloodstream, pouring through her body. The fact that she wasn't sure said it all. How many times had she heard voices, turned, and no one was there? Countless, that was how many.

"Lass, you are well?"

The voice was pleasing to her ears, deeper and more masculine than Brian's. She found her own voice and demanded, "Did you kill Jerry?"

She planted her hands on her hips, but when his eyes dropped from her face to her breasts, she lowered her hands back to her sides and tugged at her shirt.

Typical. Even an imaginary man can't find my eyes.

"Seriously?" she demanded when he wouldn't lift his gaze.

He cleared his throat as his eyes swept upward. "Um, sorry. You have breasts so beautiful they mimic the full moon in a cloudless sky." He cupped his hands, curling his fingers to the shape of a woman's breasts. In this case, *her* breasts.

"*What?*" If her subconscious was creating this man, she needed to work on her creativity.

As he gawked, eyes returning south of her chin, she took the moment to return the insulting scrutiny. His hair, longer than any man's she'd ever seen, fell halfway down his back. It was nearly white with a golden tinge. His skin was so pale; had blood ever pumped through his body? He blinked. His chest, broad and thick and muscular, rose then fell with each breath.

He must be real.

Determined to set her fears aside, she marched forward like a soldier. If there was nothing there but air when she tried to touch him, she'd drive to the hospital herself.

He didn't move as she approached, his arms still outstretched, his hands still cupped. She stopped a foot away. His face was exactly as she remembered, as if his image imbedded itself in her mind and she knew no matter how long she lived, she would never forget this face. Delusion or reality.

But that didn't answer the question of whether he was real or not.

So she pinched him.

Hard.

"Ouch. Wench, why did you do that?"

She yanked up the sleeve to find a red welt forming. "Don't call me that. It's rude."

"Rude? It's rude of me to call you a wench but you can pinch me?"

"I wanted to make sure you're real."

He reached out two fingers like he was going to pinch her back. "Are *you* real?"

She smacked his hand.

He watched her, his expression amused.

She watched him, suspicious.

He was real. Thank God, he was real.

She had felt his smooth skin between her fingers, felt the flesh give under the hard pinch, seen him yank his arm away and rub where a welt appeared. A giggle of glee erupted from her mouth, but she stopped it when it sounded more hysterical than relieved.

Then she started to cry again.

Strong arms wrapped around her and she was pulled against a chest that was as solid as a brick wall. She gulped air to protest, but somehow, the scent of him or her desperate need to be comforted overtook her senses. Despite herself, she relaxed, melting into his body, breathing in his musky scent.

Yes, he was real. His embrace was tight but not suffocating, calming her, protecting her. In fact, she had never felt so safe in all her life.

Clinging to his shirt, she could feel hard-as-steel muscle. The top of her head didn't come to his chin, but instead of feeling overwhelmed by his size, she felt soothed.

"I'm sorry to cry on you, but it's been such a bad day."

"Aye."

Bewildered by the onslaught of sensations, she turned from him. They were deep within the forest, and she was unsure from which direction she'd come. The last memory she had was staring at this man near the trailer. He ran. She followed but lost him. She had walked and walked, in circles it seemed at times, until she finally saw him standing in this clearing. How far she hiked, she had no idea.

The canopy of trees was so intertwined, they blocked the sunlight, like thick linen lying across the sky. But yet there was light coming from somewhere.

"Why are you out here?" she demanded.

He didn't respond.

She scanned the trees, the moss, the small ladybug resting on a nearby rock. Thinking was becoming difficult. Maybe she should go to the hospital for a CT scan. Maybe the blow had injured her brain after all.

"Did you kill Jerry?"

"He was going to kill you."

"Going to kill me?" Wren shuddered at his words as only someone can when discussing their own death.

"Aye."

"So you…"

"So, I rescued you."

"Rescued me."

"Aye."

"You killed him?" A canon of grief lodged in her throat.

He nodded.

"How?"

"I yanked him away from you and threw him to the concrete."

"But…but what happened to you? Where did you go when everyone showed up?" Her voice took on a whining curve, as if the higher pitch and the longer words would lure the truth out of him.

This was all becoming too much, and as hard as she tried to keep her gaze averted, it wasn't working in her favor. The faintest hint of his nipples pushed against the small shirt and held her gaze, even though she wanted to look anywhere but there.

"I have no answer for you, lass."

"No answer as to why you ran? They think I killed Jerry." She focused on the ground, desperate for her mind to clear like cleaned glass. Right now it was foggy like a thick mist. "Will you come with me to town, to the police station? You can put this whole thing to rest and just tell them what happened."

"I cannot go with you to the police station."

"Why not?"

His simple shrug was loaded with complex answers he refused to say.

"You have to. You were protecting me. You won't get into trouble, if that's what you're worried about." *What is wrong with this man?*

To help clear away a new covering of fog from her mind, she planted her gaze on his feet. Those body parts seemed to be the only place she could look and still keep focused.

"Why are you watching my feet? They are big, no?"

"What?" So much for ridding herself of confusion.

"You stare at my feet. Do you like men's feet?"

"Do I like men's feet? Did you just ask me that?"

"You are staring at my feet."

"That's because I don't want to stare at your face. Or your chest." She regretted the confession as soon as it left her mouth.

"Aye. I can understand that." He seemed unaffected, like trying not to stare at him was the most natural thing in the world.

More natural, even, than taking a drink of water when thirsty. Was he that arrogant, or just plain stupid?

"You have to come with me," she said, insisting. "If you don't, I'll tell the police where to find you, and they'll arrest you."

He shot forward like a bullet, only stopping his trajectory when he was looming over her. She stumbled backward, but he caught her by the arms, clamping his large hands around her until she cried out. Ignoring her protest, he lifted her off the ground, drawing her body to his, pinning her arms between them. Her breasts flattened against the hard wall of his chest.

He held her body, and her mind, immobile for what seemed like hours. The light behind him glowed like a night-light, and a low murmur droned throughout the forest. A hypnotic vibration seeped through her skin into her veins and coursed through her body.

Somewhere deep inside her subconscious, she knew something strange was happening but could not bring that unease forth for questioning. Instead, her heart rate calmed into still waters, and her shaking subsided. She could float away like a robin's feather on a soft spring breeze.

Then, less than a moment's breadth later, she fainted.

RIAGAN SCOOPED HER up into the cradle of his arms. She was as light as a child but with the body of a woman, a curvaceous, voluptuous woman. An hourglass-shaped woman. A woman with heavy breasts, thin waist, and hips that rounded into perfect mounds of wantonness.

Oh, but to touch those breasts. That waist. Those hips.

His hands throbbed just thinking about how parts of her body would mold to his palms. He knew not that humans were made this way.

In her faint she looked peaceful, no longer sad or scared or shaken. Thick black lashes cast dark shadows on her pale cheeks. There was no worried furrow between her brows now. Her lips, as red as the roses growing on this realm, were relaxed and plush.

He had never seen a beauty such as she.

He lowered his gaze from the smoothness of her face, down her neck, toward the swell of her chest. Just a small peek wouldn't hurt, he thought to himself, as he clasped the fabric between his fingers, ready to pull.

"Who are you?" Her voice was soft. Sweet. She knew not what his fingers were about to do.

He eased his hand back and cleared his throat.

"Who are you?" she asked again.

What do I say to this? I am an immortal druid, Protector of the Murias Cauldron?

Nay, that wouldn't work. "You can call me Ray."

"Ray?" This name was foreign to his ears as she released it from her lips.

She tried to pull away, and he lowered her gently to the ground. She crossed to the other side of the clearing, as if she didn't trust him, or herself when near him. Her arms folded into themselves, covering her chest.

"Yes, Ray is my name. And what should I call you?"

"Wren O'Hara."

"Wren? Your name is Wren?"

"Like the bird."

"Aye. Like the bird." He was silent a moment before asking, "This is a strange name, no?"

A small smile lit her face. "I guess you have to know my mother to understand why she would give me such a name."

The small smile slid away. "I want answers—that's why I'm here, not to talk about my name. What happened to you? You were there, then you were gone." He imagined her tapping her foot against the earth but she did no such thing.

He shrugged. There was no answer to give.

"Jerry was sick." Her voice crashed over the three simple words, and the portal's light flared. "He didn't deserve to die." The blue of her eyes, the same color as the Aegean, swam behind brimming tears.

For a moment, he was at a loss. He understood this wee lass not at all. The smelly man would have killed her yet she defended him?

"I meant no harm, only to protect."

She dropped her hands to her sides, and he saw them tremble.

Despite her sorrow, he wanted to touch this woman. Not only to comfort her, but to satisfy himself.

His manhood pulsed painfully as the familiar swell of his insatiable needs soared through him.

He closed the distance between them in three long strides, until he towered over her.

He stared into her face, forcing her to either stare at his chest, in the too-tight shirt, or lift her chin. The scent of her skin, evoking memories of night-blooming jasmine, filled his nostrils.

She tilted her head back, and her lips parted with the motion. Her pink tongue licked the left corner of her upper lip. He didn't think she was trying to set fire to his desire but that was exactly what she was doing.

He imagined her teeth gently, or not, nipping sensitive points on his body: his neck, his abdomen, his—

He pinched his thigh to keep control.

To touch that sweet mouth and lick the gentle corners would be a true fantasy. To have her use that mouth on him would be a sliver of heaven. Such red lips, full and inviting. He could imagine them swollen from too much kissing and knew they would plump up even more.

When one of those thick tears spilled over her lid and traveled down her smooth cheek, he crash-landed back in the moment. "How did you come to be in this forest now?"

"I, um, my mom. She lives near here."

"In the home nearby?"

Suspicion made her eyes narrow. "Yesss, why? Have you been there?"

He hoped she didn't recognize the clothes he had stolen. "No. I just passed it on my way out here."

"Why *are* you out here? The police are suspicious. They think I killed Jerry."

"What did you tell them?"

"That I didn't see anyone else, that I must've gotten knocked out."

She rubbed her arms, and he could see the skin prickled there. The forest was cold for one not used to the portal.

"What could I tell them?" she continued. "That just as Jerry was about to kick me, some phantom angel showed up and saved me, then disappeared?"

"Druid."

"What?"

"Nothing."

"Look. They think two things, neither of which is good: that I did that to Jerry or that there is a maniacal killer on the loose."

What was there to say?

Her lips trembled and she licked the corner once more. What was she trying to do? Kill him? But her thin shoulders shook and she started to cry again. Her slender hands tried to mask her tears, but they did not succeed.

Why is she crying? Such a strange human woman. Were all mortals so emotional, so erratic?

Certainly she must want to return to his arms. He gathered her back to him, thankful that the effects of the portal numbed her human mind enough that she did not question him too forcefully.

Thank the gods for small blessings and simple pleasures.

6

"The plans are in place, Master. Though there are still eleven druids to protect the Cauldron, their power is broken without Riagan. He will likely never return to the Brotherhood, and certainly not by the full moon. There should be little trouble." Gwyon forced his words to sound monotone, betraying none of the excitement simmering in his blood. He was so close to having everything he had wanted and yearned for all his life.

He had been denied the benefits of the Cauldron years ago, had been denied his chance to be a man, a warrior. And now he would finally have access to its healing powers, and he would be able to watch his immortal brothers' demise at the same time. He could ask for no more.

Gwyon became lost in thought, but when he raised his head and saw Master's hard eyes staring at him, he straightened his back and composed his expression.

"What are these plans?" Master demanded.

Gwyon swallowed, spreading his weight between his two feet. "When the full moon looms at the equinox and the veil between the worlds is thin, the power around the Cauldron will be at its most vulnerable. With Riagan gone, the band of marauders I have summoned will follow me into the cave, where we will strike to take the

Cauldron. Another band will engage the Brotherhood in battle. No one will be guarding the Cauldron with Riagan gone."

"And once I have the artifact?"

Gwyon tried not to cower under the Master's dark glare. Without Gwyon, the Master could not gain access to the Cauldron, but he found no strength in that knowledge. The Master terrified him.

"Once you have the Cauldron, you will drink from its waters. You will be immortal."

The Master's pale lips curved into a gruesome smile, or smirk, Gwyon knew not which.

"And these marauders?"

"These marauders owe you their allegiance. They would be banished to the realm of spirit were it not for your intervention. They owe you their freedom and will not disappoint."

"It is good."

Master regarded the night's sky, and Gwyon fell into his own thoughts. All he'd ever wanted in all his years was to belong to the Brotherhood, to train as a warrior druid. But that had been denied him, hadn't it? He'd been born a bastard child, with a deformity no less, and forced to work by the women's sides instead of taking his rightful place as a member of the Brotherhood of the Sacred Grove.

He could have been a valuable asset but had been refused further drink from the Cauldron's healing waters because, centuries ago, his father had already given two boys to the Brotherhood and no more were needed. He'd only been allowed to drink from it to become immortal, thus trapping him in this faulty body for eternity.

One immortal who has the old blood must remain outside the Brotherhood, his father had said.

I can't be in this broken body for eternity. Allow me to drink again and heal my body, Gwyon had pleaded. *Please.*

It is not to be. His father had turned his back on him.

Now he would exact his revenge on his brothers since his father now dwelled in the land of the fae. Even if they begged for mercy, he would not relent. The sons would pay the price of the father's decision. They deserved humiliation. They deserved death. And it would all happen at his hands.

The thoughts were so captivating, Gwyon didn't notice Master watching him. Then Master struck like an asp, and with a vise-like grip, circled Gwyon's neck, nearly snapping it like a fallen twig. One small flinch and he would suffer a broken neck. Against his screaming instincts, he held still.

"Gwyon."

He could not respond as his throat was all but closed off.

"The Cauldron and its power will be *mine*." Master spoke the words faintly, quietly, but each syllable dripped with venom and the promise of certain death.

Master released him. Gwyon collapsed onto the ground, gasping for breath as Master walked away.

WREN'S EYELIDS BATTED and fluttered. The fog swirling in her head began to clear as her sight struggled to return. Her mind hovered at the edge of awareness yet she couldn't quite remember what had just happened.

Her body moved with a gentle sway, but she knew she wasn't walking. Her cheek rested against something solid and warm, something that smelled nice, something musky and masculine.

The rhythm of movement kept lulling her back to sleep when she wanted to wake up. But when she felt a hand moving up her leg to cup her bottom, her eyes flew open and she realized she was in Ray's arms being carried like a baby.

"Stop that," she managed through a dry and dusty throat.

He moved his hand back to the underside of her knee, chuckled, and continued walking. Her mind numbed again, and she fell back into a semi-sleep.

His hot breath flowed over her face, and her skin absorbed his exhale like air. His heart thumped against her cheek. Strong, fast. She fit against him perfectly, her head imprinted between the muscles of his chest. If he never let go of her, never dropped her back into a world of insanity and disappointment, she'd be a content and happy woman.

Yes, this was what a man should be. Someone to kiss, and she could see his lips in her mind's eye, pale, pink, and full. They would be soft, she knew, yet they would hint at the man behind them—virile and powerful and masculine. Someone to hold her, his arms strong, supportive, protective. Someone to…

With a man like this, she would not be a virgin much longer. She heard herself giggle at the thought and the strong arms tugged her closer. She snuggled in closer still.

Deep within her stomach, a tingling ignited, something that Brian had never created.

Please never let me wake up. If I'm dreaming, let me drift along this beautiful current.

Then he stopped walking, and the hypnotic rhythm halted with an unexpected and unwelcome jolt. Her eyes flew open to find him staring down at her.

Could he read her thoughts? See what her dream had been? Sense her attraction?

She didn't move for several moments, then finally said, "You can put me down."

He did.

She scanned her surroundings. They were outside the trailer.

"LASS, YOU ARE very flushed." Riagan studied her through squinted eyes. "You are also very beautiful."

"You mean my chest?" Her words held a hint of sarcasm mixed with resignation.

"Your what? Do you mean your breasts?" He focused on the objects in question. "They are beautiful in their own right, for certain. Very full. They would feel nice in my hands." He cupped his hands as he had done before, flipping his gaze between them and her breasts.

The impatience on her face made him stop short in his perusal. "I meant your face. You have a beautiful face. And your cheeks. They are very red." He reached out to touch her forehead, but she swatted him away and reached for his arm, fingers ready.

"Pray, don't pinch me again." He stepped back. "I won't try to touch you. I but wanted to see if you have the fever."

She snarled at him, and he burst out laughing. *What a funny human she is.*

"You are so strange." Her arms slammed together over her chest. "I can't figure you out."

"You think I'm strange?"

"Yes."

"Well, we've proven I'm real." He rubbed the purple bruise on his arm. "Why do you question it so? I know not why you'd call me strange."

"Why do I question it? Because you've disappeared on me twice. Then the way you talk is funny. What is wrong with you?"

"What is wrong with me?"

"Yes. What is wrong with you? You better start talking or I'm going to call the police. I can't believe I haven't done that already." She rubbed her temple. "But I have a bit of headache. I'm not thinking clearly."

"Are you not well?"

"I'm fine. Just answer the questions." She pulled something black out of her pocket.

"What is that?" He leaned forward, muscles priming to snatch the object out of her hand.

"This is a phone. How do you not know what it is?" Her eyes were slits of suspicion. "*This* is how I'm going to contact the police."

"No." He reached for it.

She yanked her hand away and held the other one in front of her, fending him off. Little use that would do. He could crush that so-called phone in his bare hands if he wanted to. But then he caught a hint of her fear. "I apologize. I have many things on my mind."

"So do I, like being a murder suspect. Care to help me with that one?"

Quietly, gently, resolutely, he said, "Nay."

"Nay? What are you, a horse? Who talks like that?"

"Who talks like what? And what does a horse have to do with murder? We will say the horse killed the man?"

"What on earth are you talking about?"

"What role does Earth play here? The otherworlds are important. Not Earth."

"Excuse me?"

This was not going well. "Nothing."

"Nothing?"

"Nothing."

"What are you talking about?"

"Nothing."

She inhaled, pinched the bridge of her nose between her fingers, and exhaled.

He sensed her anger, her concern, and her anxiety.

"Why are you anxious?"

"Why am I anxious? What kind of question is that?"

He shrugged. *Can't but get into this verbal battle again. Confusing, she is.*

"Look. I'm still not completely convinced you're not a delusion."

A delusion? No, he was startlingly, shockingly real despite his desire not to be.

"Nay, I am no delusion. I am very much real."

"But why do you talk like that? Where are you from?"

So many words. "I'm, well, not from around here."

"No kidding." She shot him a look, a flare in her temper he didn't understand.

"If you try to pinch me again, lass, I will pull you over my knee and spank your little bottom until it's as red as your cheeks."

She gasped, held her breath hostage, then burst out laughing.

As the sound filled his ears, he willed his senses to decipher this enigma of a woman, to understand her, to decide if she could be the answer to his predicament. Perhaps she could fall in love with him. Well, of course she could. Women falling in love with him had never been an issue. And he could pretend the love for her, could he not? He'd never come close to experiencing the emotion that turned men weak and women senseless. But it couldn't be that difficult to pretend, could it?

Then he would be forgiven and readmitted to the Brotherhood. He could return to his post as a Protector of the Cauldron.

If the Cauldron were under such grave risk, though, why didn't the Arch Druid himself lift the terms of the punishment and allow him to resume his post? No one could get past the born Protectors of the artifact when they were all together. Why wasn't he contacted by the Arch Druid instead of being forced to fulfill the terms of his banishment in just three days?

Wren stared at him with arms crossed over her bosom—and what a beautiful bosom it was—tapping her foot against the ground, a trickle of her laughter still hanging in the air.

But an impatient lass! Know she not that there was much to think about?

"Look," she said. "I don't want to get into another argument with you—I can't understand what you say half the time anyway. But I need your help. You need to come to the police station with me and tell them what happened. I can't lose my job, especially over something I didn't do. Either come to the station or I'll have them come and find you."

Her face settled into a determined mask, and he knew she would not waver on this.

"Okay."

"Okay?"

"Aye."

She pinched the bridge of her nose again. This woman had suffered much, it seemed. She was insecure, yet compassionate and afraid. What was she afraid of?

"Okay. I will come. But not right now."

Three days until the full moon. Three days until the Cauldron faced its greatest threat since the days it had traveled across the high seas from the distant isles to settle in the druid realm. He had to get home. This woman must be the answer. He just had to decide how to capture her love.

7

Late that evening, Wren had an appointment with her therapist and friend, Michelle Jones. She had started seeing her when the stress of caring for her mother became too great. She tried not to admit her own mental stability seemed nearly as tenuous at the moment.

She knew who killed Jerry, but something she could not explain prevented her from going to the police. Anyway, he'd told her he would go after he sorted through *some personal things*. She hadn't questioned him further and accepted that it would be good enough for now.

Plus, she had other things on her mind. The voices had gotten louder throughout the day. She could almost make out distinguishable words, as opposed to the chatter she'd been hearing for the past year. At least if she could hear individual words, then she would have a better understanding of how to handle it.

Like if the voices in her head were telling her the moon was made of cheese, she could say that to her therapist. Or if the voices were telling her the blond angel was really a reincarnated Greek god, she could work with that as well.

Wren paced in the soft light of the office on Main Street. "I can feel it, Michelle. I am getting sick like my mother." Her voice echoed off the dark wooden walls, the same cheap, imitation wood that many offices in this town used. Ironic considering so many trees grew around there. She didn't mind, though. She never liked to see trees cut down. Seemed cruel somehow.

"Wren, there is no reason why we should expect you to suffer the same mental illness as your mother. Sometimes illness runs in the family; sometimes it does not. We can't jump to conclusions at this point."

"But I hear things. All the time." She fluttered her fingers around in the air. "It's like little tinkling bells, and then *voices*. I can hear their words, though I can't understand what they say."

Michelle sat across from her in an office chair with legs crossed and a yellow notepad on her lap. She flipped the cap of her pen with a manicured thumbnail as she watched Wren pace.

"Michelle, we've known each other a long time. And you know what I've gone through with Mom. For a while, these voices stopped. But now they're back. I can't sleep at night. I can't concentrate at work. I feel like someone is watching me. I can't relax, I'm so paranoid." She stopped and whirled around. The other woman's expression did not change. "It's not *normal*."

She stared into the corner of the room, her voice plummeting into desperation. "After this thing at work, with Jerry's death…"

Michelle watched her, expressionless.

"I might be seeing things, too." Should she mention Ray?

"Didn't you black out during the attack? You said you hit your head. Suffering from visual disturbances is not uncommon with a head injury. Have you spoken with your doctor?"

Wren bit back words of impatience and said instead, "I don't know. I just don't know."

She had to sort through her thoughts before expressing them to her therapist. There was no doubt she trusted Michelle—they'd been friends since grade school, and Michelle had never shown judgment of Wren or her mother. But when she held the power to have Wren committed to a mental institution, there was only so much honest dialogue she could suffer.

"Wren, you've had a very rough day."

"Sure have."

"I think it's normal that you're feeling stressed. Who wouldn't be? Your client attacked you, and then he died. You blacked out, not knowing how he died or by whose hand."

Wren was comforted by the fact that someone did not think she killed Jerry. "This is confidential, right? I mean, we've been friends a long time and you've been my therapist for nearly a year now."

Michelle's brows raised into her smooth forehead. "Is there something you're not telling me?"

Wren went to the window. The white plastic blinds were pulled shut but she pushed her fingers between two of the slats and looked out. It was dark with few streetlamps lit. A group of teenagers walked by, eating from fast-food bags. She could hear their laughter and pined for their carefree night.

"When Mom had her first breakdown, I was four. Do you remember me telling you this?"

"You've told me bits and pieces."

"I remember it like it was yesterday. She had been in the kitchen making lunch when she dropped the knife and walked out the front door."

Her mother's long wavy hair had flowed down her back, her thin, worn summer dress falling off one shoulder. Her skin was covered in freckles and her eyes were a soft green, agitated and unfocused.

"I followed her but she didn't go far, just into the nearby forest. That wasn't unusual, though. She was always walking in the woods. On this day, she took off all her clothes. There she stood. Naked. Completely naked. She lay down in the grass and started talking to herself. I mean, she carried on an entire conversation, totally oblivious to me standing there watching.

"But it was different, somehow. I mean, her conversation. I really thought she was talking to someone who was there, only that I couldn't see myself. She didn't seem crazy." Wren turned from the window. "Does this make sense? I know I was only four, but I remember it so clearly. I mean, is it possible to see things that are *real* but that other people do not?" She held her breath. She'd done it. She'd confessed her secret. What would Michelle do with it?

"Wren, you were only four. Everything is magical to a child. Through the years, you've turned that into some sort of reality. It's a defense mechanism. You could not bear to think that your mother was losing her mind so you've concocted this scenario to help explain her bizarre and delusional behavior."

Wren turned back to the window. "Oh."

Well, keeping the incident with Ray a secret was the way to go, at least until he'd gone to the police. He could prove he was real. Her reputation around town would not give her enough credibility. Guilty by association—Mom was insane, the daughter not too far behind.

Plus, she didn't want to explain why she hadn't mentioned him earlier. The police and Dr. Martin would be very upset by this omission.

"Wren?"

She fell into a nearby chair and twirled a short curl around her finger.

Michelle uncrossed and recrossed her legs. "I think you should continue on the sleeping pills. If you can start sleeping at night, and maybe coax Erika into helping more, you'll feel better. It might just be that simple."

"Erika won't help. My sister has always felt Mom is my responsibility."

A timer beeped in the corner. "Our time is up. Let's meet again next week. In the meantime, stay on the meds, unless your headaches get worse. In that case, call your doctor. We'll need to sort that out."

Wren nodded.

The older woman put her hands on Wren's shoulders, her friend now and not her therapist. "We'll work through this. Just because your mother suffers from mental illness does not mean you will too. I think you're suffering from exhaustion, plain and simple."

Wren bit her lip so hard she tasted a little drop of blood on her tongue. "But I hear things and now I'm seeing things."

"Same time next week. But call beforehand if you need anything."

Wren stepped into the dreary waiting room, just missing hitting her head on the dangling lightbulb, and went outside.

A blast of cold stung her face making her eyes water. Winter would come early this year. As if on cue, scattered, sparse snowflakes fell out of the sky. It was still autumn and early for snow but in this mountainous area, weather was unpredictable.

The night was alive with shadows as she walked down the block toward her office. No one would be there now, which was just fine. She wanted to return to the parking lot and didn't want to question why.

All but three of the lights along the street were burned out. A lone car sat in a far corner of the parking lot but she didn't recognize it as a colleague's. Behind every corner loomed darkness that promised hidden threats. Her heavy coat provided little of the warmth her body craved, and she shook inside it.

In front of her was the spot where she had first seen Jerry. Images of that morning flipped through her mind like a projector. He called her a bitch. She tried to soothe him. He yelled at her. She tried to soothe him. He hit her. He shook her. He was going to kill her.

And Ray appeared.

Just then, the same man stepped out from a shaded corner as if summoned by her mind.

She didn't know why she still questioned his existence. It was clear he was real, though even after the pinch, she hadn't really truly believed it in her heart. But if Michelle were there, she would see Wren talking to a man.

Well, not just *any* man. She would see Wren talking to a six-and-a-half-foot tall man with rippling muscles and long, nearly white hair. She would see a sharp jawline, sculpted cheekbones, and full brows. She would see a man unlike any who'd ever ventured into this small country town.

She wasn't seeing things yet. Hearing things was another story she'd tackle another day. Little giggles erupted from her throat, only slightly unhinged.

"Why are you laughing?"

Her face hardened. She was supposed to be losing her patience with him, wasn't she? "Are you following me? Or are you here to go to the police station? It's a little late in the day." She made a show of checking her watch.

His boots thudded against the concrete as he prowled forward. A lone owl hooted in the distance and a fox answered the call.

"What are you doing here?" he asked in place of an answer.

"What are *you* doing here?"

He smirked, or maybe she imagined it.

"I was just out for a stroll."

"Hmm." She wasn't sure where to focus her eyes. His chest would do just nicely but she didn't want to give him that satisfaction. His face? That was as tempting, and as rewarding, so she looked up.

"You are very tall."

"Aye."

"Aye?"

"Mmm."

She rolled her eyes and looked around. There was no evidence that anything amiss had occurred, but memories of Jerry were everywhere. In the air, in the dismal light, in the gray concrete with a spot that was darker than the surrounding area.

She had seen Jerry's spirit leave his body, and that wasn't the first time she'd seen something like that. When her grandmother died after being hit by a drunk driver, Wren, safe and uninjured in a car seat in the back, had seen her spirit lift from her body and float away.

She had never questioned it.

But she'd also never told anyone other than her mother who'd muttered something about Wren's destiny.

And now, replaying in her mind's eye, she once again saw Jerry's dead body, the blood bubbling out of his head and his still chest.

"Lass?"

She didn't answer.

"Wren?" He encircled her into those arms again as if sensing she needed his strength.

Just like Jerry's gaseous life leaving his body, the tension and stress left hers. She melted into Ray's hard chest and found the spot where her head fit and let his energy course through her trembling body.

His scent filled her nostrils and she could almost taste him, virile and alive. Something about this man was almost medicinal, able to relax her mind and body when not even the doctor's potent pills could. With each breath, the tension simmered away until finally another feeling took its place—a tingling sensation that started low in her abdomen.

She clenched her muscles against it, but it would not abate. It grew stronger and worked its way, like a slow-burning flame, through her body, riding along her bloodstream until it filled her. Heart thumping, her fingers clutched the soft cotton shirt covering his chest.

His hand rubbed the small of her back and each circular motion ignited a new flame. She melted into him like wax until he supported her weight. A whimper formed low in her throat as her hands unclasped the shirt and started traveling up his chest, toward his shoulders, prepared to wrap around his strong neck. Just as she was about to lift her head to look at this magnificent man, to study him, to absorb him, she heard her name.

"Wren?"

She froze like ice. "Brian?"

BRIAN? WHO IS *this* Brian *she speaks to?* Riagan turned as a short, thin man strode toward them. A look of confusion, and a trace of anger, shaped his uninteresting face.

"Wren?" he said again.

Riagan instantly disliked this man.

"What's going on? Who is this guy? Are you okay?"

Talk not so much, mortal man. Then he remembered he was mortal, too. *Damn.*

Wren put distance between herself and Riagan.

"Hi, Brian. Everything is fine. I, um, I'd like you to meet..." She turned, flashing surprise to see Riagan had followed her movement and now stood directly behind her like a looming wall.

"Brian, this is Ray."

Brian studied Wren then Riagan with a thin, down-turned mouth.

"Ray, this is Brian."

"Her boyfriend," he said with a sneer.

Color burst over Wren's cheeks like an explosion.

"You are a *boy*friend?" Riagan laughed robustly. He certainly was a boy compared to him, but then most men couldn't compete with his masculinity.

Wren shot him a look of warning.

Guess she wants me not to tease her boy*friend.*

Brian sidled to Wren's side and put his hand on her shoulder.

Riagan placed his hand on her other shoulder, and her pretty black curls bounced as her head spun between the two.

She edged away from both men and stood opposite, her little hands on her round hips.

"Brian, I had an appointment with Michelle, then came down here. I was going to call you later."

"What is this guy doing here, then?" He turned to Riagan. "You're not from around here, are you? You look like a woman with that long hair."

Brian's own hair was brown and cut close to his scalp. His nondescript eyes and pubescent stubble on his chin made Riagan laugh again.

"This man is your betrothed?" he stammered between breaths. "You jest, do you not?"

"No, he's not my betrothed."

"Pre-betrothed," Brian interjected. "Besides, who talks like that? Where are you from, outer space?"

"Close," he muttered. "If he is not your betrothed, then who is he?"

"I told you, man, I'm her boyfriend. We'll be *betrothed* soon enough." He looked so satisfied with himself that anger flooded through Riagan.

"Not if I have anything to do with it."

Wren whipped around, eyes flashing red. "What did you say?"

Riagan shuffled back. Big mistake. Big mistake. "Nothing. I need to go."

"Yeah, that's right. You do need to go," Brian chimed in, putting his arm around her back.

The boyfriend must use the woman's strength. No wonder he is called such.

Riagan's stomach lurched at the sight of them standing there together. The man called Brian looked weak, plain, boring, an imitation of manhood next to a Venus. But it was that man's hand, not his, on Wren's back.

He clenched his fists, then shoved them deep into the pockets of his borrowed jeans.

He turned and forced himself to walk at a steady gait until he rounded the corner. Then he took off in a sprint, building speed until he was running, nearly flying, and he wouldn't stop until he was back in the safety of the forest.

THE DRONE OF the trees signaled Riagan's arrival at the portal, but he did not notice.

Brian. What kind of name was that? And boyfriend. Bah.

His stomach clenched. Brian was not the man for her. He was not a man at all.

A boyfriend. How ridiculous.

A man is supposed to marry a woman, not be her friend. He was not much of a man, though, to be certain.

He stood outside the clearing when he next looked up.

The portal's light glowed incandescent. Existing. Beginning, and ending nowhere.

His senses suddenly burst with a thousand pricks as his hearing honed in to his surroundings. Nothing was present other than the massive trees, a small gray rabbit with a white tail, and a black crow peering at him through its beady eyes. He did not sense trouble, but something was amiss.

A light burst from within the portal.

"Brother," said a most recognizable voice.

In the clearing appeared his twin, Drake, standing upon the soft moss within a translucent mist.

"Drake." Riagan started forward.

"Do not come close to the portal. You will die if you enter. You are mortal, or did you forget?"

He halted his steps. "Drake, my brother, it is good to see you."

For the first time in all his existence, Riagan wanted to cry. He mourned losing the closeness with his brother as much as he mourned losing his immortality. When he'd been taken from his mother, Drake had been taken as well. They were all each other had.

When it came to love, that for his brother was all he'd ever truly experienced; though he knew that wasn't the love Caswallen wanted.

"Riagan, there is much trouble in the worlds."

"What speak you of, Brother? Pray, tell me. Has the Cauldron now been taken? It is not yet the equinox. Tell me, Brother."

Drake stood as still as the trees. He was Riagan's twin in all respects: long blond hair tied back with a leather strip; piercing green eyes; a long muscular physique typical of their warrior bloodline. He wore the woolen garments of Protectors of the Cauldron, as green as the lush fields of their realm, hooded and long flowing. Riagan's spirit lurched at the sight.

The rough material of his blue jeans suddenly hurt his skin, the coarseness as uncomfortable as it was unfamiliar. He tugged at the cotton shirt that stretched tight across his torso. Oxygen was thin in the air.

"Brother, the one they call Master will attempt to take the Cauldron again."

Riagan slammed his fist into his thigh. "Who is this enigma of a thief? And who is working with him? If he even thinks he can gain access to the Cauldron, then there must be a traitor within our midst."

"I know not. We of the Brotherhood have increased our vigilance. But…"

"But what?"

"We have not our full powers without you. Our barriers, though they are great, can be breached. We do not know the depth of the magic of this Master, nor with whom he works. We fear he is an enemy unlike any we have ever seen."

Riagan yearned for his old post with a ferocity that rivaled an earthquake.

"I must return." He met Drake's eye. "I must return to my post. I need to protect the Cauldron. We need to strengthen the lines. Can the Arch Druid make no exception to my punishment?"

"Nay."

His senses alight, Riagan stepped toward the portal, stopping just outside the stones. "What is it you're not telling me?"

"There is more than just trouble with the Cauldron."

"Pray to the gods, tell me." Riagan's entire body shook with the warrior's need to protect, and to kill. The ancient blood simmering in his body, the same blood as that of his forebears, ignited with this threat.

He could trace this bloodline all the way to Semias, the original druid who inhabited the worlds far before the Christ came. It had been under Semias that the Cauldron was forged from the iron of the Ural Mountains, woven with the enchantment and magic of the druids to preserve the secrets of the worlds. And it was because of this Cauldron and through Semias's bloodline that the Brotherhood of the Sacred Grove was born.

There were other revered artifacts across the worlds, but the Cauldron was the only one under the druids' protection, and the only one that granted immortality.

Riagan would rather die than see this treasure stolen.

"What is it?" he demanded.

"Caswallen has disappeared."

"What say you?"

"We know not if he is a prisoner of the Master's, if he has traveled to the fae realm for help, or if he is in meditation within the Earth. He has not been seen since the night of your banishment."

The ground beneath Riagan's feet trembled with the sudden and ferocious movement of the trees. Their limbs batted against each other and their trunks swayed with unrest.

He understood completely.

"Even if he wanted to, he could not grant you forgiveness."

Riagan growled deep within his throat like a grizzly. This was an impossible situation. Was the one indiscretion that night, nay, all those nights he'd stolen from his post to be with a lover, worth this grave risk?

"What must I do, Brother? What *can* I do?"

"You must fulfill the terms of your punishment, Riagan. Then you can cross the portal, even without the Arch Druid present, as long as you and she confess your love in front of the Council. Without the Arch Druid to allay your punishment, that is the only choice." His expression was pleading…earnest…desperate. "Fulfill the terms of the punishment, Riagan. They plan to take the Cauldron at the full moon."

The brothers locked gazes.

"You must not fail."

With that, Drake disappeared in a haze. The light flared, and Riagan shielded his eyes. The trees stopped moving as suddenly as they had started.

Three days. I can't but find love in three days' time. Insane expectations. Insane punishment.

Riagan paced the periphery of the clearing, and the portal's light shimmered.

He needed to make things right. He'd just have to figure out a way to get around the love part.

Lost in these heavy thoughts, he created a simple bed with leaves and moss, but sleep did not come the entire night. Instead, his mind whirled around images of the Cauldron, his Brotherhood, and a certain raven-haired beauty who may just hold the key to everything.

8

Wren waited for the sleep medication to dissolve into her bloodstream. She was lying in bed with Duke snoring by her side, warm and solid and comforting.

The hound had appeared on her porch years ago, half-starved for food and love. He had not been well cared for, so when she opened the door to the trailer and he walked inside, her house became his home. He'd been by her side since.

He had also been one of the brightest points in her life over the past years, and the white strands that now peppered his hair reminded her his time was drawing to a close. The vet estimated him to be about twelve, and though healthy, she knew he didn't have too many years left. Her heart wept each time she thought about life without him.

She rested her hand on his head as, at long last, the sleeping pill's numbing haze filled her.

She started to dream.

She was walking along a narrow, shallow river. Smooth gray rocks disrupted the gentle flow, causing the water, clear with just the faintest hint of blue, to bubble. There was no sun, and the sky was covered with wisps of feathery-white clouds.

Light came from somewhere, yet nowhere. Far from the river's edge, the trees grew statuesque, nearly touching trunk to trunk. They provided a barrier between the gentle peacefulness of the riverbank, reflective of the ethereal light, and the stark eeriness of the forest.

She dipped her bare toes into the water. It was cool but not cold, like a drink of chilled water with no ice.

A rustling sound leaked from the trees, and she turned. Ray appeared at the edge of the forest, handsome, beautiful, god-like. As dark as the trees and the forest were, Ray was as bright, robed in a pristine white cloak trimmed in golden thread. He watched her, and then slowly, as if floating on the shimmering air, moved forward.

She did not step to meet him. The water's soft caresses kept her rooted to the ground, strong within its tickling flow.

As he neared, she closed her eyes and inhaled, waiting for what she knew was to come, what she invited, what she yearned for.

A kiss.

He stood over her, and she tilted her head back. The curls of her raven hair fell from her face.

When he bent down, he filled her vision. She could see no light, no trees, and no clouds.

She could only see him.

She closed her eyes as he bent his head. Anticipation of the sweetness to come coursed through her and her knees threatened to buckle.

At first, he held his lips just out of reach, letting his breath seep out and wash over her face. She inhaled deeply and held still. Waiting. Desiring. Yearning.

In graceful motion, he took her face into his large palms, cupping her head. He stared into her eyes, searing himself into her mind. She could not read the emotion behind his gaze but welcomed the support of his hands as the muscles in her body slowly gave way.

He urged her mouth up to meet his and when his lips brushed against hers, her knees finally buckled, and he caught her by the arms. He tugged her to him, lifting her until he held her weight.

His lips crushed hers. She could do nothing but let herself be kissed. His lips were soft yet eager, and she opened under his probing.

When his moist tongue slipped into her mouth, she whimpered, crying under the sensation.

He licked the inside of her mouth, tasting every part of her. The hold on her arms should have hurt but didn't. She felt nothing but the hot trail of his tongue and the roaring fire low in her abdomen.

Her fingers grasped the fabric of the cloak. His kiss forced her head back but she felt nothing other than the flames tearing through her body like wildfire, cell by cell, igniting sensations that brought her to life...

Duke twitched beside her, yanking her out of the dream.

She fought against returning to the cold, lonely present, preferring the luscious expanse of her dream to harsh reality. But Duke stood at the edge of the bed now, alert and rigid, his floppy ears pinned back. She sat up, pushed her hair out of her face, and listened.

When Duke jumped off the bed and sprinted into the living room, she made her way out of bed with a resigned sigh.

Maybe I'll slip back into that dream tonight. Maybe. Hopefully. Please, God, let me return to that dream.

A noise captured her attention. Had someone knocked? Called? She glanced at the nightstand clock.

It was eight o'clock in the morning.

She yawned, stunned she'd slept all night. She shuffled her feet and rubbed her eyes. That dream had seemed so *real*.

She tripped through the bedroom door to the shrill sound of her phone ringing.

So that's what woke Duke.

Another ring reverberated through the small trailer and she hurried forward, not wanting to wake her mother, and stubbed her toe hard against the counter.

"Ouch."

Duke whined beside her. "It's okay, boy." She picked up the phone. "Hello?" She hobbled to the sink and poured a glass of water, taking a quick drink to moisten her dry throat, an unfortunate effect of the sleep meds.

"Wren, this is Dr. Martin. I've spoken with the supervisory committee at the agency, and we've agreed that you need to take an extended leave of absence. Unpaid, of course."

"What?"

"You are instructed to take an indefinite leave of absence until this situation with Jerry Smith has been resolved. You will not be paid for that time off."

"Not paid?" When had her dream become a nightmare?

"No, not paid. It is customary in situations like these."

"Situations like these? Has there ever been a situation like this before?"

"I will be in contact." He hung up the phone.

Unpaid leave? Was she being fired? They couldn't do that. What happened to innocent until proven guilty?

Wren stood at the kitchen window and pulled back the curtains, then yanked open the blind. The sun had not yet risen above the treetops and the yard was cast in creeping, sinister shadow.

The pile of unpaid bills was an inch thick, lying by the checkbook, envelopes and stamps on the counter. Each envelope held a bill, and they weren't just her bills. She also took care of her mother's finances, and the disability checks and insurance never covered enough, leaving her footing the extra cost. She barely made ends meet. Some months she didn't.

She had to find Ray today and take him to the station. There was more at stake here than just a job.

What am I going to do?

She worried at her bottom lip as she sorted the mail, putting the envelopes into piles by their payment due date.

The doorbell rang.

The clock read ten minutes after eight. She peered through the side window but saw no one at the front door. The trill of a single bell, a different sound now, clanged in her ear, and she shook her head to halt its progression into two, three, four bells, followed by two, three, four voices. Maybe it wasn't the doorbell she'd heard.

She turned on the television to listen to the news. At least it would help drown out the sounds in her head.

RIAGAN BOLTED FROM Wren's door.
Damn that wee faery for ringing the bell.
He doubled over with his hands on his knees, gulping air into his mortal lungs.
Damn this mortal body.
As he cursed the physical inferiority of his body, the tiny yellow faery floated nearby. He sensed her presence like he could sense a coming thunderstorm and wondered at her audacity in sticking around. Didn't she know how angry she'd made him?

It was early morning, and he hadn't slept. He had to move faster—the encounter with his brother proved that. The Cauldron would be at grave risk in just two days, when the full moon loomed high in the west. He studied the sky, where the white shadow of the moon lingered, not yet ready to give up its place to the sun. This was not where his interest lay, though. No, his attention, unbeknownst to the wee one, was zeroed in on the faery.

His hand shot out, and with swiftness defying his mortal body, he grabbed Oephille, closing his fingers around her diminutive body. Wings no larger than a butterfly's beat against his skin as he carried her behind the first wall of trees. Her words of anger reached his ears, but he did not care.

Out of sight of the home, he opened his hand. The faery burst forth, the sunshine orbs flashing. She opened and closed her small mouth several times as she fluttered in front of his face, hands on her tiny hips.

"Riagan Tenman, what do you think you're doing? You need her. You don't have time to play games."

"Play games? You don't even know what you're talking about, wee lass. Fly on home, faery, and leave these matters to me."

"Nay, I'll not leave them to you. You need my help."

"What I need is to return to my realm, to the Cauldron."

"Yes, but you can't until you have fulfilled the terms of your banishment, Riagan."

"Don't talk to me like I'm a wee child."

"Then don't act like a wee child."

He swiped at her bright form, but she kept well out of his reach this time.

"Have you heard word about the Cauldron? Is it safe still?"

"I know not, Riagan. But I do know that the fae king, Eogabail, summoned me to you. You must return to the Cauldron. Drake and the others cannot do this without you—the strength of the twelve is needed. The only way for you to cross the portal is to fulfill the terms of your banishment. She is your only hope."

Riagan paced as he considered her words. Oephille was right, but he had to be careful. Wren was mortal and his tale was not likely one easy to accept.

"Have you word from Caswallen?"

"Nay. Why ask you?"

Something more than the Cauldron was amiss. "Oephille, is there any other way?"

"She is your only hope. The Cauldron is in danger. We need your power."

He whipped around, and the faery flew several feet back. "What am I supposed to say? 'Hey, lady. I just killed a man for you. Now you need to confront the druid Council, profess your undying love for me, only to see me disappear from you forever. By the way, I'm centuries old and until I became a human man, I was immortal.' Insane."

"You have no other choice. You have but days. If the one known as Master obtains the Cauldron, the worlds as we know them will be forever altered. She is our only hope and you do not have time for a prolonged courtship. She must fall in love with you. You can make her do that. You know you can."

Riagan stroked his cheek and spoke more to himself than the wee faery. "If I bed this lass, that should be enough."

A light slap stung his cheek, then Oephille danced out of his reach, her rigid body showing that she meant for the slap to be anything but light.

He rubbed the skin with his fingers. "Why'd you do that?" He was tiring of this small creature.

"Bedding her is not the same as love."

Wasn't it a start? And what a fine start it would be.

"Riagan, she must love you." She fluttered closer. "And *you* must love *her*."

Love. What did that even mean? She needed to love him. That should not be difficult. Could he love her? Did he even know what love was? She was a mortal, an Earth human. Their emotions, especially those of the female species, were intertwined with the physical act of sex. Were they not?

It was obvious she enjoyed his closeness. In fact, he would bet his life on the fact that she was already attracted to him, lusting after him even. He was on the way to fulfilling the terms of his banishment and he'd yet to even kiss her. If he bedded her, wouldn't that be enough?

He'd deal with his own emotions when the time came.

What he needed right now was to get to the forest. The trees would help with this decision. Maybe they would know more about the safety of the treasure. Faeries were not always reliable. And why didn't she have word of Caswallen? The bond between the fae king and the Arch Druid was unbreakable, surpassing time and space. At least that was the way it was supposed to be.

The fae king should know where Caswallen was, or at least that he had gone missing.

"I will think about this. She does not love me, though she may well soon enough. But what about the *boy*friend?" He choked on the word. "And with only two days left, I know not if I can do this."

Riagan turned away under his show of weakness. No woman had ever been able to refuse him. Even the faery would know this. Then what troubled him?

"She may simply believe your story, Riagan. She has the old blood. Why do you think her voice was able to lure you from the forest and your deep slumber? Even without the benefit of your druid senses. There is a connection there you should not dismiss."

She has the old blood?

Was there hope at this dark hour? If the blood of the old coursed through Wren's body, she may very well believe his tale and vow to help him.

He returned to the front door, pausing before knocking. Oephille huddled by the tree line, but her voice was clear. "You must find love, Riagan. Love. Not just sex."

"Bah." He rang the bell again as Oephille disappeared into the trees.

9

The trailer had one small bathroom and Wren stood in it, staring at herself in the mirror. The reflection showed unruly hair falling over her face, eyes bright and as round as saucers. Dark shadows hovered underneath. She must be losing weight because today her cheeks seemed more pronounced, causing her lips to appear even plumper. The bruise deepened into a purplish-blue but wasn't as bad as she'd expected, and the cut was healing well.

Physically, she showed no sign of insanity though she wasn't sure what insanity should look like. With her clients, and her mother, their eyes would lose focus as they listened to the sounds in their heads. She tried to imitate her mother's lax stare, but it didn't fit her somehow.

A little solace, she supposed.

She ran the pad of her thumb over her bottom lip. The kids at school had always teased her about the size of her lips. How could famous actresses earn millions with their beautiful lips but hers welcomed ridicule?

The doorbell rang, making her jump. This time she knew it was *that* bell and not a clanging in her head. And instinct told her who it was. Ray. One final glance in the mirror showed new bursts of pink on her cheeks.

Walking down the hall on unsteady legs, she took a deep breath before she yanked open the door, prepared to confront him, to demand he visit the police or she would call them herself. But at the sight of him, memories of her dream came flooding back on a current of lust, replacing all thoughts of death and insanity. Images of his soft lips nearly made her cry out, her face scalding with embarrassment.

The man who had filled her dream now filled the doorway. A new T-shirt stretched over his torso. Where did this man buy his clothing? His powerful shoulders spread between the wooden beams of the door. And his arms, pushing out of the narrow openings of the shirt, rippled down to hands that were large and strong. He had on another pair of jeans and the same boots that she'd stared at too much already.

What was she going to say to him? She couldn't remember.

She glanced into his eyes. Was he smirking?

Oh, right.

"You," she said, stepping outside.

His eyes widened. "Me?"

"Yes, you. You. I'm on the verge of being fired from my job. Because of you."

"That is a popular word, no?"

"What?"

"Nothing. What say you of this problem with your job?"

"Why do you talk so funny?"

"I know not, lass." He slapped the back of his neck as if stung by a bee, and a flash of yellow disappeared off into the early morning light.

"What was that?" She'd seen the canary light, but the insect didn't look like a bee. *Please don't let the hallucinations start now.* "What was that?" she asked again.

Something about this man turned her mind into a nonfunctioning entity. She couldn't think. She couldn't speak. She could only stare at him, gawking like a schoolgirl. Well, it was no wonder with that shirt he wore. So she looked down from his pecs to his stomach, rippling with muscles, even through the fabric.

Brian was always talking about wanting washboard abs but Brian didn't have them. Something told her she would find them under Ray's shirt, but that wasn't the point.

The point was, a narrow waist dipped below those pecs, followed by hips housed in a pair of low-hung jeans that fit just right. From there fell long, long legs, unmistakably Herculean. The thick denim could not hide the muscular limbs pushing against the fabric.

Curls fell around her face as she once again lowered her gaze to the dirty boots. Just then Duke sauntered over to Ray and sniffed his pants with gusto, loud snorts reverberating through the air.

"He is an ugly dog."

Her gaze shot up. "He is not. How dare you."

Ray tilted his head. "You like this mutt, do you?"

"If you call him a mutt again, you're going to find this metal door with an imprint of your face in it." She rubbed Duke's head. "He's a bloodhound. And he's perfect."

The dog stared at Ray with nothing short of distaste and disdain. She mimicked that look, making sure he got the message.

But then, struck by the sudden memory of her predicament, she said, "You have to speak to the police."

As if on cue, a low grumble of thunder began, its rough greeting shaking the small trailer.

"It is going to storm." His head tilted skyward.

"It always storms here."

"Why?"

"Because of the mountains."

"Because of the portal."

"Port?"

"Portal."

"Port? We're in the mountains. There is no port here."

"Right."

"Where did you think we were?"

Ray slapped at his neck again. Wren closed her eyes and started counting under her breath, the bridge of her nose pinched between her fingers in the one way that helped her refocus after these confusing verbal exchanges.

"I know not, lass. You befuddle my thoughts, talking so fast. And you ask too many questions."

"Me?" she demanded. "You think *I* talk funny? Seriously, have you heard yourself lately? You sound like you're straight out of a Highland romance novel."

"Romance? You like romance?" His lips parted, not a lot, just a little, as if a promise was hidden behind them.

She blushed *again*.

"Is this Brian good at romance?" His voice dropped several octaves, rich and oozing like dark chocolate.

Oh my.

She pulled her bottom lip between her teeth and chewed on the side, trying to force herself to think. It was like he was able to crawl into her mind and use his powerful hands to muddle all her thoughts until they turned into a jumbled mess.

He rubbed his chin, covered in days' worth of blond scruff. She didn't know if he was trying to look sexy or was distracted by their conversation, but she found herself struggling to breathe.

She willed her chest to stop heaving, her heart to stop pounding, her mind to refocus. Just then Duke barked. It was the jolt her mind needed, and she was able to pull her thoughts back together.

"I just got a call from my supervisor, and he told me that I'm on unpaid leave. All because they think I killed Jerry. I'm sure the police will be out here to question me again, and I don't know how much more I can take. Since you are the one who was there that day, you need to talk to them. I can't lose my income."

The sky turned black and rain burst from the clouds like buckets of water, just missing them under the awning of the porch. Jagged thrashes of lightning lit the sky.

"It is early for a storm, no?" Ray surveyed the area, his brows furrowed.

The storm had come on as suddenly and as unexpectedly as the new flash of yellow by his neck.

"What *is* that?" she asked. "Are you getting bitten? I know we have a lot of bugs in the mountains, but really."

With the next flash of lightning, thunder shook the small house and a loud crack shot through the wind. A giant tree to the left split down the side, the upper half of it falling to the ground with a boom.

Wren jumped into his arms.

HER HAIR SMELLED like strawberries mixed with lavender, maybe a little vanilla, maybe a little jasmine, but organic, sweet. He inhaled, ignoring Duke's guttural growl. Through her thin back, he could feel her heart beat and knew that his own thudded against her temple. He clutched her to him. Her breasts, barely covered in a form-fitting shirt, flattened against his chest.

"Ray," she muttered, her face hidden in his chest. She tried to pull away. Duke growled again, this time louder, more threatening, but Riagan held her fast. He did not want to hold her against her will but found he could not let go. Her small body writhed against him, but it only made him use his strength more.

Maybe it was the thrashing wind, his punishment, or the troubles that lay ahead, but suddenly, anger pulsed through him like the force of the storm. It was all becoming too much. He could not do what was asked of him. Riagan would never be able to fulfill this punishment. He was incapable of love. Period.

And here was this woman, pushing against his chest as he held her short, voluptuous body. He should have ignored her voice and left her to her fate. Damn this woman.

He gave her no freedom to move. The scent of fear filled the air. He wanted to take her now, against her will if it came to that. Maybe Oephille was wrong. Maybe taking her body would fulfill the terms of his banishment. It was a so-called act of love, was it not?

Then he could give in to the intense throbbing of his body and satiate this deep burning need, so intense he'd never felt it for any other woman. By pushing her against the wall, he could then free his arms to rip her clothing off and see her womanly curves displayed before him. Then he would touch her, and he knew she would enjoy it. All women he'd had did. Then he could take her and she would be his.

"Ray," she said, gasping.

Then the mutt bit him on the leg, not enough to break the skin, but enough to give fair warning. The animal yanked at his jeans and wouldn't release them until he released Wren. He dropped his arms and stared at her as he struggled to gather his wits. The thunder rumbled again, shaking the windows.

"That damned dog bit me."

"Serves you right. You don't hold a woman against her will." She backed through the door and into the home, stopping several feet from him. Her arms were held out, staying his approach, warning and weary.

She looked afraid. But he also saw something else. Was it desire? Energy emanated off her skin in tidal waves, but he could not read its origins.

The dog growled another warning and sat on his haunches between them.

"I apologize." He felt like someone had pulled his plug and drained him of every ounce of energy. The task at hand was too great. He could not do this.

"Ray, are you okay?" The look of fear was replaced by concern. Such a gentle soul, she was. How could she care about his welfare? Did she not know how close he came to taking her against her will?

She backed farther away until she stood by a red sofa, Duke by her side. The dog nearly came up to her hip bone. His long floppy ears and droopy eyes seemed strange on a dog that would obviously attack him if he touched Wren again. If the situation were not so dire, he would have laughed at the mutt's attempt to intimidate him.

"I know not, lass. I know not." His sigh was heavy, weighted.

"Tell me, and maybe I can help. You look so sad."

Her expression was pleading, as if the pain his soul felt reverberated through the air and filled her as well. There was something about this woman he couldn't quite understand. She cared for those who sought to harm her.

But *could* she help him? *Would* she? Was this even worth the try?

Riagan glanced at the surrounding trees as feelings he didn't understand funneled through him. The trees thrashed, mirroring the unrest he felt in his soul.

Wren did not seem bothered by the early morning storm—perhaps it was normal for this area—but he didn't like it. The worlds were unsettled by more than just lightning and thunder.

With a deep breath and gathered resolve, he stepped inside. "We need to talk."

She motioned to a chair on the opposite side of the room. "Sit down. Would you like some tea?"

"No and no. I prefer to stand to tell this tale." He was surprised to find his hands shaking. "Actually, yes. I would like some tea, and I will help."

She shrugged and turned toward the kitchen. Welcoming the distraction, he gaped at the way her hips, in a perfect-fitting pair of black cotton pants, swayed as she moved. Her bottom, tight and high, clenched and unclenched with the motion of her legs. *Ooh, delicious.*

He fell into step behind her, drawn forward by the motion of those hips. They were like magnets and his body jerked, alive and ready. He felt no need to control her now, to take her against her will. However powerful that urge had been, it subsided, leaving in its wake the absolute knowledge that a woman like this should be savored for a long, long time.

Just as he reached out to clasp those hips in his hands, the sudden memory that she didn't live alone deflated him like a balloon. "Where is your mother? You live with her, do you not?"

"She's in bed. She wakes up at ten o'clock."

"At exactly ten o'clock?"

"Yes, nearly every morning. She, well, she suffers from a mental illness. Two actually."

"Two mental illnesses?" He tried not to gawk at her bouncing breasts as she retrieved loose tea from a little ceramic jar.

"Yes. Two. Schizophrenia and obsessive compulsive disorder. She hears voices no one else hears, which is the schizophrenia, and the obsessive-compulsive disorder makes her rigid, uncompromising. Getting up at exactly ten every morning is one symptom of that."

"Oh. Wouldn't the storm wake her? Or the mutt's barking—" He broke off the question at the dirty look she shot him.

"Doubt it."

Their kitchen was tiny, white, and clean, almost sterile. There were a handful of cabinets, a small stovetop, and a refrigerator that had rust along the hinges. There was a counter where several envelopes lay scattered though upon closer look, they appeared to be organized into stacks.

"What are these?" he asked, stalling.

As Wren poured water into a kettle, she glanced over her shoulder. "Bills."

"Bills? What are bills?"

"Bills. You know, you have to pay for things, like electricity." Her blue eyes nearly disappeared behind narrowed lids. "Gas, phone, water."

"But there are many more bills here than what you list."

"You're very perceptive." Sarcasm molded her words like little clay swords. "My mother is ill so I also take care of her bills, along with my own."

"And this is why you are so concerned about your job."

"Yes. I can't lose my income. Or my health insurance."

"Health insurance?"

"Yes. Health insurance. For when I have my own breakdown." Her voice became so soft he could barely hear her. Something told him she spoke to herself and not for his benefit. "When I have my own breakdown," she said again. "If I haven't already."

The whistle on the tea kettle blew and she lifted the cobalt blue pot off the burner. Steam rose from the cup as she poured the water.

So she thinks she will have the same problems as her mother.

Riagan felt a strange flicker of an unknown emotion deep within his gut, almost an urge to take care of this wee lass, to help her bear the burden of life, to protect her from life's traumas.

He also had an urge to lick the nipples that pierced the T-shirt. He'd not seen a pair of breasts such as those even on an immortal. They must be caressed. They simply must. So he sat on his hands on the stool near the counter and bit the inside of his cheek. Hard.

Wren handed him a mug. "It's hot."

Before she finished speaking, he was gulping the scalding liquid, ignoring the burn of his tongue and throat.

Newly mortal, he had not had an appetite and had not realized his thirst until the tea washed down his throat.

"Are you hungry?" She watched him set the empty mug on the counter.

"Famished."

"I don't have a lot here, but I'll make you something."

"I thank you." His stomach growled as if on cue.

While she set about preparing him what looked like a meat sandwich, he gathered all the willpower he possessed.

"We need to talk," he stated flatly.

"Um, okay."

Duke lumbered over to stand by her leg, as if knowing what was to come and knowing he needed to offer his support. The mutt was perceptive, if not more than a little annoying.

But just then Riagan heard a shuffling noise and he glanced at the clock. Ten o'clock on the dot. Gods, Wren's mother was precise. And she was also as naked as the day she was born. Wren rushed forward faster than he'd ever seen a human move.

"Mama!"

10

Wren grabbed her mother's thin shoulders, turned her around, and marched her back into the bedroom. "Mama, we have a guest. You have to put clothes on."

"Okay, sweetheart."

"I'll make you some tea. Once you get dressed, come on out."

Wren shut the door to her mother's bedroom and walked down the hall, hoping her cheeks were not as red as they felt. She wasn't embarrassed of her mother, more like chagrined *for* her mother. She should have been more careful in making sure her mother was properly dressed when the clock hit nine fifty-nine.

Riagan was studying pictures on the wall and seemed oblivious to what had happened, though she knew he'd seen her mother. Naked.

"Who is this?" He pointed to a photo Wren had taken at Erika's twenty-fifth birthday dinner. Her sister was glaring into the camera over a plate piled high with food. Wren had gone out of her way to make her sister's favorite meal of fried chicken and dumplings, but Erika said they'd have been better off going to the local Chinese restaurant in town, which was known for its horrible dishes as well as food poisoning. Wren shut away the memory of her hurt feelings and forced her attention back to the picture, which Ray was tapping with a long finger.

"That's Erika. My older sister."

"Hmm. You look nothing alike."

"No, we don't. She used to tease me and tell me that I was Snow White and that Mom wasn't really my mom."

"She is mean, this sister?"

"All siblings can be mean, right?"

"Nay. My brother and I never fought. He is my twin. His name is Drake."

"Are you identical?"

Two six-foot-five-inch blond-haired men with rippling muscles and enticing accents. Oh, what a dream.

"Aye, nearly," he answered.

Lost in her little sidebar of a daydream, she forgot what question he was answering. "Nearly what?" Damn his good looks for making it impossible to think.

"We are identical. No one would be able to tell us apart by looking at us, but we know the difference."

"Oh, Lord," she muttered, and he laughed. "And is he your only sibling?"

Ray stiffened, his jaw clenched.

"What is it? What's wrong?"

He turned from the pictures and headed toward the door. "I have a half brother."

She was about to ask more questions when her mother returned. This time she wore a calf-length dress with a plastic strand of green ivy vine woven through her hair. Lipstick was smeared across her mouth.

"Mama," she began when her mother shuffled into the kitchen. "This is Ray. Ray, this is my mother, Annie O'Hara."

Her mom's mouth fell open. She gawked at him before demanding enthusiastically, "The time has come, then?"

Ray glanced from her mother to Wren.

Wren shrugged. "The time has come for what?"

"Destiny. The time has come to fulfill your destiny." Her eyes danced with a delight Wren did not understand or share.

"Wren, Mom. Call me Wren. And it's time to fulfill my destiny? What are you talking about?"

"Who is he?" Annie's mood changed like a sideswipe.

"Ray is a…friend. He's new to the area." She glanced at Ray, but he was staring at her mother, a morose and miserable expression on his handsome face.

"I'm going for a walk. I need to see if they're here." Her mother made for the door.

"Mama, you have to eat breakfast and take your medicine. Where is your pillbox? I couldn't find it this morning."

She didn't answer but instead demanded of Ray, "Did you know her name is Destiny?"

"Destiny? I did not."

"Call me Wren."

"Do you know why I named her Wren?"

Without waiting for an answer, she plunged on. "When I was a little girl, I used to catch wrens. I had a huge wooden cage built just for them. I could leave the door open, though. Even if they flew away, they always came back. The little people liked them too."

She cupped her hand imitating how she used to hold the birds. "They would fly right into my hand, eat from my palm, sit on my shoulder. At one point I had at least twenty that lived in my cage and hundreds that lived in the woods. I could go walking in the forest, and they would follow me."

The smile on her face was serene and peaceful, evidence of yet another mood change. Then she frowned. "They all flew away and I don't know what happened to them. They don't come around anymore. Maybe they're with the faeries." She turned to Wren. "But now I have my very own wren and she'll never leave me."

Annie walked toward Wren with her arms outstretched, like she was going to embrace her, then stopped mid-stride, turned to the living room, and fell into her chair. Wren tiptoed over and reached into the pocket of her mother's robe where she found the medicine box. The pills she'd watched her mom take before work yesterday were in there. She must have spit them out after Wren left. *Oh no.*

"What are those?" Ray asked.

Wren massaged her temples as the dull ache of a headache threatened to grow roots behind her eye. "Her medicine. Excuse me, but I need to call her doctor."

"Why?"

Wren ignored his question and headed back into the kitchen. Ray followed her, so close she could feel the vibrations off his skin. She had to stare at the phone a full minute before her mind could re-register what she needed to do. Call the doctor. Right.

Just then, Kelly showed up for her biweekly visit, letting herself into the home without knocking. Duke greeted her with a sloppy lick of her knee. She patted him on the head like he was an old friend, then pulled a bone out of her purse and gave it to him.

"Hi, Kelly," Wren greeted.

"Wren." Kelly gave her a quick hug then turned to stone when she saw Ray.

"Oh, I'm sorry. Ray, this is Kelly. Kelly, Ray."

Ray muffled a *hello*, but Kelly said nothing, gawking like she was seeing Fabio or some other male model in the flesh.

"Kelly?" Wren prompted.

"I'm sorry." Kelly shook her head more violently than was normal. She walked over to Ray and held out her hand. "Hi."

Ray smiled, and Kelly's knees buckled. She caught herself on the table with her other hand, then scurried into the kitchen. With hands on the counter, she leaned forward, gazing at him from afar.

Oh come on. He's not that good-looking. Well, maybe he is, but really? Despite herself, Wren cracked a smile.

"He should've come earlier," her mother muttered. "You can't wait till the equinox to get shit done."

"Did she miss another dose?" Kelly asked, unnecessarily.

"Yep. With what's been going on at work, I haven't been as diligent about checking her pillbox. She'd been doing so well."

"Need some soup," her mother quipped. "The faeries told me they'd bring me soup. The kind with the little berries from the forest. Now I don't have no soup."

Wren sighed and found Ray staring at her. "What?" she demanded, prepared to defend her mother against any ill speak.

"Your mother says interesting things, does she not?"

"Yes, she does. That's part of her illness."

Kelly studied the pillbox, counting under her breath. "I think she needs to go into the hospital, Wren, just to tweak her meds and get her stabilized. She shouldn't have deteriorated this much so fast. Maybe she needs a different dose." Kelly stopped talking to stare at Ray again who was simply too large a presence to be in the small kitchen.

Wren returned to her mother and gently shook her. "Mama, Kelly's here, and we think it would be a good idea for you to go to the hospital for a few days. Is that okay?"

"I'm tired, honey. I am."

Ray moved into the living room, casting uncertain glances at Kelly who was staring at him like he was something not quite human.

"Kelly, can you call the ambulance?" Wren tried to swallow the aggravation she was starting to feel.

"Yes." She tore her eyes from Ray long enough to get her cell phone. She dialed, then talked for a few moments before flipping the phone shut. "Done. They'll need you to sign the papers." Her gaze settled back on Ray.

"Okay." Wren's voice was louder than necessary. "Thanks for your help."

No one spoke for a long time while Wren packed her mother a bag and set it by the door. She turned to find Kelly slowly inching her way toward Ray like a cat on the prowl. He seemed oblivious, more fascinated by Annie than the nurse. The whole thing irritated her. "You can wait outside if you want."

With a brisk nod, Ray turned and slipped through the metal door, letting it slam shut behind him.

Kelly's shoulders slumped as she watched him descend off the porch and pass out of sight. The rain stopped and the thunder could be heard rolling off into the distance.

Once the ambulance arrived, Wren signed the paperwork after they loaded her mother inside. Before she could say good-bye, her mother fell asleep, snoring softly.

With Ray nowhere to be seen, Kelly seemed more her old self and gave Wren a big hug. "I'm so sorry to hear what happened at work. Let me know if you need anything."

"Thanks, Kelly. I appreciate that. And thanks for all your help with Mom."

After Kelly left, Wren went onto the small wooden porch and scanned the property. Clouds spread across the sky, gray and ominous, hanging low on the horizon, obscuring the peaks of the mountain range. Little sunlight passed through, and the air was cool. She shivered and was about to go inside for a sweater when Ray stepped out from behind an enormous tree that grew along the side of house.

He started across the yard, his gaze locked on hers. Something in him had changed since he was last in the trailer, and uncertainty erupted through her body.

She swallowed a flash of fear as his purposeful steps carried him forward, toward her. His hands were not clenched but his body was tight, like he was about to explode from some pent-up emotion. He didn't look angry but resolute, determined. And for whatever reason, she had the feeling that she was at the heart of this new, alarming focus. She felt like a helpless doe about to be devoured by a starved lion.

The grass crunching under his booted feet was the only sound. She wanted to rub her arms to warm her body but found she couldn't move. The expanse of Ray's chest broadened as he approached, making him seem bigger somehow, threatening. With each step, more and more of her breath left her body until she felt dizzy.

He stopped at the bottom stair, five steps away from her. Sweat broke out over her palms as he climbed, slowly and one by one. Not once had he averted his lock on her face. Would he catch her again if she fainted?

Heat emanated off his body and the air surrounding her rose in temperature until it was almost too hot. He was too close. With each of his breaths, electric shocks fired off him, pricking her own skin, turning her chilled and bumpy skin into a heated wet blanket.

She dug her nails into the rail and couldn't help but pant at his closeness. Breathing became difficult. Ray moved toward her, lifting his arms, prepared to do *something*. Would he pull her to him again?

Or would he hurt her, beat her, kill her? She really did not know this man very well.

But she found herself gently yet firmly gathered into his arms. Her head found the now familiar indentation and settled there like a magnet. His arms—long, powerful, intense—wrapped around her small frame and supported her weight, her fears, her uncertainties. And she realized this was just what she needed and wanted—to be held. To just be held.

THE LASS FELL into his arms with no hesitation, and it felt good to have her there. Always one who preferred the act of sex over anything else, Riagan was surprised to find that he could hold a woman close and not be fighting off the urge to take her.

The desire was there, to be certain—no man could be near a woman such as this and not think of taking her to his bed. But for right here, right now, he was content to hold the suffering lass. That may have been the strangest thing that had happened so far.

After several moments, when he was sure her strength had returned, he asked, "How fares your mother?"

With a sigh, she removed herself from his arms and stared at her fingernails. Would she cry if she tried to speak? He had little doubt she would. His arms were ready to pull her back against him at the first sign of her need.

Instead, she spoke. "Why were you in the forest that day?"

Shocked by her question, he realized there was a yearning in her, but he was uncertain what it was for. The first rays of the day's sun finally broke through the cloud cover and shone down upon the dead grass.

He placed his hands on her shoulders, forcing her to face him, to acknowledge him and his closeness. She tilted her head back and met his eyes. Her shoulders shook under his touch, and he realized she not only fought the emotions about her mother but fought the ones about him as well. She was falling for him but wanted it not.

He straightened, tall and erect, until he towered over her. He had little time left and there was certainly no time for romantic games. With a glimmer of hope, he forced himself to focus on his goal—to fulfill the terms of his punishment and return to the Brotherhood—and pushed aside any other feelings that threatened. The full moon would rise soon, and he had no time to waste.

He studied her expression, trying to gauge her willingness. If she could but fall in love with him, then he could cross the portal, save the Cauldron, and redeem himself for past mistakes. But of course she'd fall in love with him—that had never been a problem for him in the past. But could he get her to do so with so short of time left?

And what about her? Was she supposed to be the one to have her heart broken so he could regain immortality and his place in the Brotherhood?

He liked the idea not.

I do not want to hurt this lass. I have grown but a bit fond of her, I have.

He gazed toward the forest, where the portal's light shone like a dim glimmer of hope. With the full moon so close, the veil between the worlds was already thinning.

He squelched an emotion he chose not to recognize and coldness settled into his body, the coldness of the warrior druid he was. Resolve built in his body like the bricks of one of the empty buildings on her Main Street. Just the way he'd been taught.

Fluttering along the tree line danced the faery, her sunshine colors flashing against the brightening sky. She blended in with the rays, and he doubted Wren could see her. But Riagan could see the troublemaker well. She flitted around, and the trees swayed behind her, their limbs intertwined and waving like the ocean.

"It is time, Riagan." The faery's voice carried to him, and he understood.

He returned his gaze to Wren. He felt like he'd not had a woman in centuries. If he were to claim her body, her heart would be his. He didn't know how he knew this, but he did, as he knew having her would be the pinnacle of his existence.

He was suddenly overcome with an urgent yearning he could not control. The tenderness he'd shown moments ago, whilst cradling her in sorrow, was gone. In its place was the need to fulfill his destiny. And his destiny lay with the Cauldron.

He clamped down on her shoulders until she cried out, opening her cherry lips in protest. He silenced her words with the force of his own mouth, desperate and bold. Even the softest of heather that powdered the landscape of his homeland could not compare to the plush pillows of her mouth.

He yanked her to him and barely noticed she struggled. She was so much smaller, weaker than he that he didn't feel the push against his chest, the writhing of her petite frame. Her fight just served to create more delicious friction against his alert and responsive body.

He increased the pressure against her mouth and groaned as her soft lips gave under his aggressive probing. Licking the inside of her mouth was like tasting the sweetest, ripest fruit in all the land. Her tongue was warm, wet, and he could not temper the way he flicked it with his own.

Her mouth was unlike any taste he'd experienced upon his realm—sweet, light as honey and berries.

With one hand, he gripped her mass of curls and tugged her head back from his, breaking the kiss to taste the skin on her neck. He brought his lips to the pulsing spot right under her ear, and then he extended his tongue and tasted her. He licked her collarbone to the sharp line of her jaw. He readjusted her head how he willed and held her immobile with the strength of his other arm.

"Stop," she said whimpering.

He ignored the plea. The stress of the past days was cast aside, and an animal emerged in its place.

"Please," she whispered.

He nibbled along her neck and sucked the tip of her ear between his teeth. She tried to shake him off.

He growled low in his throat and shoved her against the side of the home. She beat against his chest with her small hands, and he snorted, grabbing her wrists and thrusting them over her head. He held them easily with one hand while the other ran down her raised arm and traveled to her breast. He'd wanted to touch her since the day in the parking lot and nearly came with the feel of her now.

His lips moved back to her mouth and this time she hesitated, her fight reduced. She wanted his kiss. She may try to fight it, but that simple parting of her moist lips told him she welcomed this invasion. He thrust his hips against her and she cried out, a mixture of fear and desire filling her voice.

"Lass," he said, breathing into her ear, "I want you."

She struggled anew. "Stop."

But he didn't.

"Stop. You're scaring me."

He heard her voice, but it sounded far away as he massaged her large breast in his hand and licked the corner of her mouth. The breast fit his hand perfectly, and he knew his hand would forever remain ready to cup it again. In fact, he never wanted to let her go. Her smell, taste, the feel of her was overwhelming, imprinting itself in his mind, against his skin, within his soul.

He'd never responded to a woman like this and it was too delicious to bear. He wanted her, to take her body fully and completely, to feel her underneath him as he brought pleasure to the both of them with his ancient rhythm.

But then a whip-like slap against his neck made him pull back. "Ouch."

She wiggled out of his arms and moved to the far banister. Her full breasts heaved with each breath, nipples taut against her shirt. He couldn't control his urge to wrap his big hands around their soft plumpness again, and he lunged forward, trapping her against the railing before she had time to move.

He cupped her breasts in his hands, ready to die with the feel of such perfection.

"Ouch." Something slapped his neck again, and he stumbled back. Was it that damned faery again? But the slap was too hard for such a wee creature. What was it then?

Lingering near the tree line was Oephille, anger causing her brightness to pulse. He raised his gaze to the tree by her side, whose longest sinewy limb hovered just over his head.

Damned trees. They were supposed to be friends.

But when he looked back at Wren, stunningly, hauntingly beautiful…achingly, tenderly vulnerable, he realized he'd been about to make an enormous mistake. Forcing the lass would not achieve anything other than brief respite for the desperate hunger in his loins, and desperate it was. No, it would take more than that.

But how his body ached. His manhood pushed painfully against his too-tight jeans. He throbbed all over, understanding well how the fire in his body could usurp the logic in his mind.

Wren's slender arms folded over her chest, and she stared at him, mouth open, eyes wide. She appeared more bewildered now than angry.

"I'm sorry, lass." And he meant it. Well, at least part of him did. What was going on here? This wee woman had a strange effect on him, and he liked it not. He didn't recognize himself, and that was dangerous. He had to stay focused on his goal.

She remained silent, watching him like a weary calf who had just survived an attack by a grizzly bear.

He raised his hands and shrugged his shoulders. She stood before him, captivating and ethereal, perfect and scared.

Her lips parted as though she were about to speak, but then she stepped forward, closing the space between them. She did not touch him but looked directly into his eyes. Hers were soft and pleading. For what?

Then he knew.

She panted and her mouth opened again. He bent his head toward hers. She did not pull away. He inhaled her scent and brought his lips to hers. Soft, so soft were her lips, like bundles of silk.

He moved his hands from her shoulders to the bare skin of her neck and cradled her face. He was gentle now, tender. The urgent needs of his body were now controlled under the desperate timing of his predicament. He had not frightened her earlier as he'd thought. No, he could tell she wanted him to kiss her, to hold her. So he pulled her closer, then closer still. He needed her to love him and love him true. And from her reaction to this kiss, she was already halfway there.

She lifted her arms and placed her hands on the outside of his arms. He flexed his muscles and heard the thread of his shirt give. She squeezed his arms and made the softest moan, deep in her throat.

It took all the power of his ancient resolve not to carry her inside and to the bed. He wanted to mate with this woman so badly he could taste the salty pleasure of sex like he could taste her fruity sweetness.

But he had her where he needed her.

Falling for him.

11

Wren broke away from the kiss and turned toward the forest. It was dark, cast in shadow, the trees looming like long, cylindrical giants.

"Where did you come from?" She heard strain and uncertainty in her voice. "I don't understand what is going on here. Who are you?"

Somehow this man had entered her life, saved her life, and now had altered her life. Not only did she not know who he was, but she had no idea who she was anymore.

She was content with Brian, if not happy. He was safe, secure, and would make a good husband. He would care for her when her own mental break came, if it hadn't already. But here she was, kissing this man who had killed her client, gotten her suspended from her job, and nearly forced her against her will. She didn't recognize herself.

When he didn't respond, she wrapped her arms around her stomach. "I think you should leave."

"Wren?"

"What?"

"We need to talk."

"Are you actually going to give me the answers I want? Come with me to the police station?" Somehow, she knew that was not what he had in mind.

"About something else."

"What then?"

Just as his lips parted to speak, a minivan lurched up the driveway, interrupting the moment. Something told her she should be glad for the distraction, even though it was her sister. As she slammed on the brakes, her five children piled out of the car and ran toward the house.

"Auntie Wren," the children, in various stages of filth, screamed. She glanced at Ray. His mouth hung open as he stared at the onslaught of children.

Wren welcomed each dirty child into her arms. "Hey, guys."

Erika, overweight and unwashed, lumbered behind the kids. "Who are you?" she demanded as she reached the porch, picking her teeth with a chipped pink fingernail.

"I am Ray."

"Ray?" Her beady eyes flipped to Wren. "What happened to Brian?" She sneered at his name—she had never liked Brian. In fact, Erika had never liked anyone.

"Nothing happened to Brian. He's working."

With a huff, Erika pushed into the trailer. Wren followed, with Ray close behind. The kids ran into the kitchen, yanking cookies and prepackaged cakes out of one of the top cabinets. Within minutes, they settled down in front of the television and began shoving food into their mouths, crumbs flying.

"Did Mom go to the hospital again or something?" Oreo crumbs, nestled in the corners of Erika's mouth, spewed forth as she spoke.

"Yes. Kelly called an ambulance a couple of hours ago. She stopped taking her meds."

"Humph." Erika shoved another cookie in her mouth, chugged a soda, then burped loudly.

Wren took a deep breath and listened for Ray's comment, but he said nothing. He stood behind her left shoulder, very close, but not touching. She couldn't help but wonder what he was thinking. First her mother and now her sister. Brian accepted these women in her life with no comment. But she really knew nothing of Ray. What would he think?

Her heart tugged as she looked at her nieces and nephews. Then she glanced at Erika, who was cleaning her ear with a bobby pin. She had never been close to her sister, and it wasn't because they were only a year apart in age. Erika had never liked her and never tried to hide that fact. She had teased Wren relentlessly as a child, mocking her looks by calling her Snow White with a hateful sneer while rallying the kids on the playground to do the same. No one treated her like the princess the name symbolized, for sure.

Ray laid a hand on her shoulder and the weight of it sent an intoxicating mix of calmness and miniature shocks through her body. She closed her eyes, letting the sensation overcome her. As her head lolled back, a soft moan escaped her lips. Her body leaned toward his, drawn by his heat. She settled her head against his chest and forgot everything bad in her life.

"Let's go." She was suddenly eager for space and slid outside.

She walked down the porch steps, the memory of the kiss threatening to make her stop, pull this enigma of a man toward her, and make him kiss her again. She continued well into the yard, desperate for privacy from prying eyes.

Something in her was changing. It was like Ray had entered her body, taken her nerves, and rearranged them to make a completely different person. She was calmer, that was certain. But she also felt alive in a way she never had before. Each living cell of her skin pulsed with a new energy, and she saw the world through a different lens than ever before. She didn't know if it was for better or worse.

She'd been frightened when he held her and wouldn't let her go. The kiss had been too harsh, too demanding. But when he'd pulled away, disappointment washed over her in waves, and she'd returned to him for more.

Kissing Brian never felt like that. They'd shared their first kiss when they were sixteen, and little had changed since that first uncomfortable, sloppy meeting of their lips.

In high school, he'd tried to coax her into sleeping with him, but she'd held back. When she left for college, she had boyfriends but never had sex with any of them. She was just never interested enough to risk so much.

Then, as an adult, she returned to this area, and to Brian. She still wasn't interested in sex, and his born-again Christian sensibility wasn't either.

She'd gotten off the hook.

But now, well. Being kissed by Ray had pierced her body with a million sugar-coated, sweet-scented arrows. For the first time ever in her life, she wanted more.

How much more?

Everything, a voice whispered in her head.

Ray placed a hand on the small of her back and steered her toward the truck, out of view of the trailer's windows. She went willingly.

What am I doing? What about Brian?

But Brian was forgotten as Ray stopped at the driver's side door and pushed her against the cool metal. Her heart felt like it was about to burst open like a lit package of Fourth of July fireworks.

He put his hands on either side of her shoulders and leaned down. She could have ducked underneath his arms to escape, but she didn't want to. No, she wanted to be kissed again.

He leaned in and inhaled her scent—she'd never experienced anything so sexy—and her knees gave out. Catching her by the arms, his hands clamped above her elbows. He pulled her forward, crushing her against his solid chest. Never had she felt like such a woman, and her body lit like a torch soaked in gasoline.

Tingling sensations shot through her and she suppressed a giggle of glee, lest he think she was laughing at him. She would do nothing to cause him to stop this intense exploration of her mouth.

He prodded her lips apart with a hot, moist tongue, and she obeyed his unspoken request. Using his body as a weight to hold her in place, she could barely breathe, barely wanted to breathe. He was large, so much bigger than she, and she felt, for the first time ever, what it was to be out of her mind with passion.

She arched her back, knowing her breasts would mold to his hardened chest. A puff of air shot out of his mouth and she smiled, sensing how turned on he was, relishing in the simple fact that she was the cause of his arousal. Her breasts had always been a source of chagrin for her, with men spending far more time staring at them than looking at her face. How could she never have known how incredible they were? That they held the ability to bring a grown man to a whimpering mass? If Ray had opened his eyes, he would have seen a very womanly, cat-like grin pull at her lips as his kiss burned against them.

She clutched his arms, moaning at the strength coursing through his body, at the fire awakening hers.

With this man, nothing else mattered. Nothing.

RIAGAN KEPT HER flat against the smooth metal of the truck with his body, bracing himself with his hands beside her shoulders, the coolness of the truck a welcome salve for the burning of his body.

He positioned his hardness against her, relishing in the light whimper that came from deep within her throat. The lass wanted him, that much was certain. And what was also as certain was that he wanted her, too.

He moved his hips side to side, up and down, forcing himself to keep the grinding gentle. He slid his hand into her hair. The silky strands wrapped around his fingers as if capturing him in a web. He ran his tongue along her teeth, the rim inside her lips, her tongue.

He was almost too hot, too boiling from her touch, like an active, virile volcano. He held her head firm for his kiss, his touch. She could not pull back even if she wanted to.

It didn't seem that she did.

He moved his other hand down to the small of her back. His palm fit well over the narrow expanse. But then her buttocks jutted out underneath in the most sensual swell. He cupped her bottom in his hand as she nibbled his lip.

He ran his hand under the soft mound and clenched. Then he trailed his hand up her side, following the womanly curves that were so perfectly placed she could've been born of the angels.

Then he found her breast. She jolted at the intimacy of his touch, but he held her head fast and she surrendered. He massaged the blessed pillow as her hands ran up and down his arms, making soft scratches with her nails along the way.

The other breast was every bit as inviting, nearly throbbing under his expert touch. A thick handful of his hair was clasped in her hand. Nails dug into his arms sending erotic flashes of pain through his veins.

It hurt but felt so good.

Finally releasing her mouth, he trailed licks toward her neck after she tilted her head back to give him access. Her sweet perfume was more noticeable against the throbbing veins under her ear, and his hips pushed harder.

That scent wafted through his blood, imprinting itself in his memory. He would never forget that scent. Ever.

His hips moved faster and she clutched him, trying to keep balanced against the truck.

Lust consumed him. He could devour this woman—the feel of her skin, the smell of her breath, the sound of her voice. Everything about her whirled in a haze as his body took full command of the situation. He wanted this woman.

He wanted her now. "Let's go into the forest."

She moved her hips in rhythm with his. "Ray?"

"Come with me."

She tried to pull away. "Ray."

His hips continued the slow gyration against hers.

"Ray, please. Stop."

"Stop?" He knew his breath was hot in her ear. "Stop? You don't want me?"

"My sister. Her children."

"They are busy eating cookies." Licking her neck would change her mind and he flicked his tongue over her skin, expecting a whimper but receiving another "Stop."

This time he pulled back.

She slid down the truck. He faced her, his hands clenched and his body aching. She stood with her back to the forest and didn't seem to notice the portal's brilliant light shining.

"Not here. Not like this. Not in front of my nieces and nephews." Her eyes were hardened now, resolute. Then she said quietly, as if to herself, "Maybe not at all," as if she was trying to decide whether to give herself to him or not.

He saw the desire in her eyes, smelled the sweet scent wafting off her skin. She wanted him, there was no doubt, but she was also refusing him.

Riagan wanted to scream. Why, exactly, he was no longer certain.

12

Ray stalked off into the forest and somehow she wasn't surprised. That was the only place he ever went. He didn't seem angry at her, but frustration was written all over his face. She didn't mean to be a tease but this was new to her. She'd never felt the desire to throw herself at a man before. Was this normal?

Had she hit her head so hard that it changed some fundamental part of her? Life as she knew it seemed so distant, so remote, so obscure. Work. Jerry. Her mom, now safely in the hospital. It was all a dream. The only reality that mattered now was the man standing at the edge of the forest watching her with an expression she could not read.

And she didn't even know him.

When he turned and bolted into the forest, tears welled in her eyes. Was she sad because he'd left? Sad because he hadn't come back and taken the virginity she was so willing to give? Or was she sad because deep down she knew her behavior was the result of her mental breakdown?

When Erika and the children tumbled out of the house, Wren wiped her eyes then planted a smile on her face. Her sister would never notice it didn't reach her eyes.

"Bye," Erika said with a grunt. The kids ran to Wren, and she hugged them all. Then she helped buckle the younger ones in their car seats and blew kisses. Erika threw her an impatient glare and peeled away.

Wren watched until the van lurched out of sight, then, seeing no sign of Ray, went back into the now quiet trailer. She cleaned up the mess they left behind and went into the kitchen to make another cup of tea.

Duke pawed at her ankle. "Hi, boy. You want a bone?"

Duke's chocolate eyes watched her, as if judging her mental competence for himself. He didn't respond to the offer of a bone.

She rubbed his head. "You'll still be my best guy, even if I am committed to the psych ward."

Duke shook his big head as if he was disagreeing with her, his velvety black ears flapping with the motion. She gave him a bone anyway, though he didn't touch it.

Instead of tea, Wren decided wine would work better, much better, and she poured a generous glass. Chamomile, be damned.

Wren settled onto the sofa with a blanket pulled over her shoulders. Chatter rang in her ears like a noisy movie theater.

With a gulp of wine, she burrowed under the worn cotton of the quilt. She took another quick swallow and tried not to retch at the burning in the back of her throat.

Brian never made her feel the way Ray did. She had never had the urge to take their relationship further, had always assumed sex would be about procreation with her husband and never about passion. But now, the fire that had started in her lower abdomen and erupted through her body shattered every notion she'd ever possessed.

Her eyes lost focus as she slipped into memories of how Ray's mouth, body, heat felt. The way he moved her head to every angle he wished—altering, changing, improving his access—made her want to dart into the forest and launch herself at him like a spear.

And that was just because of the kiss. Not to mention how his large and hard body molded against hers. How his hips moved in a rhythm that was foreign to her yet delicious and more welcome than a warm bath. How his eyes could pierce her into place with the passion that dwelled behind them.

She took several more sips, eager for the mind-numbing effects as the heat in her body grew to uncomfortable proportions, like she was sitting in a dryer set on high. Duke was curled up on the other end of the couch, his head on his paws, his eyes, wide and alert, studying her. A few more sips and her mind quieted, her muscles relaxing like they hadn't in weeks. Maybe she should give up the sleeping pills and just drink.

Then, like the blast of a foghorn on a quiet lake, the doorbell trilled, and she jumped, half-asleep, half-intoxicated. Wine tipped out of the glass, spilling down the front of her shirt.

She snatched up the quilt to wipe off her clothes, then stumbled to the door. Ray stood on the other side of the peephole, and her pulse shot into the stratosphere. In one gulp, she downed the rest of the wine, not-so-smoothly set the glass on the table, then flung open the door.

Staring at her was six and a half feet of pure, masculine, Adonis-esque male.

With a level of effort to rival a pro bicyclist, she tried to steady her breath, fearing her thumping heart could be heard all the way in town.

It didn't work.

"Can I come in?" Ray asked.

The sun was beginning its descent behind the mountains, casting shades of pink and purple across the mountains' skyline. It was too early for the fog to roll in but the clouds lay low, casting a gray veil over the horizon. The shadow of a beard covered the hard lines of Ray's jaw, and she was surprised she hadn't noticed it earlier.

So handsome.

So raw.

So turn my insides into a rich chocolate mousse.

She motioned him in.

Ray filled the room until she felt sure it would implode with his size, his energy. He was much larger than just his physical body should allow. He was a big man, for sure, with his great height and broad shoulders, but he also exuded so much energy, so much *masculine* energy, it consumed the entire trailer. Maybe they would all simply combust from the pressure.

With a flick of his hand, he pushed the door shut. Staring at him, watching as he took one step, then another in her direction, she suddenly felt fragile, desirous, and immobile—from fear or expectation, she didn't know.

He looked like a warrior with bloodlust.

She was no match for him and was not sure she wanted to be.

As he pursued her across the room, she backed up, and up, until she hit the wall. She couldn't move to the right or left. He was coming right toward her, locking her in place with such intensity behind those green eyes, she felt frozen.

Then he stopped, inches from her body. She didn't look up, couldn't look up, for if she did, she knew she would give herself to him right then and there.

He cupped her chin in his long muscular fingers and forced her head back. With his other hand, he grasped her waist. She started to protest but her words were stalled before they even left her lips. She wanted this man and wouldn't question why.

RIAGAN CLOSED HIS mouth over Wren's, stifling the soft, halfhearted protest he knew lingered there. He also knew she would allow the kiss, wanted it. Desire radiated off her body like a vibration, creating a silky white aura that enveloped them both.

He needed this woman like his mortal body needed air to breathe.

He forced her lips to part as desire surged through him. She parted them readily, giving him the taste of sweetened wine kissed by the fresh mountain air—air that he suddenly needed more than anything else he'd ever needed in his life.

He deepened the kiss, his tongue dancing farther into her mouth, forcing her head back as he pushed against her. Her tongue was wet, soft, and a perfect match for his.

Did she kiss her boyfriend like this?

The thought made him crazy, and he grabbed her wrists, pushing her hands over her head, moving his hips over hers. Even if she wanted to protest, there was nothing she could do. But the way she met his kiss told him she did not want him to stop.

He ground against her, nearly bringing himself to the edge, but he wanted more. A woman like her deserved more than quick lovemaking. He needed to take his time.

A lot of time.

But then, like a bolt of lightning, he realized he didn't have time. He had no time. The air was sucked out of him like a vacuum, leaving him withered, leathered, and sucked dry.

He dropped her arms. "I have to talk to you."

He edged back. His hands tingled with desire to cup her magnificent breasts, to massage and kiss them to distraction, but the black, ominous cloud of the worlds' fates overshadowed even the most powerful passion he felt for this woman.

"I need your help."

She studied him, her back still against the wall as if seeking support. "With what?"

As his mind fought to gather and coordinate the right words, his eyes focused on the perfect female who stood across from him. Her breasts pushed against a thin shirt, stained by what looked like wine. Her pants hung low on deliciously curvaceous hips. Her lips, red as a cherry ripe for the picking, were closed now, but moist and swollen. Her skin, alabaster. Her eyes, glassy blue. Her hair, as black as midnight.

He could not control himself around her, and forgot all about the full moon, the Brotherhood, the Cauldron. At this moment, he knew nothing but her. A primal instinct he could not control was now controlling him.

With one long stride, he was before her again, crushing her lips. She opened under the probing of his tongue, and he entered into her moist mouth again, this time more slowly.

The small of her back became lost in the long expanse of his arms. Her hands thrust deep into his hair and drew his body down toward hers. Stooping his sizable frame to meet her was difficult, and he could not feel the full press of her body with her feet on the ground.

Clutching her tight and firm buttocks, he lifted her off the ground. As her legs wrapped around his waist, he marveled that she could be so light. The muscles of her legs contracted against his torso as she squeezed, sending a rush of desire through him. His hands clasped underneath her, the expanse of his palms covering her bottom, his fingertips close to her most sensitive area.

"Where is your bed?" His voice was hoarse and deep.

With her head tilted back, she nodded toward the right. In a mere five strides, they were in the bedroom, and with a booted foot, he kicked the door closed. Wren's delectable fragrance hovered everywhere inside the small space. The lamp on her nightstand cast enough light across the darkening room to make her pale skin luminous and her eyes glow.

She looked like a dream, a fantasy, a prayer.

An angel.

With a gentle, caring swoop, he laid her down on the bed. Her Aegean eyes gazed at him through half-closed lids, the dark lashes long and full and sultry. She looked so trusting, so innocent, so lusty and desirous. This woman was many things, to be certain.

He lay down beside her, holding his weight on an elbow. The skin of her neck was warm beneath his probing tongue. He cupped one of those delicious breasts and it filled his palm. He squeezed and released each breast in turn as he licked her collarbone. Finally, he pulled up her shirt, unable to resist the sight of those precious gems any longer.

She wore black lace undergarments that made him insane, covering her body just enough to leave him wanting. He undid the front clasp of the top piece with a single motion and murmured his approval. Staring down, drinking in their perfection, he knew already how these fabulous mounds felt in his hands. Now he wanted to know how they would taste in his mouth.

So he took a hardened nipple between his teeth and sucked gently, her hips lifting off the bed in response. He never wanted to release these ripe peaks. Ever.

Sharp nails dug into his shoulder as he sought the other nipple.

"Ray." She clawed at his shirt. "Take this off."

He reared back and yanked it off, grateful for his warrior physique. He wanted this woman to appreciate his body the way he appreciated hers and was glad he had much to offer.

The light reflected off her white skin, perfectly unblemished, utterly smooth, and tantalizingly fresh. He licked her breast like he would lick an ice-cream cone.

His fingers ran over her taut abdomen, tracing the cut of her waist, the swell of her hip. At the top of her pants, he paused for a second before easing underneath.

She sucked in her stomach to allow him better access and his entire hand disappeared. His fingers brushed against the lace, then tickled their way underneath the fabric until he felt the encroaching heat of her. He paused, listening to her breath, gauging the tension in her body. She exuded nothing but arousal, and his hand continued its progression through the silky curls toward the wet, burning part of her body he so desperately wanted to possess.

When his finger entered her, she cried out, and he swallowed the sound with his mouth. He licked the inside of her lips with a rhythm that matched his hand's motion as he moved his finger, slowly…slowly. This woman deserved the most treasured lovemaking he could provide, and he savored her like a thirst-ravaged man savors a trickle of water.

Soon her pants became too restrictive, so he stood and yanked them off. Black lace panties molded over perfectly rounded hips, and he stopped for a moment to absorb the sight of this ethereal beauty lying before him.

He then removed his jeans, and allowed her burning gaze a moment to, hopefully, appreciate what she saw. At the edge of the bed, he paused, naked and exposed and erect.

"Lass." His need for her turned his voice raspy and wanting.

Her eyes, glassy and iridescent, stared at his body as he gazed down at hers. Her body was surely molded from Venus herself. There was no flaw with this woman, and he had to have her. He had to take her.

Now.

13

Reason left her body as desire consumed it. Even without touch, as he stood staring at her and she at him, her skin became alight like a million stars were exploding over it, showering her with their burning flame.

When he returned to his place beside her, her hands grasped him closer, as if he could float away at a moment's notice. Every place his tongue or fingers or palm touched her pulsed with an energy she'd never experienced before.

She was on fire, this man's skin burning under her touch. Blood pumped through her body, swelling her lips, her nipples, the sensitive area between her legs. Physical reactions she would never have expected now consumed her as the most natural response to the most erotic moment of her life.

The muscles in Ray's arms were ridges of hardness beneath her fingers, and she could not resist touching them, running her fingers over the hills and crevices. When she used her nails, he moaned low in his throat.

The urge to welcome him into her body was uncontrollable and unlike any feeling she'd ever had. Maybe that was why she was still a virgin, waiting for a moment like this, a moment when she knew without a doubt that she wanted her body merged with another's.

She was ready to give herself to this man, to give him her virginity, and, surprisingly, her heart. To give him everything.

"Do you want me to make love to you, lass? To show you how it feels to have a man's love?"

Those sultry words, rolling off his hot tongue in his growling and strange way of speech, made her legs part as if of their own volition. She did not care how wanton she was acting, and he did not seem to care either. Rather, he stared down at her parted legs, at the exposure left in their wake, and he started to pant.

Never could she have imagined a hunger like she had now.

"Yes. Make love to me."

He lowered onto her. The muscles in her stomach knotted and tensed in delicious anticipation as he pushed her thighs farther apart with his leg. Trailing one hand from her breasts to the top of her thighs made her shudder, and when he reinserted his finger between her legs, her body rode the gentle motion. She wanted to be possessed by him, consumed by him.

The sensation washed over her like a thousand shocks. Hot breath flowed over her neck and her skin drank it in. Silky strands of his hair tickled her face and she inhaled.

His expert fingers explored every inch of her exposed body, finding pleasure points she never knew existed. Her body shook with the force of his touch as he brought her to the edge of what would be the first man-given orgasm she'd ever had.

Blood pumped through her body, pooling between her legs as his relentless pursuit of her pleasure culminated in a soul-bursting orgasm that shook her to her core.

He silenced her cries with his mouth, swallowing her ecstasy with a hot kiss. Waves rippled through her body and tears filled her eyes. Such delicious pleasure. She'd never felt anything like it in all her life.

Then he nudged her legs farther apart, urging her to open to him, which she did willingly, begging. With his hands on either side of her face, he looked directly into her eyes. No—into her soul. She knew her expression was pleading, desperate.

He inserted the tip of his erection into her body. Cries hovered just below the surface as he tried to fill her beyond capacity. He was too big. His body was too large, even though he'd only just begun to enter her. Involuntarily, she tried to clamp her legs together against the intrusion.

"Relax, lass. Relax, and I will fit."

Before she could tense again, he pushed all the way inside her body, and she was so completely full of him, so utterly, wholly consumed by him that there was nothing left of her.

She was his.

WREN QUIVERED BENEATH him and Riagan inched back to see what expression her face held. The lamp's soft glow cast shadows through the otherwise dark room and reflected off her porcelain skin. Knowing women as he did, he knew the look on her face, and it was one of complete and total satisfaction.

He had satisfied this woman. And she had much satisfied him. Waves of contentment washed over him, and he resisted the urge to leap off the bed and dance a jig. Never had he been so affected by a partner's pleasure.

Instead he kissed her, relishing the chills that peppered her arms, running over her abdomen, and to the tips of her toes. He left her warm body briefly as he grabbed a blanket, heavy and soft. Then he spread the quilt around them as she snuggled into the crook of his arm. She laid her head in the middle of his chest where she fit so perfectly. The *second* place she fit so perfectly.

With a wispy motion, she caressed his chest, tracing the muscles with her fingertips.

"How fare you?" he whispered.

Wren sighed, contentment making the sound feathery light. "You have such an odd way of talking."

Smoothing the curls from her forehead, he kissed her eyes, her nose, and her mouth.

"You are well?" he asked again.

"I feel amazing."

He stared at the pattern on the ceiling. There was no way to know this woman would be untouched, a virgin. Yet, he'd seen the blood-speckled sheets when he grabbed the blanket, and he'd felt the barrier give when he'd entered her. No surprise her boyfriend would not be man enough for her, but he had not expected her to be a maiden still.

What did this mean?

He wasn't sure, but his mind was fractured, full of flashes of thoughts and images that would not merge into anything comprehensible. Still basking in post-coital bliss, he forced his mind quiet. For now, at least.

He didn't know if it was the Earth's oxygen that heightened the pleasure or the direness of the situation. Making love to Wren had changed something within him, but he wasn't sure what. He felt different, altered, as if the union of their bodies had taken the chemistry of his body and rearranged it. What the result was, he knew not.

Wren's breathing slowed, and he thought she was asleep. But then she spoke, so softly he almost missed it. "I think I'm falling in love with you." She giggled through a sigh. "And I don't even know you."

He clutched her tight as he listened to her breath deepen in slumber.

She loves me. Could this be real? Have I fulfilled the terms of my banishment?

Elation did not follow this realization.

A cold bitterness seeped into his heart and filled it to capacity.

What does this mean for her?

As her body relaxed into deeper sleep, he could almost feel her melting into his skin, her heat replacing the iciness that was now threatening to consume him.

Thank the gods she was asleep because she couldn't see the pain on his face.

Would he return to the Brotherhood and she remain a mortal here on Earth? Would she return to Brian and try to make a life with that boring excuse of a man?

The thought of her lying in Brian's arms as she now lay in his made him rage.

Nay. She belongs not with that boy.

But where did she belong? She didn't belong with Riagan, either. Being a member of the Brotherhood meant being alone and isolated, focused solely on the Cauldron. His realm was no place for her, even if—

But no, all he wanted was to return to his realm and protect the Cauldron. That was all he knew how to do. Yes, that was all he wanted.

Or was it?

Feelings unfamiliar to him—maybe sadness, maybe melancholy—settled into his soul, but he did not know why. He favored this wee lass, that was certain. But caring for her was an emotion he had no room for. If she was to be the sacrifice in this, then so be it. Right?

The dog's snores wafted into the room from just outside the closed door, mixing with Wren's soft breaths. She was so delicate, had already been through so much. She accepted things without question.

A trait of the Protector of the Murias Cauldron was to exude strength and competence at all times, to be the ultimate Protector. He knew he had that effect on this sensitive woman. She would have no control in his presence.

But now it seemed that her trust was to be used against her because there was no other way. A born Protector of the Cauldron was always such and could not sway from that designation.

Riagan had to return. There was no other choice.

Wren breathed a soft gasp and he forced himself to loosen his grip.

She need only accompany me to the Council and fulfill the terms of this banishment.

He swallowed hard and caressed her arm, willing his fingertips to lock in the memory of how she felt beneath them.

He would hold her this night, make love to her in the morn, then take her to the portal where he would channel the Council. She would profess her love and he would leave her forever.

He had sacrificed his Brotherhood and the Cauldron for a lover's union before. Now he would have to sacrifice a woman's love for his Brotherhood and the Cauldron. He was glad for the night so that no one could see the tear that slid down his cheek.

The moon outside was a nearly perfect orb—bright, white, and magical. Would that the night should never end.

EARLY THE NEXT morning, the lass rubbed her head against his chest, and he hugged her close to his warm body. He ran a hand through her curls and she moaned, then stretched like a Cheshire cat. His body grew in response and he flipped her onto her back.

She watched him through veiled eyes as he rose up on his hands to gaze upon her nakedness. The delicate hourglass shape of her body stood out against the light-colored sheets.

He bent and kissed the skin of her stomach.

She purred.

With hands deep in his hair, she drew him upward until their mouths met. She tasted so warm and sweet, like dew on a spring morn.

He took his time with her, running hands over her smooth body, cupping her breasts, her buttocks, tickling her thighs.

When he could stand it no longer, he entered her in one swift movement, and her lusty moan stamped itself in his mind. He would never forget the sound she made when their bodies became one.

Her hips rode the movement of his body, her confidence no longer that of a virgin. Small hands clutched his back and he forced himself to take it slow, knowing she would be sore. He hoped her nails would leave scars in his skin, evidence of the passion they had shared. A reminder, when he was far from her, that she had indeed existed.

He staked his claim on her body, on her soul, just as she wrapped herself around him. He would always be her first. Always.

They cried out together, shaking from more than just exertion. He grazed his cheek along hers and rubbed, surprised to feel moisture there. Too afraid to gaze upon the tears that escaped her eyes, too afraid to acknowledge they were tears of happiness and love, he held her close, his own face buried in the pillow.

After several moments of piecing together his rigid resolve, he felt strong again, emotionally and physically. He fell to his back and she snuggled into the crook of his arm, wiggling in as close to him as she could. He inhaled the scent of her hair.

Then she rose up on her elbow and gazed down at him. She looked like a wild minx, pale, hair disheveled, untamed, and for the moment, satiated. He realized that he'd never hold her again. Never breathe in her scent. Never cup those perfect breasts or kiss those ruby lips.

Before a sob formed in his gut, he shut down those thoughts and channeled his warrior teachings. He'd need all his strength for what he was about to do.

Suddenly a flush spread across her cheeks and she lay back down, hiding her face.

"What is it, lass?"

She giggled. "Nothing." After a pause she said, "Did you sleep well?"

He'd tell her not that he hadn't slept at all. But he did have to tell her the truth, and tell her the full truth, he would. He owed her that much and now was the time. "Well enough," he started. "You?"

"Hmm," was her reply.

"Wren?"

"Yes?"

He ran a hand up and down her arm, bringing chills to her smooth skin. "I need your help."

"Okay."

So trusting. Guilt pierced his heart with a pain worse than a dagger's blade. At first he didn't recognize the emotion. Then when the knowledge of what he was feeling dawned on him, it made him feel even worse. Too many emotions on this realm, for certain. Being a mortal brought too much trouble, too much pain.

"Have you ever felt that life isn't what it seems? That there are other forces out there, outside of what textbooks convey to you, what preachers preach to you, what others tell you?"

Her muscles tensed, and he knew he'd hit a nerve.

"What are you talking about?" Her voice barely rose above a breath.

"Wren," he started, but struggled to go on. He was about to shatter every truth she'd ever known. "I have much to tell you. You must understand there are things I will say that you will cast aside as delusional. Insane."

She tried to sit up, but he held her down. He could not risk looking her in the eye.

"Open your mind to all that you have been told is myth, magic, fairy tale."

She remained quiet. He continued, though her petite body shook beside him.

"My name is not Ray. It's Riagan Tenman, son of Ragda, and Protector of the Murias Cauldron."

She stiffened.

"I am an immortal druid of the Brotherhood of the Sacred Grove, born in the year 453 AD. I am one of twelve sworn Protectors of the Murias Cauldron, who was punished for an indiscretion and was banished by our Arch Druid to the realm of man."

His ability to speak dropped off like it had been chopped by an ax.

How did he explain to her that he was supposed to find love? To have a woman fall in love with him, and he had chosen her for the task?

The other part of the banishment was that he was to find love too. *Was* he in love?

In truth, he wouldn't know what love was if it bit him on the arse. No, he wasn't in love. That was something he'd never felt—would never feel in his life. But he *did* care about her. Yes, he cared about her, and a great deal at that, which was shocking considering how little time they'd spent together.

His level of caring for the lass should be enough for the Council. His teachings couldn't beat an emotion completely out of him, then wither away for him to suddenly be able to feel that emotion again, could they?

"I have to remain on this realm until I find someone who loves me and whom I love in return. Then my banishment will be lifted and I can return to my rightful place as Protector of the Cauldron."

There. That was believable, no? He'd not wanted words to pour out of his mouth in this way but it was done. The truth was out.

She jerked out of his arms, catapulting herself off the bed. A broad brushstroke of fury colored her features. A good reaction, this was not.

"Lass…"

"Get out." Her chest heaved.

He sat up. "Nay. I'll not leave until you've listened to me. Then you'll understand. Open your mind, Wren. There is more here than you have been taught. This is no delusion, no hallucination. You are not ill."

She gawked at him.

"Right now the Cauldron is at risk. There will be an attempt to steal it tomorrow night. I must return to my Brotherhood and assume my position as Protector, for if the Cauldron is taken, all mysteries of the worlds will be lost from us forever and will be in the hands of him who they call Master."

By the gods, this jumble of words is not how I wanted to tell her. Shush, Riagan, shush. She is frightened and you speak too much.

Then she started to giggle, a high-pitched disturbing sound, for certain. Duke whined behind the closed door and scratched to get in.

Then her face fell into an expression of stone. "Get out."

"But he will enslave the humans. Destroy the Earth as you know it." He paused, pleading. "He will become immortal."

"Get out."

"Lass, please."

"GET OUT!" She flung open the door, and Duke rushed in, growling by her feet. Slobber oozed over his pink lips and his enormous eyes bulged.

"OUT!"

Och, but that did not go well.

Her voice was crazed and the dog's growl mimicked it perfectly.

What have I done? This was not supposed to be her reaction. Oephille said she has the old blood. Why does she then react this way?

Her eyes darkened in rage.

I'm in trouble.

He slid out of the bed and grabbed his jeans. "Wren, please. You must listen to me. I know that you know there is more to this life than what you see before you. You are special, Wren. I…I…" He struggled to finish the sentence, suddenly aware of how very true the statement was. "I need you."

"Get out before I kill you and then let my dog devour you from head to toe."

He fled the trailer, his mind reeling.

14

Wren's teeth chattered as if she was standing, naked, on an iceberg far out in the ocean. She stood in the doorway to her bedroom staring at the blood-spotted sheets, evidence of the loss of her virginity, and rock-solid proof of her naiveté, her insanity.

Sobs wrenched up through her body. She raced into the bathroom then vomited into the toilet.

The image of Jerry's dead body and Ray's halo flashed before her and she heaved. Bracing herself against the cold bowl, she could not stop the pictures of the past days playing in her mind like a projector, pounding her with relentless force.

Jerry's dead body.

Dr. Martin's accusing eyes.

Her mother's blank stare.

Ray's constant, unexplained presence.

The signs were there—she was losing her mind. The signs had started long before Jerry's death with the creeping awareness of the voices, and kept hurling evidence after evidence at her, and she had refused to see it.

Well, those blood-stained sheets made sure she could see it now.

How could she have trusted this stranger? Had she been so desperate that she'd given herself to a man she didn't know, a man who'd killed her client? She'd given *this* man her virginity? Maybe even her sanity?

Then she saw him as he was when he came to her last night—soft, tender, and prepared to make love to her till morning light. Her stomach tightened with the memory of his body with its rippling muscles pumping with desire—desire for *her*. When he moved inside her, he had lured her into his captivity. Would she ever be able to escape?

She turned her head and gazed at the bed through the open door. The blood mocked her, reinforcing the notion that she was not able to care for herself, that she was just two steps away from becoming her mother. She knew the road well and also knew that she was traveling down it at warp speed.

At this point she would welcome the break from reality. Life was too difficult. Holding on to her sanity was too much of a struggle. She wouldn't fight it any longer.

She didn't want to fight any longer.

A second later, she had her keys in her fist and was sprinting toward the truck.

A gray mass was oozing its way into her mind like a disease, obliterating coherent thoughts, replacing them with nothingness as black and as deep and as finite as a cavernous pit.

She slammed the door and locked it. Chatter erupted in her head so loud, she clutched her ears.

"Stop. Please. I can't take it." Sobs poured out of her in waves of anguish.

She gasped for air as if she were drowning. Fighting with the key and the ignition, she finally managed to start the truck. Its roar to life did nothing to quiet the chorus in her head.

She steered onto the road and floored the gas, making the truck jerk and stall as it struggled to increase speed. Shadows fell across the road, but she didn't bother to turn on the headlights. She went faster and faster, the truck slowly gaining momentum, the tires screeching around the sharp curves.

Run, Wren. Run.

From the past. From the present. From the future.

From the madness that will swallow you alive.

She pushed the pedal harder and fought to control the wobbling steering wheel. No other cars were out, but it wouldn't have mattered anyway.

Ray. Blond, powerful, beautiful Ray. Angel with the halo.

Why had he come here? To torment her? That was too hateful to consider. But why else? Was this really all just a hallucination?

Her clients, and her mother, always acted like the voices and visions were so real. Maybe that's what all of this was. Maybe once she was medicated, these hallucinations would be phased out and a young woman in a stupor of medicated existence would be what was left.

A light mist began to fall, but she didn't turn on the wipers, keeping her foot pushed down on the pedal, forcing the truck to skid and slide around the turns.

Images of Ray flipped to images of blood-stained sheets. Those flashed to images of her mother, then of herself in ten years, slivers of madness shaping her days.

A road sign, yellow and reflective, warned of dangerous curves ahead. She chuckled and gripped the wheel as she took the first turn, the curve so sharp it was almost ninety degrees. The back wheels lost traction and the truck swerved. She didn't let up on the gas, though, and all wheels slid on the wet surface, sending the truck into a tailspin. She forgot about Duke, her mother, Ray, her madness.

She forgot about everything.

The truck lost control. Wren lost control. She smiled to herself as the truck hurtled toward the massive tree in front of her.

RIAGAN COLLAPSED NEAR the portal. His human, mortal heart struggled to beat as the veil thinned, time barreling toward the equinox. The air held too little oxygen, and he felt like he'd just climbed to the top of the Pyrenees.

The trees were alive, swaying restlessly, their long limbs undulating in harmonious and foreboding rhythm. He would have welcomed their advice but they were silent. Far off in the distance, bells chimed the fae realm's preparation for the full moon.

Despair marched through his body like a band of maniacal, bloodthirsty warriors.

"This is impossible. What is the point of all of this?" He yanked at the strands of his hair as he wailed to the trees. "Damn the Arch Druid. Damn him for this punishment. I have made many mistakes, it is certain, but I did not deserve this."

Was there ever any hope that he could return home? Or was this all a cruel joke? He had never been expected to find love, had he? They'd made sure of that when he was a babe. He'd been a fool to think there was even a chance at redemption.

The Arch Druid had set him up to impossible demands—banished to the realm of man until he found love, a silly and impossible punishment.

And he'd failed, just like the Arch Druid expected.

Even though he had suspicions, cold, hard realization crashed over him like a waterfall of ice. He was never meant to return. He'd been given a punishment that he could never fulfill. Ever. And that was why he'd been given it, wasn't it?

He struggled for the breath that would keep his human, mortal body alive. Never meant to return. Of course. But why?

Riagan passed the rest of the day and night in turmoil—his mind at turns furious and focused, then confused, wavering and uncertain. Never in all his years had a situation such as this come to pass: an attempt to steal the Cauldron, followed by a severe and unwarranted punishment, only to discover that the punishment was never to be alleviated. He was doomed.

AT FIRST LIGHT, on the day of the autumnal equinox, Riagan was still staring into the portal, as he had been doing the entire night. If only its light would resolve all his problems to dusty nothingness.

Alas, it was not to be. Nothing changed other than the fact that his legs were stiff and his feet were numb and his mind was a juxtaposed hodgepodge of puzzle pieces.

With effort, he lifted to his feet. Desperate to get the blood pumping through his veins again, he started walking in a circle, then in a line, then straight toward Wren's trailer. What he would do once he got there, he knew not.

15

"Master!" Gwyon spoke in quiet, rushed words, shuffling forward, hiding his pain behind excitement. "It is time." He wrenched his hands together as he leaned against an enormous stone.

Master forked his long gray fingers under his chin. "You have missed something."

Gwyon's mind pitched and stumbled and staggered. What could he have missed? He'd traveled all the realms, done due diligence in gathering the best band of marauders to help him take the Cauldron. He had searched far and wide, then far and wide again to ensure there were no obstacles in their path. He had missed naught.

But Master's gray eyes didn't blink, and Gwyon leaned against the stone, not wanting to show fear but unable to show strength.

"Why do you think you were sent to the realm of man all those times?"

A cold, prickly sweat broke out on Gwyon's neck, dripping onto his back in icy droplets. He had thought it strange to travel thus, but had not questioned it. There were many quirks, if they could be called such, about Master that he had not questioned. Indeed, he'd done his job. Hadn't he?

"I had my suspicions but intended for you to confirm or refute them."

"But something was missed?" The effort it took for Gwyon to utter those words was paramount to skipping up the side of a glacier.

"There has been a break in the veil of magic, courtesy of the pending equinox when all shadows clear, and now I see."

Gwyon swallowed. "See what, Master?"

"A Redeemer."

"A Redeemer?" It felt as if a crater had beamed him in the chest. "Impossible."

Master's eyes lit like a flare. "You question me?"

"No, Master." He swallowed. "Please tell me what I am to do."

"A human woman is the link, the mother of the Redeemer. Find her, and kill her. Once you do, the veil will dissipate and you will see clearly the Redeemer. Then kill her."

Two murders? Gwyon had never considered the possibility. Hurt his brothers, yes. He was prepared for such. Drink from the Cauldron. Again, yes. He wanted to be healed. But kill two women on the realm of man?

"How will I find these women, Master?"

"One has hair of red. The other, the Redeemer, hair of black. In that order, they must be eliminated."

THE YELLOW LIGHT was blinding, searing her pupils through her closed lids. Wren tried to shield her eyes but couldn't move her leaden arms. She struggled to sit up but was being held down, though she couldn't tell why or how. Where was she?

Bells clanged louder than if she were lying on the floor of a church during Christmas Eve choir practice.

At long last, there was a lull in the serenade but that was promptly replaced by chattering voices. They sounded like an agitated pack of chipmunks.

If she could have, she would have covered her ears.

A second later, the voices narrowed and thinned until only one voice remained, and she swore it spoke her name.

Destiny.

Her lids fluttered, but the flashes of light were too bright, the glare overpowering her vision. Several moments later, several attempts later, she managed to force her eyes to remain open for more than a second, to zero in on the reason for the light, and she saw a small butterfly flapping its wings inches from her face.

No, it wasn't a butterfly. It was bursting with colors brighter and richer than a rainbow, with sunshine yellow glowing all around.

She blinked again.

She saw a face, an ethereally beautiful face, tiny as a silver coin, hovering in front of her nose.

There were arms and legs and a body below this face—resembling a small child's doll dressed in vibrant, glowing yellow. But the doll was alive. How did she know this? By its own blinking eyes and moving lips as if it was trying to say something.

Wren blinked again, holding her lids closed while she counted to five before she opened them again.

Her breath caught.

It was a faery.

WREN WAVERED IN and out of consciousness. Was this what it was like in Hell? Unable to awaken, yet unable to die; able to hear, but unable to communicate in any other way? Seeing images of faeries, knowing her mother had visions of little winged ones during bouts of psychosis, and knowing she was following down the same tumultuous path?

She tried to move her fingers but they wouldn't budge. Nor would her toes and feet cooperate. Her blood was filled with concrete, and she slipped back into the void, to a world where she was covered with thick, black, oozing tar that left her mind unable to gain its freedom.

Then she awoke, popping into the world of awareness as if she were a jack-in-the-box. She opened her eyes, squinting against whitewashed walls.

"So, you're awake, are you?"

That voice. Wren lifted her gaze, and there he was peering over her. Dr. Rick Martin.

"Where am I?" Her mouth felt like it was stuffed with cotton.

With a deep breath, he exhaled and his breath washed over her face. He still smelled of tobacco and mint. Not a pleasant memory.

"You are in the hospital."

"Why?" Her voice was hoarse, cracked, and sore. Something was pushing against her chin, something that kept her from lowering her face.

"Because you tried to kill yourself." The matter-of-fact words hit her like bricks hurled from close range. The image of the massive tree flashed before her.

"How long have I been here?"

"Now, now. That's enough talk. You need your rest." He held up a long syringe and pulled the IV between his fingers.

"No, I don't want to be medicated." Fear of the tar pit gripped her mind. She tried to lift her hand but with the previous medicine still coursing through her body, it was impossible.

"I can't move my hands," she whispered, trying to hang on to any thread of consciousness.

"You are in a straitjacket. As you know, we use those for dangerous patients. And you, Destiny O'Hara, are very dangerous."

With that, he left the room, and she once again tumbled into the void, wondering why he'd called her by a name no one used but her mother.

16

Riagan stood beside the trailer, gazing at the moon. He ignored the ten-ton weight that had settled in his chest after he'd watched Wren's truck drive around a corner and pass out of sight. Now here he was, a mortal, banned from his Brotherhood because of his selfish needs. He'd taken for granted the fact that no one had ever attempted to steal the Cauldron in all the moons it had been under the Brotherhood's protection.

Now he'd found a woman, and she loved him, and he should be able to return to his realm. But where did that leave her? Him?

Her love of him was only half the terms. The other half was that *he* had to find love as well. Anger simmered through his blood like a scalding liquid, igniting every cell it touched. Impossible punishment.

He wouldn't know what love was even if he was in the throes of it. This was not fair. He didn't deserve this. She didn't deserve this.

His fingers curled into his palms, and he beat them against his thighs. "She doesn't belong on this realm. But she doesn't belong with me, either."

Wren would marry and have children. She would continue to dote on that droopy dog, and knowing she had such a loyal friend was one small bit of comfort. But who would protect her?

He would be protecting the Cauldron, gods willing. Or he would be dead. A life as a mortal on Earth would be unbearable, especially if Wren would have nothing to do with him. Making love to her all his mortal days would be the only way he would willingly pass the time.

But now he wasn't protecting anything—not the Cauldron, not Wren.

What happened to Caswallen? He'd never disappeared like this before. Ray murmured an ancient spell of protection for the aged druid, but the words fell flat on his tongue.

The first stars were just appearing in the sky, and the moon, white and glowing, was taking its place from the sun. With a disgruntled sigh, he headed toward the forest. He would return to where he belonged, or he would die trying. The best thing for Wren would be to marry Brian and forget about him.

Teeth clenched against the hollow pit in his stomach, he pushed ahead, blinking back moisture he refused to acknowledge was there.

The entire forest, beginning with the first trees that lined the periphery of the wood to as far back as his eyes could see, swayed in unison. They had not shown their ancient secret this far from the portal as of yet. Magic of the otherworlds hung in the air so thick he could taste it. Familiar yet distant, sweet yet metallic.

And where was Oephille? He hadn't seen her since the day prior. Then, as if summoned by his thoughts, a flash of sunshine glitter flew by his eyes.

He didn't bother to grab her. If she had found him, then she wanted something.

"Riagan." She smelled like a ripe honeydew melon.

"Yes?"

"She's hurt."

"Wren? Speak you of Wren?" He swiped at her.

"Yes, I speak of Destiny."

"Who?"

"Wren."

"She is hurt? She can't be."

"She is."

"Pray you speak foul. What are you talking about?"

Oephille flew out of reach, but he could hear her loud and clear. "Wren is hurt, Riagan."

"Where is she?" His body swelled with fear.

Oephille hovered without speaking.

"Where is she?" He swiped a large hand across the air again but still missed the faery.

"In the hospital."

"The hospital? Why?"

"She crashed her truck."

"Her truck?" Riagan had watched her peel away but did not see anything happen other than that. Truthfully, he'd been lost in his own thoughts.

"Her truck hit a tree, Riagan, and she is injured. She is in the hospital."

"Pray, is she okay? How fares she?"

"Her body is fine. Her mind..."

His gut clenched into a ball so tight, he knew it would take years to unfurl. "Her mind?" he whispered.

"She tried to kill herself. She is broken."

Riagan understood the words the faery spoke. He knew what each one meant, but somehow, he still couldn't comprehend. Wren tried to kill herself?

The faery lost its yellow glamour in the wake of what she spoke. She no longer glittered; her eyes no longer shone. She still kept a safe distance from him, and he didn't blame her one bit. He wanted to kill her, to sever this tragic line of speech coming from her vibrantly colored lips.

"She tried to take her life?" Maybe he'd misunderstood.

"Yes, Riagan. She drove her truck into a tree."

"Drove her truck into a tree?" He wanted to quit repeating her words but couldn't.

"Aye."

"But, it could've been an accident, could it not?" That was the answer.

"It was no accident."

Terror consumed him and he swiped at Oephille again. She flew to the nearest tree branch and sat upon it, inches out of his reach.

"How do you know?" Answering the moment's direness, his muscles coiled with tension as if preparing for a fight.

Oephille fluttered farther away, but her words felt like a hammer to his skull despite the distance. "I was there, Riagan. I was in the truck with her. She pushed her foot on the gas and drove straight for that tree. She wanted to kill herself."

Wanted…to…kill…herself.

"You must go to her, Riagan. Bring her back from this void. Make her understand there is more to her life than fear. Make her understand her destiny."

Go to her. Her destiny.

"What is her destiny?"

"Go to her, Riagan. Pull her back from the brink."

But wasn't he the one who put her there? Who had cast the final blow to what was left of her fragile sanity?

The realization that he had led Wren to this point hit him with gale-force winds.

He buckled under the weight, falling to his knees, wailing.

He was unaware of anything other than overwhelming pain—suffocating, life-ending pain.

"Oephille, help her. Please. I can't—I'm no good for her. Please."

He pulled himself to his feet and dashed into the forest.

The rhythmic pounding of his boots reverberated through him, and he counted his steps to avoid thinking of Wren—alone, frightened, hurt.

What had he done to her?

He sprinted as fast as he could, running from the faery, from Wren, from the devastation he left in his wake. Running as fast as he could before the cold, hard truth settled in his conscience and never left, for if it did and he truly knew what he'd lost, he would die from the tragedy of it.

As he neared the portal, the trees' rhythm turned from slow, sinuous movements into thrashing wildness. He shielded his face with his arms against the limbs. If a hurricane were coming, it would present no less chaos. The moon's pull against the veil took all the oxygen out of the air, and his mortal body struggled. He staggered forward. It was time to end this.

He gasped for breath, his arms covered in scrapes and scratches. Small beads of blood spotted his skin. He stood to his full height and pushed long strands of hair away from his face. He wore another pair of blue jeans and a T-shirt from Annie's closet, but the mortal human clothes felt stifling. His skin felt raw and the clothes scratched worse than the thrashing trees. He'd never belonged on this realm, and this was just one more proof.

The light of the portal was so bright as he came upon it, it was blinding, and he closed his eyes, waiting for the pupils to adjust.

When he opened them again, he surveyed the clearing. There was no sign of the ring of stones or Drake or the Brotherhood. They would be busy, though he had to admit, part of him hoped, *willed* that Drake, or Caswallen, would be here waiting for him, telling him this was all a nightmare, a mistake, and they needed him at once in the Grove.

Fury made his limbs shake. There was much he didn't understand, and he didn't know how to find the answers.

It was clear Wren carried the old blood within her veins, but how diluted was it?

Riagan fell against the tree as it halted its wild movement to cradle him against its side. Just then the light dimmed to a soft, hazy glow. There before him stood the Arch Druid, Caswallen, clad in the crimson judgment robe. Around his waist was the belt of woven golden thread with the Arch Druid's sickle, the symbol of his high office, hanging down his thigh.

"Caswallen?" Riagan's breath was ragged with relief. Caswallen could grant him pardon, and there was time yet to return to the Cauldron.

Riagan fell to his knee and bowed his head. Surrounding them, the trees dipped their broad canopies in greeting.

"Riagan, son of Ragda Tenman, why came you to this sacred place?" If Riagan didn't know this man's voice better than any other's, he would have sworn it was a child speaking.

"Arch Druid, I come to ask pardon, to return to my post as Protector of the Murias Cauldron, to protect our most ancient and precious artifact from imminent threat."

"Have you fulfilled the terms of your banishment?"

Riagan did not find comfort in the elder's tone.

Wren had professed her love for him.

And, yes, he cared for her as well.

But love? He couldn't feel love.

He thought of the petite woman, with her raven-colored hair, as dark as the coal that grew under these mountains, her eyes that betrayed her emotions and thoughts as clearly as if she'd spoken them aloud. She had trusted him all along.

And what had he done?

Sent her spiraling down the path toward lunacy, right alongside her bizarre mother.

The pain he'd caused her was now his pain, too. But he didn't know if it was love.

Besides, it didn't matter now. He forced his mind from Wren. "Caswallen, the hour draws upon us. The Cauldron is at risk. Know you this not? Where have you been?"

He squashed any more thought of the enigma of love. This was the time to be a warrior, not a lover. He had to return to his homeland. If evil won the Cauldron, it would affect Earth as well. If it affected Earth, it would also affect Wren.

Materializing before him was the entire druid Council, eleven warrior druids, clad in ceremonial red robes. Around each of their waists hung the sickle that druids of the Sacred Grove were sworn to bear at all times.

Riagan scanned the faces of his Brotherhood, absorbing each familiar feature with longing. And there in the midst was Drake.

Their eyes locked for the briefest of moments. The trees settled into a wavering unrest, limbs undulating overhead.

We welcome you, they droned to the Council.

The Arch Druid bowed his head, then looked back at Riagan.

The nearest tree reached down a limb and laid it on his shoulder. The trees were ancient friends of the druids—kind, protective, supportive. He felt raw, grateful for their friendship, relieved that the end of this entire ordeal was upon them.

Caswallen spoke. "Riagan, son of Ragda, why came you here if you have not fulfilled the terms?"

With a deep inhale, Riagan began, "I have come here on this night when the veil between the worlds is thinnest, when the full moon holds court high in the night sky, to tell you…" He took a deep breath, steeling his mind and his body as the limb tightened on his shoulder, "That it is time to stop this nonsense and save the Cauldron."

There was a gasp among the Brotherhood. It was forbidden to show disrespect to the elder, but Riagan found he cared not for the old ways. There was no time for this. It was time to fight, not maintain protocol. A strange feeling of liberation settled around him, igniting his cause with fire.

Gray eyes froze on his face, but he stared back without flinching. "Caswallen, we swore an oath to our forebears to protect the Murias Cauldron with our lives. We have no time to wait here, on this realm, engaged in silly love talk."

Chatter erupted among the Brotherhood. Many nodded. They must see the insanity to this situation, and the direness. Why couldn't the Arch Druid?

"Caswallen, have you no idea the threat that lies in wait? There will be another attempt on the Cauldron tonight. Know you this not?" The tree's limb was heavy on his shoulder.

Whispers continued through the line of druids as they discussed the situation amongst themselves. Caswallen remained calm and silent. Only the hardness behind his eyes betrayed his displeasure. No, it was more than that. Something sinister lingered behind his gaze.

The Arch Druid lifted his pale hand, the long fingers protruding like thin twigs from his palm, and waved it. The druids quieted, though their eyes remained unsettled. Drake's were full of tears. Why?

If the entire Council were here, who was protecting the Cauldron? Mayhaps the Arch Druid had read it in the waters and knew they would return to their realm in time to protect the ancient artifact.

Still, it was a great risk and Riagan's blood pumped hard and fast.

Caswallen paced the clearing, as if pondering the state of the village's wheat supply versus Riagan's fate. "You want to return to our realm?"

"Aye, I have been punished enough. There are more important issues at stake than whether or not I can find love. As we both know, I cannot."

Caswallen flashed a smirk but then cleared his throat and the expression vanished.

"Your predecessors made sure of that, did they not?" Riagan held the end of the tree limb, welcoming its strength. Gods knew he had none for himself. Something was amiss and he feared he might not figure it out until it was too late.

The faces of his Brothers mirrored the confusion and concern that he knew lined his own, but the Arch Druid's eyes remained cold, distant, yet satisfied in some obscure way.

"What about this woman? This woman whom you saved from imminent death, bedded, then helped to turn into a hospital patient in a psychiatric ward?"

A sickening surge of nausea started at Riagan's toes and worked its way up through his body. He swallowed against it and stood tall. How did the Arch Druid know about Wren?

Where had Caswallen been? kept repeating itself in Riagan's mind.

"You are a danger to the Brotherhood, to others. I will have to rectify your actions here on Earth, won't I? I will have to deal with this human woman you have toyed with and left broken."

"Deal with her?"

"I will need to end her life."

Wren's image flashed before him and he became suspended in time, no longer at the Council before the Arch Druid, by this ancient and wise tree. No, he was with her and only her. She was in his arms again, her head nestled into his chest. He could smell the sweet scent of her wild black hair as it tickled his chin, the small of her back, lost in his long arms as he held her tight to him.

He was hit with a sudden longing he did not understand. Mixed within this foreign emotion was an equally strong urge to bring an end to this Council, immediately.

He thought of Wren's face, soft and satisfied in slumber after their lovemaking. He had been a danger to her. That much was true. Would leaving her now and returning to the druid realm be the right answer? Maybe it was right for the Cauldron and the Brotherhood, but was it the right thing to do for Wren? When did her welfare get to be the main concern?

Whatever happened to him could happen, but he needed to get the Arch Druid off Earth and away from Wren. The message behind Caswallen's eyes when he spoke of her left him with a blackened sense of foreboding.

Emboldened by his revelation, he stood up straighter, broader, manifesting himself into the druid he always was. The Protector.

As he scanned the faces of his Brotherhood, he knew what he had to do. Saving the Cauldron wasn't the greatest priority anymore. Saving Wren was.

"I choose to remain a mortal. I will remain upon Earth. Be gone and protect the Cauldron the best you can."

A gasp erupted through the line of warriors.

"No," whispered Drake, his green eyes swimming.

The Arch Druid chuckled, an ugly sound that caused the trees to beat a wild, prompt rhythm.

Caswallen lifted his bony hand, forking his fingers at Riagan.

WREN DRAGGED HERSELF from the cavernous blackness again only to realize her greatest fear was unfolding like an accordion. She suddenly knew the meaning of terror at its purest.

She blinked to moisten her dry eyes. It was dark outside the windows, and the moon was hovering between the slats in the blinds like a white pearl.

She blinked again and a flash of yellow appeared in the corner of her eye. As if on cue, the little creature fluttered into view, bursting with the most blinding rays Wren had ever seen. The sun would not be so bright even if one were to fly directly into it.

"Destiny?"

The faery speaks. Was this what her mother heard? It sounded so *real*.

"Destiny?" she repeated. "Look at me."

Am I in Hell?

"You are no such place."

Did the faery just read my mind?

"Destiny, try to focus."

"Wren." Her throat felt like it had lost a fight with sandpaper.

"Wren, listen to me," the little creature continued. "The hour is late. The veil is thin. Riagan needs you. Go to him."

"Ray?" she mouthed. There was something she felt like she was supposed to remember about the owner of that name but couldn't.

"You must come with me."

"I can't." The medicine must have been on time-release because the tar was infiltrating her mind again. She was having trouble thinking. Speaking. "The straps…" she muttered. "I can't move."

"I will free you."

"But how?" She wasn't sure if she actually spoke the words or just thought them. Before she could try to speak again, she plummeted into the awaiting black cavity of unconsciousness.

17

Wren stumbled out of the truck of an acquaintance who had happened to be in the hospital parking lot when she fled out a side door. She thanked him, slammed the door, then darted toward the steps of the trailer.

It was a struggle to make her legs move. They were heavy, immobile with the effects of the powerful medicines she'd been given. She almost tripped over a tree root as she hurried toward the steps.

"Destiny," a deep booming voice said.

She stopped, her nails cutting into the wooden banister. It couldn't be. What was Dr. Martin doing here, and how had he gotten here so fast?

Why did he keep calling her by her first name?

"Destiny." This time it was a command, and she found herself turning, willing the shaking in her lips to calm. Her sixth sense flared.

"Dr. Martin?"

He struggled toward her, leaning heavily on his cane. The full moon's light was so bright it could still be daytime.

"I see you have left the hospital without my permission." His black eyes were like coal. "Though I'd love to know how you got out of that straitjacket."

She couldn't tell him a little faery had helped her, so she said nothing.

He shuffled toward the stairs and unease pricked her skin. His eyes seemed unfocused, shifting from her to the sky to the forest. There was something unstable, and frightening, about his presence.

"What are you doing here?" Her words dripped with the hatred she felt toward this man, masking the underlying fear.

"I did not sign off on your release."

She eased up another step.

He followed. "I should call the police."

His threat hung in the air. He wouldn't call the police to report that she'd left the hospital. No, he would also bring up Jerry's death. He would call the police to report a *suspected murderer* had left the hospital. Against doctor's orders at that.

A glint of metal reflected the moonlight as he moved. It was a small dagger, half hidden behind his back.

Fear turned to terror, and she lunged for the door. The knob twisted in her hand. He reached forward and almost caught her arm but tripped over his cane. He did catch her ankle, though, and clutched it, clamping down with surprising strength. He yanked, and she lost her balance, falling to her knee.

She kicked out. He twisted her ankle. She kicked again.

An unholy howl shattered the night air as Duke appeared from behind the house and charged toward the doctor. He growled louder than a tiger as tan pants ripped between his razor-sharp teeth.

Wren jerked free from Dr. Martin's grasp, then threw open the door that Kelly hadn't locked. She hurled herself inside, Duke on her heels. She forced the dead bolt with shaking hands.

Dr. Martin slammed his fists against the wood. "Destiny! You can't run from me!"

Wren's teeth chattered as she peeked through the peephole. Terror simmered in her like a growing disease. Dr. Martin leaned into the door and tried to stare back at her through the small glass circle. He yanked on the knob.

On silent feet, she eased into the middle of the living room. There was no other door to the trailer so she was safe for now. The windows were always locked so that wasn't an issue. She glanced at the phone in the kitchen. Should she call the police?

She hesitated. It was her word against his. Besides, she was the one who was a murder suspect and had just left a psych ward without release. He was the respected psychiatrist.

What did he want? Why would he want to hurt her?

The blinds and curtains were shut tight. For once, the noise in her head held silent, freeing up space and energy for her to decide what to do. Duke remained plastered by her side, as loyal as ever. Sounds of his heavy breathing were the only thing she could hear.

She glanced at him and did a double take. Her dog seemed larger, as if he'd been filled with water or pumped up like a hot-air balloon. He was an eighty-pound dog that now looked at least one hundred twenty.

Oh God, don't let me hallucinate now. Especially not over the one thing that brings me the most comfort.

Duke sniffed her knee, licked it once as if comforting her, then started padding around the trailer. He sniffed below each window and around the door. When he was finished with his rounds, he returned to Wren's side and sat on his haunches.

After several moments, Dr. Martin's cane scooted across the worn wooden porch with a screech, and she could tell he was moving from the door. Then she heard his cane—*thud thud thud*—as he went down the stairs.

Duke raised to all fours. He galloped into the kitchen and released a ferocious bark underneath the window. The hairs on her body rose to a spiky peak.

Against the screaming in her head to stay where she was, or to go hide in the bedroom, she forced her feet to move, one at a time, into the kitchen. With breath held, she peered through the slits in the blinds and saw Dr. Martin struggling to pull a ladder from the run-down shed behind the trailer. In one hand he held a hammer. Was he going to bust through the window? Why would he want to do this? There was something more to his actions than just her leaving the hospital.

She watched the scene unfold but refused to believe it was real. What should she do? Fight him? Escape into the forest? What did he *want*?

Duke growled low and menacingly, his nose pushed through the blinds. She could see his bared teeth. This dog would fight to the death for her, and if he would fight for her, then she would fight too. She scanned the kitchen for a knife, trying to jog her memory as to where she hid them from her mother.

Then she remembered that they were above the refrigerator, but before she pulled a stool over, she heard the sound of a truck coming up the drive. She peered through the blind and saw Brian's familiar pickup truck lurching toward the trailer.

Her heart caught in her throat. She glanced between Dr. Martin and Brian. She could tell the doctor heard the car because he shuffled out of sight behind the shed.

Brian didn't seem to see him and beeped his horn as he put the truck in park. Never had she been so happy to see him.

He hopped out of the truck and took the stairs two at a time. Wren flung the door open and fell into his arms. "Brian, thank God."

"Wren, you're shaking. Have you already heard?" His brown eyes filled with concern.

Wren wiggled away from him, then yanked at his elbow. She locked the door behind them and peeked out the window. Brian stood in the living room, watching her, his dark brows lifted. She ran back into the kitchen and peered out the slit in the blinds.

"Heard what?"

"About your mother."

"What about my mother?"

"I was at the station when we got the call."

Blood plummeted to Wren's toes as she stood there, pooling at her feet making her light-headed and dizzy.

"What call?"

"That she's gone missing."

"What? She's in the hospital. She can't go missing from a hospital."

"She has, Wren. The police are looking for her now. I'm sorry."

Her mother had left the hospital? She pulled out her cell phone and saw several missed calls from Kelly. Wren felt detached, as if her spirit was floating in space and her body was just a shell on Earth.

"I'm sure they'll find her," he said. "They're looking in town and surrounding areas now."

She wondered if surrounding areas encompassed the forest around the trailer, or if it was too remote? If they were smart, they would start there, she thought to herself, but Wren didn't say anything. She would find her mother herself, and that way there would be no need to involve the authorities. The last thing she wanted was for her mother to be put into a home because Wren couldn't care for her.

This was nothing unusual, she told herself. Her mother often talked about running away, finding far-off, obscure friends, leaving Earth, but Wren wrote the talk off as another hallucination, another quirk of schizophrenia. In truth, Annie often disappeared when Wren wasn't looking, and if she was found, it was deep in the forest. If she wasn't, well, she always returned.

There was no reason this time would be any different.

Wren thought of Ray and suddenly yearned for him like a salve for a burn. She did not question why. Her instincts told her to find him, that maybe his insane words could add sanity to this situation, and she would listen to those instincts. Besides, nothing else made sense in her life.

"Brian, we need to talk."

Duke sat by her leg, and she rubbed his furry head which now came up to her waist. She scoured his body only to find paws that had widened again, legs that had lengthened, and a body that had expanded to even greater girth.

She blinked.

Brian seemed to notice as well. "How much have you been feeding that dog?" He tried to force a smile, but it slid away as he met her gaze.

She tossed her curls to clear her head. "Brian, I—I'm not the woman for you."

"What?"

"I can't do this anymore."

Wren felt the burn of his eyes on her, but she could not look up. He was a good man and deserved better than what she could give him. She looked at Duke instead and couldn't help but wonder what he had eaten. *Had* she fed him too much? Duke shook his head, as if telling her that his size had nothing to do with her overfilling his food bowl.

"Wren?"

"I need to leave this area for a while."

"What about your mother?"

"Kelly will call me when they find her."

He lifted his arm toward her but stopped before making contact. What did her expression tell him? She could only imagine.

He turned his back to her. Then, without a word, he left the trailer. He rotated to face her once more from the driveway but did not wave.

Wren turned to Duke. "She might be in the forest."

The dog's head bobbed up and down. Up and down.

"Ray will be there too."

Again, the large head moved.

"I must hurry."

Duke pushed against her thigh, urging her toward the door.

TWO DRUIDS RESTRAINED Drake, hands clamped around his struggling arms. "You can't do this, Caswallen. We need him."

The Arch Druid turned to Drake and flicked his index finger. Drake fell against the Brothers as if stunned by a gun.

"He has decided his fate, has he not? He has opted for a mortal life. He has opted to try and save the woman he almost killed."

Riagan studied the man standing across the clearing. He looked like the same Arch Druid who had taught him folklore and magic for the past years. The man before him had the same gaunt, thin frame, always swallowed beneath the fabric of the robes. His hands were long, veiny and white, resembling more ghost than man. But there was a change, in more than just his curt, cold attitude. Nay, there was a change behind his eyes, a change in his soul.

Riagan met his brother's blazing gaze. "Aye. This is how it must be, Drake. You must find another to fill my place as one of the Protectors, if it is not lost from us on this night."

"Who would that be, pray tell?" Drake said, wailing. "We need *you*. We have no other in our bloodline." He fought against those holding him, despair storming his handsome features.

"Aye, Brother. We have another."

Their gazes locked. "Gwyon."

Drake's mouth fell open. "Gwyon?"

"Aye. He is our father's blood-born son and will carry the gene. Let him take my place."

"But, Riagan. He can't."

Riagan fought a choke that threatened to spill upward and suffocate him. He needed all of his strength—he was losing everything that was dear to him, save for Wren. The best for everyone would be to move on. Without him. He would remain on Earth and watch over Wren, even if it was from afar.

And the Brotherhood, well, yes, there was another and it was time to make amends—to make amends to a little babe who was born with crooked feet and denied a place in the Brotherhood.

Gwyon hadn't even been given a chance. With two sons, strong and physically perfect, already given to the Brotherhood, there was no need for another. Thus, when he was born, Gwyon was allowed to drink from the Cauldron's waters for immortality, but not for healing. And he was the one who needed it.

Where was he now? Would he want a chance to finally belong? The image of Gwyon's sad dark eyes following every move he and the Brothers made grabbed Riagan's heart and twisted it into a braid. He should have been given a chance. No man of their powerful bloodline, crooked feet or not, deserved to be treated like one of the women who did the weaving and wash. This was the least he could do.

"Yes, he can. Bring him into the Brotherhood, teach him the ancient wisdom. When he has learned all that his mind and soul can learn, lead him to the Cauldron and let him drink. Then he can take his place among the Brotherhood where he belongs."

"Impossible." Caswallen's expression held satisfaction. Certainty. "One must remain outside the Brotherhood who has the gene. He cannot become a member."

Drake yanked free of the strong hands that held him. "But brother, you have found true love, have you not? We do not need a replacement."

Another ugly chuckle erupted from the Arch Druid's lips and all turned, confusion set upon every brow. "He doesn't know how to love. Each Arch Druid has made sure of that. None of you can love."

"What?" Drake demanded, not understanding what Riagan already knew. At least his assumption was confirmed. He was never meant to fulfill the terms of his banishment. He was never meant to return.

"Riagan, son of Ragda, you have not fulfilled the terms of your punishment. You will remain a mortal upon this earth just as you asked. And so it shall be." Caswallen raised his thin arm and forked his fingers toward Riagan again. The robe fell away, revealing skin so white it was gray.

Then a voice, soft and vulnerable, said, "No."

Wren stood at the edge of the clearing, Oephille sitting on her shoulder, and a massive oak tree standing at her back.

WREN FORCED HERSELF to stay rooted to the ground, imagining herself one of the surrounding trees, despite the frightening and intimidating stares of the massive men in front of her. The soft flutter of the faery's wings beat against her cheek, and the rough bark against her back was welcome support.

There was an acrid scent deep within this forest that she couldn't place. It smelled like something burning, something metallic, something stranger than any smell she'd ever encountered.

In an arc along one side of the clearing stood several men, all wearing identical, flowing red robes. One looked exactly like Ray, and she knew that must be the brother he spoke of. A step in front was an older man with long gray hair and pasty, pale skin. He glared at her through eyes as cold and harsh as the Arctic Circle. She gasped at the hatred she saw there. Evil, pure evil was all she could think.

Her hands sought the bark of the tree.

She felt a flash of relief that she did not see her mother in the midst of these men. Where she was, though, Wren would have to tackle after she was finished here—whatever that meant.

The limb wrapped around her hand and gently squeezed. She felt instantly better, as if the tree gave her some of the oxygen that seemed all but void in this strange place.

Ray stared at her as if trying to figure out if she was a dream come true or a nightmare most feared.

She should say something, but it was Ray who spoke first. "Wren?"

She wanted to smile, or at least look less terrified, but her facial muscles would not work. So she just stood there, more uncertain and alarmed than she had ever been in her life.

Ray's body bulged with what she imagined was unshed energy, making him look even bigger than before, if that were possible. He finally pulled his gaze from hers and swung it between her and the man with the cold eyes.

"Who presents themselves at this sacred Council?" demanded the older man. He must be the Arch Druid Ray had mentioned that day when he told her who he really was, the day when she believed she'd lost her mind and traveled straight to Hell on an express train. Now, with this ominous man before her, she wondered if *this* was not Hell.

The tree nudged her shoulder. She cleared her throat and tried to answer, but it came out as a dry, coarse groan. She coughed then said, "My name is Wren O'Hara."

She stepped forward, Ray suddenly by her side.

A flash of what looked like shock crossed the older man's face but was quickly replaced with a leer oozing with hatred.

"Why have you come here, Wren O'Hara?" His voice, just a hint deeper than her seven-year-old nephew's, did not sound pleased. Didn't he want Ray to return to his home? To protect this Cauldron?

Somehow she got the impression he did not. In fact, rage contorted his features and she stepped back, suddenly gripped by terror.

"Have strength, Wren." The tiny faery's words were crystal clear and sounded exactly like the voices she'd been hearing these past months. It was a wonder she hadn't understood them all along.

The rough twigs of the tree's limbs lay over her shoulder like hands. Without them, she didn't think she could speak, but she absorbed the strength of this powerful mass and said, "My business is to say that…" She turned to Ray. His eyes glowed like green jade lit from within.

"I…I've come to say that…" What had she come to say? That her reality on Earth was becoming unbearable so better to live in the land of insanity? Or that she actually believed Ray's words and wanted to help?

With her eyes boring into Ray's, she stated, "I have fallen in love with this man, Ra—I mean, Riagan T-T-Tenman." She hoped she pronounced his name correctly, realizing it was more of a fit for him. A simple and easy name like Ray didn't merge with such a complex and powerful man.

Breath seeped out of Riagan's chest as if he'd just been deflated. She couldn't tell if he was moved by her words or if he found them a bore.

She turned back to the ancient-looking man standing before her. He met her gaze unflinchingly, and she recoiled. Never had she seen a face so ashen gray on a person who was alive. Well, she didn't know if he was alive or not. Hadn't Riagan mentioned something about being immortal? Jerry had had the same color after his spirit left his body.

The surrounding light flared. Where did it come from? The silvery glow cast an eerie sheen across the clearing.

Riagan grasped her by the shoulders and turned her toward him. He lifted her face with his finger. "You love me? You love me true?"

He cradled her face in his large palms and looked into her eyes, as if searching to the depths of her soul for the answer. "It wasn't just because we made love?"

"It wasn't because of that." Tears welled in her eyes and the Council was all but forgotten. "I just love you."

"Wren." His face contorted as if he were in pain.

Wasn't this what he wanted to hear? Didn't she need to love him? But he needed to love her back, didn't he?

Her heart sank like a cinder block. He didn't love her.

He needed to love her in return and he didn't.

She wanted to cry and bit her lower lip to prevent the trembling. What had she expected?

His solid arm wrapped around her shoulder, pulling her into his chest. His heartbeat was strong and fast, his body tense. Despite the fact that she'd confessed her love and he didn't respond, his embrace told her he would protect her no matter what. It lessened the weight of despair threatening to stop her heart, though only a little.

But when the Arch Druid cackled out a sound to rival an evil witch's, she knew she'd need his protection at this moment more than his love.

18

"Riagan." The Arch Druid's voice sliced through the forest causing the trees to beat against one another, unsettled and agitated. "Does your friend understand you have to feel love, too, for you to fulfill the terms of your banishment? Does she know why you were banished in the first place?"

Riagan clasped Wren so close, he could tell she struggled to breathe. He needed to keep her nearby, though. Danger permeated the forest like a foul odor.

The semicircle of men watched, alert. He knew they were eager to have their Brotherhood restored to its ultimate power. How could Caswallen justify otherwise?

Wren's shoulders shook, but he did not release his grip.

Caswallen clasped his hands in front of his concave stomach. "Whatever the case, Riagan, it is too late."

"No, it's not," whispered one of his Brothers.

Drake stepped forward, his red robe blinding against the lightness of his hair. "What say you, Caswallen? He needs to return to his Brotherhood where he belongs." Drake lowered his voice, but his words dripped with fury. "Need I remind you that the hour of attack is upon us?"

The Arch Druid regarded Drake with ice in his eyes before slowly turning to Riagan.

"You did not fulfill the terms. There will be no forgiveness."

Riagan wished Wren had not come, that she was back at her run-down trailer with her boy of a future fiancé and her funny-looking mutt. She had already sacrificed too much for him. He did not want her to sacrifice her life, and by the way Caswallen was studying her, the seriousness of his intent was growing more obvious with each passing minute.

The Arch Druid lifted his hands and pushed the hood back until it fell below his shoulders. His face was ugly, altered within a sneer Riagan had never seen before.

"It is too late. The Murias Cauldron is, as we speak, being taken. You have lost, and you will die a mortal. Along with your mortal lover."

CASWALLEN LUNGED FOR Wren as he pulled a dagger from inside his robe. The moon's light reflected off its long blade, like a beacon calling for her life. One thrust would kill her, that was clear.

Wren could see this, but somehow felt disconnected, as if she was watching from a limb high in one of these giant oaks. Everything moved slowly, sluggishly.

She tried to lift her hand to fend off the attack but couldn't. Was it the medicine still coursing through her body, was she still in the straitjacket, or was this all just a dream?

When she felt Riagan's hard shove into the tree, the impact awoke her from whatever strange hold she was under. With the breath knocked out of her, the tree's bark opened like a cavernous black mouth and wrapped around her body. She tried to scream, but she could hear no sound other than the vibrations of the wood.

She could see out, though, as clearly as she had when she was by Riagan's side. He crouched with his back to her, arms spread wide. His shirt ripped in several places as his body grew in size, much like Duke's had done.

Riagan grabbed for Caswallen's dagger, but missed, and it sliced through his palm. Blood ran down his hand and over his arm, too red against the paleness of his skin. He didn't seem to notice because he crouched low again, his powerful legs bent, ready to spring. He raised his arms, palms opened toward the elder.

The two men circled each other—one crouched, one upright. Beads of sweat covered Riagan's brow, but the Arch Druid was as calm as shallow water, his face hardened, focused on his goal, which, she thought with a shudder, was to kill.

Then, with a sudden burst of what sounded like thunder, a bulbous black mass burst forth from the center of the clearing. Within a heartbeat, the mass splintered into a band of black-as-night creatures with long talons and sharp teeth that dripped with saliva. A second later, they spread out to surround the clearing and those in it.

Drake's voice boomed, "We fight!"

With one hand, each druid removed a dagger from beneath his cloak. With the other, they pulled out a sword. The whoosh of their synchronized movement blew the hair around her face as they sliced at the oncoming creatures.

"Brother," Drake yelled.

Riagan lifted his left hand, palm open, ready to accept the sword he seemed to know his brother was throwing. His long fingers closed around the hilt like it was a limb of his own body, and he made two swift slices through the air. Then he crouched again. His broad back rippled with tension, his eyes never leaving his target.

The Brotherhood formed a circle, their backs toward the middle, their long arms thrust outward with weapons ready. Wren could feel their power even from within the depth of the tree, the only tree that did not thrash and beat to the rhythm of battle.

The creatures rushed forward, eyes wild and glowing red like they were lit by inner fire. They weaved between the surrounding trees, popping in and out of view, until they surrounded the smaller, tighter group of druids. The warriors did not flinch. The power emanating from them wavered through the air like bursts of orange, red, and black, like a fireworks display.

Riagan and Caswallen were oblivious to these monsters and circled each other like birds of prey until a piercing war cry erupted and everyone turned. Wren covered her ears, but that didn't stop her from hearing the most painful wail she'd ever heard. When she looked to see who, or what, made that sound, she saw an enormous black crow sitting on a nearby tree's heavy branch. Its shining black beak was opened wide, obscuring its entire face with its haunting deep pit.

The bird halted its call and everything was quiet. The crow expanded its broad wings, at least eight feet wide. Its eyes were round as saucers and orange, bright, glowing. The creature scanned the clearing, then flew to the Earth's floor where it positioned itself along the periphery as if it were about to referee a football game.

After a lightning-quick flick of its long wing, the battle began.

The creatures broke apart and rushed the circle of druids. The druids crouched in unison, not to the ground but as if compacting their bodies into an impenetrable wall. The slice of metal against flesh sent shivers into the tree and through her body.

Riagan thrust forward and Caswallen lunged right. With a fluid swipe, Riagan's dagger sliced the elder's cloak and blood oozed over the fabric, darkening the already red hue. The druid grabbed the hilt of Riagan's dagger, then yanked Riagan toward him. The Arch Druid was powerful for such a thin, sickly looking man. The tree shook around her and she knew its fear.

Riagan, with a pull of his arm that ripped the entire side of his shirt, broke free of the druid's hold and crouched again, muscles pulsing. His back, broad and strong, heaved with his breath.

She looked up to see the moon, full and enormous, looming through a newly formed opening in the trees' canopy, like a spectator at a sporting event. The crow sat immobile but alert—an ominous black mass that would have been difficult to ignore were it not for the life-and-death battle unfolding in front of her.

Then she saw a familiar shadow weaving along the tree line. She strained to see past the men, but it disappeared behind a massive trunk before it reappeared and the moonlight reflected off the canine form.

Duke.

"Duke, run," she screamed, but her warning cry was swallowed up by the sounds of battle.

He must have heard her, though, because he swiveled his bulk in her direction, his large chocolate eyes focused and alert. He inclined his head at her but stayed at the edge of the battle, positioned like a sentry. If it were even possible, he seemed bigger here in the forest—like a small horse more than a large dog. Was she hallucinating again?

The sounds of creatures dying yanked her attention back to the battle. It was a hateful sound—one of fury, disaster, desperation. She thought this would be a massacre, that there was no way the small number of druids could win against so many. But the circle of warrior druids had not broken, had not shrunk. In fact, they had broadened the space of their circle, and their arms flew with slices faster than strikes of lightning. Enemy after enemy charged toward them and fell.

With each jab of the dagger or whip of the sword, another monster died, only to be replaced by another until she realized they replenished instantly. How, she did not know.

There was no frustration on the faces of the warriors, though. Their motions were as crisp and lethal as when the battle began. Riagan's brother fought three men at once, whirling in a deadly dance as his weapons flew through the air, slicing through fur and skin, piercing organs, causing death. The others were just as efficient.

Riagan made an arc with his dagger, forcing the Arch Druid back on his heels. The elder was not finished, though, and lunged toward Riagan, just missing his throat. Wren could hear the whistle of the Arch Druid's sword as it whirled through the air. Riagan darted behind the elder's back and thrust his dagger, cutting through Caswallen's robe.

As Caswallen stumbled, two creatures came after Riagan, pushing him back toward the tree where she was held. Sweat glistened off his skin like crystals. He did not appear winded but focused, lethal. His white knuckles circled around the hilt of his dagger, whose tip dripped with blood.

The creatures sprang forward, and Riagan moved so fast she could no longer see his arms. He whirled with the force of a hurricane—slicing, jabbing, and killing.

Two more appeared.

Riagan's body didn't seem real, he was moving so fast. He stabbed through creature after creature in one fluid movement until each fell upon the ground, dead.

Just as he stopped and turned toward Wren, another stream of blackness burst from behind the trees. Would they ever stop?

The Arch Druid crouched before Riagan who was huffing now, heaving with exertion.

Duke wove in and out of the trees, his eyes flipping from Riagan to Wren. He came to her side and sat, alert.

Just when it looked like Riagan was fading and the Arch Druid was gathering renewed energy, the tree's longest limb reached down and pushed the Arch Druid, knocking him off balance.

The crow cawed. She heard a chuckle and glanced down at Duke. Was he smirking?

Riagan lunged forward and with one powerful thrust of his dagger, pierced the shoulder, missing the heart by inches. Caswallen gasped. With a blood-curdling battle cry, Riagan yanked the dagger back and positioned himself to attack again.

The Arch Druid didn't falter. He stood with his mouth open and his eyes wide. If possible, he turned a shade more ashen gray but he did not fall. Riagan watched, ready to strike again. Duke rose to all fours.

Caswallen laughed, a coyote-like cry as the trees moaned their own monotone wail of distress. The ebony monsters, those still alive and standing, stopped midfight. The druids tightened their defensive circle, backs facing inward, arms facing outward, tightly woven. Blood dripped from sword and dagger.

Then all at once, the enemy, with Caswallen leading, morphed together into one dark mass, losing all shape and distinction. The globule hovered in the air, right in the middle of the circle of warriors, then dispersed like a mass of flies.

The warriors turned to Riagan, whose shirt was soaked with perspiration, dyed red with blood. The tree let Wren go and she rushed forward, her arms circling Riagan as he fell to the ground, either in a faint or dead. Duke went to his side and sniffed the hair on his head.

Riagan's twin darted toward them, swinging out the sides of his cloak until they were all covered by its soft thread. He started to chant, words she didn't understand. Before she could question him, she was sucked inside a black void. She couldn't see. All she heard was a deafening drone. If she screamed, she couldn't hear it.

Then she was falling. With Riagan wrapped in her arms, she couldn't reach out, couldn't stop her plummeting. Down…down…down until she lost consciousness.

19

There she was, a hazy apparition, floating above his head. An angel. A goddess. A dream.

Hmm…death becomes me. If this is the afterlife, I will take a hundred.

"Riagan?" Her voice was soft and sensual, caressing his skin with silky threads.

"Riagan."

I could melt into that gentle cadence and linger for eternity.

"Riagan!"

Och, but that is melodious no longer.

"Riagan Tenman, if that truly is your name, open your eyes right now and look at me, or I'll pinch your arm."

Well, I don't want to open my eyes if that's the way my afterlife dream goes. Now this must be Hell. Humph.

His lids popped open.

Her lips split into a smile.

"That's better," she crooned. "Can you speak?"

"Wren?" His eyes closed again and his body went limp.

"Riagan?" The shrill of her voice hurt his ears. She slapped at his cheeks. He wanted her to stop but couldn't wake up enough to say so.

"Damn it, Riagan, open your eyes."

They flew open. "Yell at me not, lass. I have a headache."

"Oh, Riagan." She pulled him to her breast and hugged him tight. Now he knew he'd died and gone to Heaven. He nuzzled deeper into her breasts to where he could scarcely breathe. But with breasts like these, he didn't need oxygen.

"Can you speak?" she asked.

His mouth tasted like metal and was as dry as a dandelion on a scorching summer day.

"Are you okay? How are you feeling? Are you badly hurt?"

Her white shirt had fallen from her skin as she bent forward and he had a perfect view of her plump breasts. He lifted his head and licked the bare skin that swelled out from the thin cotton.

Then his head hit the ground.

"Not funny," she quipped.

He struggled to sit up. "What happened?" he croaked.

Drake popped into view.

"Drake, have you died as well?"

"Died?" Confusion flashed across Drake's face, then he shook his head. "Died? Neither of us is dead, you ancient oaf."

Wren leaned forward and her plump breasts grazed his cheek again. He could not resist another lick, and this time she did not pull away. Then he buried his head between those two delicious orbs and inhaled. She giggled, and he grazed his teeth over her exposed skin.

With each nibble, his mind fought for clarity. Had he hit his head? The last thing he remembered was the fight with Caswallen in the clearing. Wren had showed up and confessed her love for him, and Caswallen had deemed it too late, saying the Cauldron was being taken soon.

He sought the familiar forest of Earth but was met with an even more familiar scene—the druid realm. Bolting upright, he demanded, "Brother, how did I return to this realm? Did Caswallen forgive me after all? Has this all been but a dream?"

Wren's brows pursed and her generous mouth formed into a perfect cherry, as if she wanted to interrupt and say something but didn't know what.

Then he knew. He had crossed the portal. By the gods, he'd crossed the portal. And *Wren* was here?

"Where is Caswallen? What has happened? How long have I been out? How did Wren cross?"

"Cross what?" she asked.

Drake held his hand up to stop the onslaught of questions. "You have been out but a minute Earth's time—"

"Earth's time? What does that mean?" Wren asked, interrupting. "I thought I fainted. Where are—?" She stared at the unfamiliar surroundings.

Drake spoke to Riagan, his voice strained. "Right after you fainted, I was able to grab you, and I pulled you and your lady through." He stared into Riagan's eyes, a message there that his pained head wouldn't let through. "There were no problems."

"No problems?" Riagan struggled to understand. "But, I did not confess."

Drake held his palm up. "There is no time to explain that which you already suspect. But you must rise, Brother. It is time. We must protect the Cauldron."

"I fainted?" Riagan still wondered what his brother was trying to say.

"Didn't *I* faint?" Wren's brows drew together.

"Hush. Both of you. I will explain later."

Riagan struggled to stand, but his legs felt like leaden logs. "I cannot, Brother. You must go without me."

"Aye. It takes time for your entire form to return, but you must come."

Riagan looked at Wren. "How did you cross?"

"How did I cross what? Where the hell are we?"

"Come, we must hurry," Drake said. "Wren, can you support him on that side, and I'll take the brunt of his weight on this side?"

"This makes no sense," she muttered as she scooped underneath his arm and helped Drake stand him up.

Riagan stared at her, but she faced forward as they pushed ahead. She glowed in this world, like a flickering candle. He found it difficult to look away from her luminous skin, but he did, and found himself staring at her hair. Had it grown?

"Focus, Brother. You must channel your mind to the task ahead. They have not taken the Cauldron yet but lie in wait, ready to strike at midnight. It is but nearly the hour and you, we, must be ready."

"The Cauldron? By the gods, where is the Brotherhood?" Riagan whipped out of their arms, spinning in a three sixty.

"I sense them but admit I have not seen them yet."

"So they crossed?"

"I believe so. Pray that they are at their posts spanning the realm. You are the Protector who defends the Cauldron at its resting place, though. If the one they call Master is already on this realm, and I suspect he is, then you are the most important one at this moment."

"Yes." Riagan straightened, unsupported. He'd been born to protect the ancient artifact, and he would not defy his heritage again. And with this lady by his side, he felt invincible.

He would answer the question of how he, and Wren, crossed the portal later. Wren was safe enough by his side. Now, it was time to save the Cauldron.

RIAGAN SHOOK OFF the effects of the battle much the same way Duke shook off water. He rose to his full height, erect and proud, his long body somehow more grand and powerful than she remembered. The mortal clothes tugged where the seams were not already ripped as his muscles seemed to expand and his height grew.

Riagan was changing, there was no denying that. He flexed and unflexed his hands; his face hardened into a line of will and determination. It was at once terrifying and awesome to behold.

Wren stumbled as she tried to gather her wits and close her mouth, which she knew was dangling open like an unhinged window screen after a hurricane.

His skin was beautiful, like carved white marble. She reached out a hand to caress it, for surely he was a mirage.

Just as she leaned into him, someone grabbed her wrist and yanked. It was Drake, staring hard into her face. She tried again to shut her mouth but wasn't certain of success.

"We must hurry," Drake urged.

"What?" she sputtered. Riagan's scent wove around her like silk ribbon—a heady mixture of musk, vanilla, and some undefined masculine notes that made her head feel as if it were a balloon about to float away to Heaven.

As soon as Drake lessened his grasp, she moved forward again. Riagan stood before her as a powerful warrior druid, an immortal druid. Her safe place in the middle of his chest was far above her head now. She reached up to caress it, wanting to make sure it was still there, but Drake grabbed her chin and turned her face toward his.

"There will be time for that later, lass."

She felt like she was drowning in a vat of warm, sweet olive oil. The world in front of her became hazy, and Drake's voice came from somewhere far away. She was lusciously sandwiched between two of the most masculine bodies ever created, grateful they were taking over this situation because for some reason, she couldn't even remember her name. Tingling shot through her body, and every cell she was made of burst alive.

Somewhere far away, in the very distant place where her brain could still think, she sensed tension in the air, urgency pulsing through the two men at her sides. When she put her hands on each of their arms, she couldn't help but move them up and down, relishing the severe undulations of their magnificent muscles, the sheer power held beneath the skin.

One of the men growled, and she lifted her chin to find Riagan glaring at his brother, whose face was set in a smirk. Her hands stopped mid-rub, and Riagan grabbed her wrist, yanking her far away from his brother. He put his arm around her waist, hugging her against him, then propelled her forward, keeping her several feet from Drake.

For someone who didn't love her, he surely was jealous.

Feeling overly satisfied, she forced herself to look ahead. "Where—where on Earth are we?"

"We are not on Earth, Wren." He squeezed her side. "Open your mind."

Not on Earth? All she remembered was the Arch Druid disappearing. Then the tree had released her from its hold. She'd knelt before Riagan and cradled him until he awoke. That was just a few moments ago. When did they have the time to leave Earth? Many strange things were happening, that was for sure.

"Well, where are we? Have I been here before? And where's Duke? He was in the forest with us."

"Shh," Riagan said gently. "We must be quiet. I'm not sure even I understand all that has happened."

They ducked behind a thirty-foot tree that was wide enough to shield them. The light was a mixture of radiant blue and somber gray, part shimmery, part staid. The sound of rushing water came from nearby, but she could see no river. They were surrounded by trees, thousands upon thousands of trees, larger and grander than those in the forest behind her trailer.

They were, in fact, enormous both in height and width. Their bark was as smooth as glass, though deep brown in color like normal trees. The limbs, though too high above her head to touch, glistened in the obscure light, and she felt sure they would be of the same glassy material. The leaves, the smallest the size of a dinner plate and the largest at least as big as a chair's seat, shimmered high above her head, not like glitter, but as if she could see life pumping through their veins.

She'd never seen anything so beautiful, well, except for the two men flanking her sides. They were certainly beautiful…and masculine…and powerful…and ethereal. Her stomach flipped each time she looked from one to the other. If she died now, in the midst of this male perfection, she would die a very happy woman.

Just then the sound of pounding feet merged with the noise from the water, jolting her into the moment. Coming from the left was a group of men, the Arch Druid at the helm. They marched in a perfect V formation with silver swords in one hand and large sickles in the other. Each person, if that's what they were, was clad in head-to-toe black, making her think of ninjas from a Japanese action flick. Even their faces were covered with black masks, with only slits open for their eyes.

Drake and Riagan laid large palms on her shoulders, pushing her down into a crouched position as they followed suit.

"Drake," Riagan whispered, "Caswallen is the one known as Master?"

"Aye."

"They are one and the same?"

"Aye."

"Did you suspect?"

"Nay, brother. The worlds have been unsettled since the night you were banned. But who could have foreseen this? As you know, we of the Brotherhood may be immortal but we are not privy to the sight." He paused for a moment, then continued. "If only I'd known."

"I don't understand," Wren began. "Well, I don't understand anything, but why is the Arch Druid after the Cauldron? I mean, is he now the enemy? And what is the sight? Is that like seeing things? Telling the future?"

Riagan gazed down at her. "Aye. He must be after immortality. By gaining access to the Cauldron, he can drink from its waters and become thus."

"It is likely. I have no other explanation," Drake agreed.

After the group disappeared in the distance, to where she did not know, the brothers took her by her arms, lifting her to her feet. The trio followed a worn trail until the sound of the river filled Wren's ears, rushing and alive.

They started to climb a steep slope, the grade making movement difficult, but they pushed ahead until they came to a small lookout high on a mountainside. There, they hunched down behind a gray stone boulder. Below, the black-clad men stood in a circle, their arms uplifted, their palms touching at the pinkie finger until they merged as one. There was no sign of the rest of the Brotherhood.

Looming like a massive white orb was the full moon, just off to their right, hovering like a crystal ball. So enormous and close, Wren could hit it with a rock. "Oh. My. God."

Riagan's hand clamped down over her mouth before she could say more.

Now she knew she was hallucinating. The moon consumed a quarter of the night sky with its radiant white presence. She could see the cavernous beaches and the soaring mountains. She knew if she walked forward, she would be able to touch it.

"Riagan," she began, but he gave her a gentle shake.

"You must be quiet."

She nodded, and he loosened his grip.

The sounds of chanting wafted up with a breeze, and she was able to focus on the small, black group below as they lifted their heads. The moon's glow reflected off their faces, ghostly in the gray light.

Wren shuddered. "Where is the Cauldron?"

Riagan pointed to the left. She had been so consumed by the moon she hadn't noticed the waterfall. It was enormous too, at least three stories high, with a narrow yet powerful overflow of water rushing down the rock face of a mountain. Was everything here supersized?

The water cascaded into a pool at the bottom of the mountain, but the place where it landed seemed undersized for the amount of water pouring into it. A gentle river also flowed into the pool and she wondered if it accommodated the massive amount of water from the fall. Or was there something else down there? Somewhere else the water went?

Caswallen's men dropped their arms and turned as a single unit toward the waterfall. They moved forward, almost gliding across the moss-covered ground. Riagan and Drake were tense and so was she.

Something was about to happen.

But what?

20

Riagan, Wren, and Drake watched as the group, led by Caswallen, stepped into the water that pooled at the bottom of the waterfall. The men walked in a single-file line, easing into the water as if walking down stairs. When their heads submerged and there was no ripple of water, Riagan flashed a silent plea at Wren to remain with his brother. After he received her quiet nod of agreement, his gaze turned to Drake. A separate silent message passed between them in which Riagan pleaded for Drake to forgo going to his post, to remain by Wren's side. Drake agreed, knowing it was Riagan who needed to be nearest the Cauldron at this direst of moments.

Riagan slid down the mountain.

He was several paces behind the last man in the group and knew he moved with the quietness of a spider. Riagan said a prayer of thanks to the gods for giving him back his full druid powers when he crossed the portal.

The water numbed the soles of his feet, ice cold, but so welcome. This was the pool he knew well. He had not only been born near this very spot, but the cave to the Cauldron lay just behind this waterfall, deeply imbedded into the rock face.

Were he not so focused, like a viper on its prey, he would have cried tears of joy and jubilation at returning home. His stomach churned when he thought of the Arch Druid's betrayal. How could he change to the side of evil and void his most sacred vows? When did he become the Master? It must've happened right under their unassuming noses.

Caswallen had been born into the Arch Druid's role, been trained for it his entire life, was chosen by the gods as the one who would become the next leader of this group of warriors. What did this mean for the Brotherhood of the Sacred Grove? They had never encountered such a betrayal, and Riagan was not sure how they would recover or survive.

His muscles coiled and constricted as he submerged beneath the water, but he shut his mind to anything other than the Cauldron. Its powerful presence lured him forward, obscuring all other thoughts as it beckoned him to cross the mile underwater to get to its dwelling place.

He maintained his gait to match that of Caswallen and the others, careful not to fall behind, but as careful not to plunge ahead. Did they detect his presence? He knew the spell of invisibility, which not only made him physically invisible but also made the energy he emitted invisible. Caswallen would know how to counter that spell, but as the group continued forward, he doubted he'd see use for it. Caswallen likely thought Riagan was dead or stuck upon the Earth as a mortal.

He likely thought the first half of his goal was achieved.

The water was a cool, transparent green, almost like looking through a piece of sea glass. These waters were enchanted, brought forth from the lakes of the Isle before the great storm obliterated that sacred place. Even through transport, the waters, carried in oak barrels in the hulls of great wooden ships, maintained their magical, protective powers. Only within a pool such as this could an artifact as revered as the Murias Cauldron remain protected, and only through an enchanted river could men be submerged for so long without breath.

Just ahead, a neon glow lit the water. The entrance to the cave. The Cauldron. Caswallen's men had made it. But so had he.

He slipped around the side to come at the Cauldron from a narrow passageway he'd carved into the side of the rock face, a passage even the Arch Druid didn't know of. He'd carved that hidden door to sneak out and meet his lovers.

A stab of pain shot through his heart, and he closed his eyes. So much had been sacrificed for his wanton desires. But then he thought of Wren and pushed ahead, determination igniting his every warrior sense.

As he passed the opening, he eased the door shut so that no water seeped into the passageway. His lungs filled with the air that pumped deep into the cave through a narrow hole that had been drilled from the top of the mountain.

The pounding thud of multiple footsteps reverberated off the rock face, telling Riagan the enemy was closer than he thought. He stole along the black, smooth wall, ancient instincts telling him the way since he'd not lit the lantern.

It did not take long until the green light of the Cauldron blazed from a pit deep within. He quickened his steps, and moments later relief flooded over him to see the ancient artifact nestled in its groove. Safe. Sound. Secure.

The treasure, pristine black and shiny, sat humbly in a small recess built into the wall. The Cauldron was merely eight inches in height, and in no way portrayed the amount of power housed within its unpretentious bowl.

The sounds of his enemy grew, causing his heartbeat to spike.

Riagan knew not what he was to encounter, but he was ready. It all came down to this: he was a sworn Protector of the Murias Cauldron and by the gods, he would protect it.

He planted his large body in front of the artifact and waited.

A breath later, Caswallen's men appeared through the blackened walls.

The Arch Druid stopped feet from Riagan and the others fell in behind him, forming a tight-knit semicircle.

Riagan braced himself.

"Riagan Tenman, son of Ragda." Caswallen's brows rose in shock then fell in fury. Was he surprised to see Riagan? It was obvious he was. It took only seconds for him to compose himself, though. "You have lost, Riagan. Your Brothers are engaged in combat across the realm and unable to assist you. You have failed in your task. Surrender the artifact or blood will be drawn on this night." His eyes pierced Riagan's. "Your blood, your brother's, and the woman's."

Riagan's muscles pulled tighter than the strings of a bow. He scanned the men. Their swords were not drawn, nor were their daggers.

So he will use magic to obtain the Cauldron—the magic of the wise and learned Arch Druid.

But how did he and his men pass through the water into the cave? He was not a Protector. He was not immortal. He could only pass through if a member of the Brotherhood escorted him.

Who then is the traitor? He scanned the faces. His mind felt foggy, unclear, weighed down by the uncertainty pulsing through him.

There is something I am not seeing.

Riagan rose to his full height and braced himself. For what he was uncertain.

Eyes locked on Caswallen, he did not see the arrow as it came whizzing through the air, lethal in its precision.

A jolt of pain shot through his body as the arrow's tip, fired from close range in the shadows, pierced his shoulder. He gasped, once, then fell like a stone.

WREN WATCHED RIAGAN burst out of the water, onto the shore, then rise to the soft ground. His legs moved so fast she could not distinguish one from the other, though the bright crimson sheen of blood traveling down from his shoulder, over his bicep, and toward his wrist was as visible as the grandiose moon to her side.

"The Cauldron's been taken." Riagan's voice boomed like a drum. "And the Brotherhood are engaged in battle across the realm. There is no one to help."

The Cauldron? Taken?

Drake dove over the edge of their hideout and was beside his brother a second later.

A black mass moved in the distance, passing by the moon like a shadow. Wren could not detect individual forms but knew that it was the Arch Druid and his band of black-clothed men. As they neared, she could see a glowing green light coming from within the group. The Cauldron.

She jumped when a cool hand fell on her shoulder from behind, clamping down, taking away her ability to bolt away, or to even turn and look. Whoever the stranger was bent down and spoke into her ear.

She was struck mute by the soft cadence of the foreign tongue he spoke in, and by the distant yet real feeling she'd heard this voice before.

His hand was cold, like ice held within a thin towel. Strength poured from this hand through the skin on her shoulder and began to work its way through her body. With this touch and this voice, something in her began to change, like the uncoiling of a rope.

Destiny. Destiny. Destiny.

His words washed over her—a cleansing, purifying bath. From the top of her head, over her skin, traveling down her torso, legs, and down to her toes, the change seeped inside her body and altered everything about her.

She could *feel* this transformation, but she wasn't frightened. She was curious in a detached, pondering sort of way.

Her mind gradually numbed until she could hear nothing except the man's voice, though she didn't understand a word he said. Riagan and Drake became distant memories. The rush of the water vanished. She was falling, falling, falling.

Then from somewhere very far away, she felt herself awaken.

Suddenly she could see again, though now everything took on a glittery shimmer and her vision became clear, acute, and precise. She could see every minute detail for as far as the landscape carried.

When she gazed upon the twin brothers standing below her, she realized Riagan *glowed*. His skin was translucent, more alluring than even the Earth-sized moon nestled against the skyline. Her heart surged with a trillion bursts of energy, encompassing her entire body, making her tremble inside and out. She started to move forward, her skin tingling. She had to get to Riagan. She didn't question why, or what force was at work inside of her body, mind, and soul. She just knew she had to move to his side.

Before she could, the stranger clamped on her again and this time spoke in her native tongue. "There will be time later. Save the Cauldron now."

When she turned to identify the person who kept speaking into her ear, no one was there. The words had succeeded in forcing her mind to focus, though, as if she'd finally discovered her one true mission in life, and she narrowed in on the black mass flowing toward the brothers.

She could taste their evil, like a revolting mixture of coppery metallic nestled within rot.

Somehow she flew down the mountainside, whether in air or by foot she did not know, and halted in front of the group. The black band had morphed into individuals again, Caswallen at the helm. They nearly ran into her, she appeared so suddenly.

In the deepest recess of her mind, Wren knew it was she who stood in front of the men, that it was she whom they stared at now. But the part of her that *felt* like Wren remained a twinkling light buried inside. This other part—bolder, stronger, mightier—was a part of herself she recognized as lying dormant, always there and present but unacknowledged and inactive.

Until now.

Her body expanded, bursting upward into great height until she towered above the men. She took a moment of pleasure in the look of fear in their eyes.

Then a voice, hers but yet not, carried through the air, bouncing off the mountain and obliterating the sound of the nearby waterfall. "Who dares disturb the peace of the Murias Cauldron?"

Fright filled the men's eyes, and she would have chuckled in her mortal form. She filled the air, nearly suffocating them, and she relished her power. Drake and Riagan stood by the water's edge—two warriors pulsing with their ancient energy—and she found the beat merged in harmony with her own. They were allies in this fight.

Caswallen's face glowed green above the Cauldron's light. Without a word, he lifted his ashen hand and forked his long fingers, the bones visible and veins purple. He thrust his fingers toward her.

Instinctively, she lifted her own hand, which glowed golden in the dim light. Caswallen's magic stung her palm like the wrong end of a bee, but her own energy turned his efforts into a puff of smoke. She watched, enchanted and accepting, as the power dissipated into the air.

What else is this new body capable of?

As Caswallen gathered his power for another attack, she silenced her mind, putting part of herself to sleep, allowing her instincts to take control.

The Arch Druid would be a worthy opponent, but she felt no fear. She would fight to the death to protect that which needed protection. Why she suddenly cared so much, she did not question.

Caswallen's body burst upward, as if trying to mimic her size. The surge in his power pricked her skin like pelts of hard rain as he loomed in front of her. She could feel his power—dark, menacing, threatening.

She gathered her strength inward, pulling from all corners of her spirit, assembling her powers like she was assembling a tower. The power was immense and her body trembled with its force.

Caswallen gathered his strength as well, and though she knew it was not as potent as her own, his power was fresh and alive, whereas hers had been dormant—for how long, she knew not.

Their eyes locked. Her body tensed in preparation, and she fought the urge to cower under his gray stare. His eyes were like deep pits of nothingness, a void of dead matter that reflected all the black, negative, hateful energy of the worlds. How could this man have been the Brotherhood's leader? Did they not see the menace that lingered within his thin frame?

How many of us will it consume if I do not win? What will happen if I do not retrieve the Cauldron?

Caswallen whipped his hand up and a lightning bolt, flashing with electricity, flew at her so fast she almost missed the chance to protect herself. But her instincts, though long silent, were alive. With her forearm, she covered her chest. The bolt of energy burned the cloak she now wore. Her skin singed but the flash of pain vanished within a second.

The Cauldron's green light flared in his arms. Drake crouched down, ready to strike. Riagan held his gaze steady on her, ready to defend and protect, and she felt his alliance. The vibrations from his body poured through his stare and added to her strength.

The other men present did not move but watched with guarded yet detached expressions as they were little involved. This was a battle between her and the Arch Druid, and not of their responsibility.

She raised her arm, as if she were not about to kill an ancient but rather to pet a puppy.

But death was her intention.

She forked her fingers and white sizzling light burst forth, slamming into Caswallen's chest, hurling him backward. Surprised that he'd not defended himself, she felt a quick surge of hope that her powers were indeed greater than his. If she were quicker, more powerful, the odds were in their favor.

And she was determined.

Caswallen slammed into the ground. The glowing Cauldron stayed nestled in the crook of his elbow like a football, flaring with each burst of magic.

He snarled, his gray teeth long and piercing, like lethal daggers hanging in his mouth.

She smiled back at him with her white teeth and ruby red lips. Her smile was hypnotic, she knew, and she held him immobile with its light.

Someone clad in a robe of green stumbled forward, then struggled to stand upright in front of the Arch Druid, shielding the Master's body with his own. Where he had come from, she could not say.

"You'll not harm Master!" His voice was frantic, cracked.

She knew this man but was not sure how. His identity lay just outside her reach and she did not have time to pull it forward. "Who are you? Who protects this traitor with his life?" Her voice echoed off the mountains.

The man watched her from eyes as black as the rocks behind the waterfall. Was he one of the Brotherhood? If so, why did he protect Caswallen?

Before she could say more, the elder druid's hand closed around the younger man's shoulder, his fingers whitening as he squeezed into the man's flesh.

"Watch me kill her, my pet," he said, his voice raspy in pitch.

She raised her hands to fend off oncoming blows as Caswallen hurled a boulder-sized ball of fire at her. The heat of the passing orb burned her cheeks and sent her hair flying around her face. Somewhere to the right she heard one of the men scream in terror or in fury.

She mumbled words her old self didn't understand, and the fireball burst into a million pieces, dying on the moist rocky ground. A small sigh of relief escaped her, but she forced her mind to refocus. Weakness would not help her now.

Before the Arch Druid could regroup, she flicked her fingers, a simple, inconsequential flip of her digits that would have gone unnoticed save for the power it exerted. The Arch Druid screamed, releasing his captive before falling to the ground in a heap. There he remained, alive, she knew, but stunned and immobile.

She swiveled her gaze to the cowering man with the black eyes.

GWYON'S KNEES SHOOK and his teeth chattered. The magic in the Grove was overwhelming, filling his lungs to where he could not breathe. He gasped for the air that seemed to have been consumed by the fireball.

With his destiny only inches away in Caswallen's fallen grasp, he tried to stand upright. He had not brought forth his walking sticks from his shelter behind the trees. They were supposed to have had the Cauldron by now, to have drunk from its waters and been healed. Master had not seemed to understand that they needed to drink from its waters *before* enlisting in battle.

He hoped the elder's mistake did not prove fatal.

Gwyon could almost taste the cool waters that would grant him all that he'd ever wanted, and his lips twitched in anticipation.

Only this woman stood in his way.

She loomed before him, and somewhere deep within him registered what a beautiful sight she was. He'd never seen hair so black, almost blue. Smooth and the curls long and silky. The strands fell well down her back, almost to her hips, and around her shoulders. She could have worn it as a dress if it were but a few inches longer. Her skin was as white as chalk, and her eyes as blue as the deepest oceans. He had to tear his eyes away and remember all that she represented was all that he hated.

She lifted her hand and motioned him forward. He dared not move, but watched her, trying to decide on his next action. Caswallen had gone silent, and Gwyon didn't know if he was dead, defeated, or regaining his strength for another attack. He wanted to turn and see but rotating a body such as his was no easy task.

The woman's eyes were hypnotic, and he found he could not look away even if he wanted to. They swam within her pale face. He was falling, falling, falling and he could not catch himself. A gentle smile tugged at her crimson lips though she did not smirk. Her expression was kind, welcoming, comforting. Somewhere deep inside him, a voice screamed to look away.

But under her stare, he could do nothing. He was tired, more tired than he'd ever been in his life. Resentment floated away like a thread of cotton along the breeze. He felt alien now, like he didn't know who he was. But he wasn't angry and that was the strangest feeling of all. He'd carried that anger since the day of his birth and to have it suddenly gone was strange—and liberating.

Suspended in a haze, Gwyon didn't realize Caswallen had risen until he clamped a bony hand around his neck, slowly crushing his windpipe.

21

Gwyon fell to his knees, an ear-piercing scream erupting from his pale lips. Riagan watched Caswallen's fingers tighten around his half brother's neck, his knuckles whitening with the force. Caswallen thrust Gwyon to the ground, slamming his crippled body into the soft moss. Gwyon lay motionless, but gasping. With his left hand still holding the Cauldron, Caswallen slipped a hand into his cloak.

He removed a sword, the sharp blade glinting in the moonlight, the iron hilt reflecting pure gold overlay. When the weapon caught the gleam of the Cauldron, the blade shone brightly. From its pointed tip dripped lethal poison.

The woman, who looked like Wren but didn't look like Wren, widened her eyes, though her smile remained. If there was fear within her soul, she didn't show it and he didn't sense it as she lifted her arms to fend off another impending attack.

Caswallen lifted the sword high above his head, one long hand clasped around the jeweled hilt. The cloak's sleeves fell back to reveal a thin, gray arm that appeared too weak to yield such a heavy object.

But it wasn't. With one loud gasp and powerful swing, the Arch Druid brought the sword down, aimed right at Wren's heart. Rage surged through Riagan like the force of a tornado. The man who was Riagan became the warrior who was Protector, and fury shook every cell in his body. Stealing the Cauldron was one thing but trying to murder this woman was another.

He would die before he let that happen.

Riagan sprang forward from his place beside Drake, shaking off his brother's restraining hand, and threw himself in between the sword's lethal blade and Wren.

The last thing he remembered was the shining tip hurtling toward his chest and the terrified scream of the female behind him.

THE SWORD LIFTED over the Arch Druid's head and everything slowed. As the tip came down toward her, she could read the spell of finality and mortality engraved along the side. Riagan jerked forward. Somehow, in the midst of his sudden movement, her body retreated, snapping back to the woman she knew herself to be—pathetic, weak, earthly. What happened to her strength?

She raised her hands, prepared to fend off this attack, praying the blade would slash her and not him, but Riagan was too fast. His mouth opened, like he was yelling at someone, but no sound came out. His smooth muscles rippled with exertion. Every vein in his arms pulsed. His blond hair swung around him like a million silky tentacles, wrapping around his shoulders, flying behind his head.

Her heart constricted as his warrior body continued forward with an agility that defied his size. His feet left the ground, his body lifted, hurtling sideways. His shirt hung in tatters from the sheer breadth of his shoulders.

Before she could blink, he leapt in front of the Arch Druid, his body toppling through the air into the sword's lethal path. The poisoned tip sliced through his shoulder, piercing that gorgeous unblemished skin, pulled taut with his struggle. Fresh blood oozed over the dried blood from the earlier wound.

Long strands of his hair fell to the mossy ground in wisps of gold as the sword continued its trajectory. Somewhere in the distance she heard Drake scream.

Or was that heart-wrenching cry hers?

Riagan's body plummeted to the ground, his expression changing from determination to agony. His eyes narrowed to slits and his mouth twisted. No more blood bubbled forth at his shoulder where the blade had sliced into his body, and she watched the skin seal, locking in what she knew would be fatal poison.

When his massive body finally struck the ground, a loud thud shook the land under her feet. Drake lunged forward to grab the Cauldron from Caswallen but a voice, clear and steady, spoke, as if from the heavens. "Touch not the Cauldron, Drake. Your soul will burn."

All eyes darted toward the voice but there was no one there. Wren recognized it as the same voice that had spoken to her at the lookout, right before she'd transformed into someone she no longer knew. The voice sounded like it was being broadcast over an intercom, but she doubted there was such a system for that here. She looked around anyway as the voice declared, "Only the Redeemer can retrieve the Cauldron once it's been taken."

She watched Drake jerk back, inclining his head to the unknown voice. Muscles tight, veins visible under the pale skin, Drake glared at Caswallen. With her prior strength gone, Wren felt a stab of fear. Where was that new Wren when she needed her?

Caswallen held the Cauldron tight within his arm and stared at Wren. Without averting his gaze, he ordered, "Gwyon, kill her." His voice was high pitched like a siren.

But Gwyon did not respond. With a roar of anger, Caswallen stabilized the sword with both hands wrapped around the hilt, allowing the Cauldron to drop to the ground.

Wren's body started to shake. She felt cheated. Without the power of the previous moments, she felt naked, exposed. What had happened? Riagan remained silent by her feet, but with the sword pointed at her heart, she was too afraid to kneel by his side.

Was everything lost then? The Arch Druid would win. In the process, he would kill Riagan, possibly Drake, and her. Who was the man behind the phantom voice and could he be of help to them at this direst moment?

She stole a glance at Riagan. He was pale, and she was relieved that she did not see the gaseous spirit leaving his body. He was still alive but unconscious, the poison likely coursing through his blood. If he died, she had nothing to live for. Even if he didn't feel the same toward her, she loved him. With her heart and her soul, with the entire strength of her being, she had fallen in love with this man. Was there a future for her if he died? Wandering aimlessly through this strange and alternate universe? Or worse, returning to her trailer in the mountains, her life, as dismal as it was?

Without him by her side?

She met Caswallen's eyes again.

He didn't lift the sword to bring it down upon her. Rather, he pulled his elbow back, the hilt secured in his bony hand. He intended to thrust forward, straight into her heart until it slid through the pumping organ, severing her life.

Her teeth started to chatter.

The black-clad men disappeared like a whisper upon the wind, and she didn't know if they would return in greater numbers or be gone for good. It did not seem likely she would be around to discover the answer.

Gwyon huddled nearby, his eyes vacant and his expression lax like he was in a trance.

Drake stood rooted in front of Riagan, just to Wren's side.

Then, as if the cosmos had snapped its fingers, Caswallen lunged and the Cauldron's light flared, and Wren watched the blade shoot forward. She closed her eyes, prepared for what was to come, not sure that if Riagan was dead already that she wanted to live anyway.

A loud, outraged hiss made her eyes fly open. Crouched before her was Riagan, fully alert, as if he'd been taking a quick nap instead of battling the fatal poison. His skin was red with fury, and she stumbled back, suddenly afraid of the power emanating from him.

With lightning speed and warp precision, he grabbed the sword's hilt, clamping down his fingers over the Arch Druid's in mid-thrust. He yanked with a powerful grunt and an intense ripple of his muscles, jerking the elder toward him with the force. Caught off balance, Caswallen stumbled.

Riagan used the momentum to pull Caswallen into his chest, then locked his left arm around the elder's neck. Caswallen choked. Riagan did not lessen his grip. With his right hand, he wrenched the sword away and held it out before them, pointing the tip back toward the elder's heart.

With a piercing war cry that made Wren clutch her ears and release her own scream, Riagan thrust the blade into Caswallen's chest, far enough to sever Caswallen's life force but not far enough to sever his own. Blood, an unholy crimson-black color, thick and viscous, gurgled up through the Arch Druid's mouth and spilled over his lips. An instant later, his lips sealed shut, as did the skin surrounding the sword's point. The poison was locked in his body, pooling in his dying heart.

The Cauldron's light burst into pure white light, consuming the space around them.

Riagan released Caswallen and he collapsed in a lifeless, crumpled heap. As she stood there watching—horrified, confused, in shock—his body changed to dust and blew away with the wind. The only remnants of evil were the cloak, covered now in blood, and the sword that landed on the ground. Poison continued its slow, deadly drip off the tip. No one moved to touch it.

A voice behind them shouted, "No!"

Wren whirled around to see Gwyon coming at her, surprisingly agile atop his misshapen feet. His hands were outstretched, his dark eyes wide, crazed, inhuman. Too consumed with Caswallen's demise, she had let down her guard, hadn't even heard him behind her. But now he was upon her, his hands grasping her arms, pulling her toward him, taking her hostage.

"I am a warrior. I am a warrior too!" he shouted.

Riagan panted in front of them, sweat glistening off his forehead. His shirt hung in tatters over his moist torso. His eyes were like darts, focused on his target, his muscles massive, bulging.

Gwyon's arm was around her throat, and she could feel that he was supporting part of his weight on her shoulders. It would have been funny if he didn't have a dagger pointed at her throat, the tip nudging her jugular. Perspiration broke out on her brow.

"Get the Cauldron," Gwyon demanded.

"What?" she shrieked.

"No!" yelled Riagan. "She will burn if she touches the Cauldron. Wren, don't."

The point of the dagger pressed into her neck, and she felt the give of her skin. Gwyon's arm shook, and that scared her even more. He seemed out of his mind, insane. There was no telling what he would do—or make her do.

"I will kill her, Riagan. I will kill her now. Let her grab the Cauldron, then you can have her." His monotonous voice sent shivers up her spine.

"Gwyon, she will burn if she touches the Cauldron. There must be another way." A bead of sweat slid over his temple.

Drake rested a hand on Riagan's shoulder. "Brother. Do not fret."

Riagan ignored him.

Gwyon smirked. "Another way? Another way, Brother-mine? There could have been another way years ago, could there not?"

Riagan was quiet for several moments. "Aye," he offered. "There could have been."

Wren felt the trickle of her own blood, warm against her neck. The Cauldron sat upon the ground where Caswallen had dropped it. It seemed so simple, so nonthreatening. Would it really burn her if she touched it?

Riagan growled low in his throat like an enraged animal and crouched to the ground. Drake moved in front of the Cauldron, ready to protect, careful not to touch.

As if standing had taken its toll, Gwyon swayed, stumbling over his own feet. Wren lost her balance. The blade sliced into her neck again, not deep, but enough to hurt. She cried out.

Riagan lunged forward.

Gwyon righted himself just in time to reposition the knife.

Drake grabbed Riagan by the arm and held him fast.

Gwyon laughed in her ear, his rough beard scraping her cheek like a bristle pad.

Then there was a sound of something huge and determined and menacing crashing through the forest. Surely it was a monster, a great grizzly or an elephant. As limbs snapped and trunks were pushed out of the way, a shadow wove through the forest toward them.

Wren knew her eyes were wide with fright. She would take Gwyon any day compared to what was coming.

But as the animal bounded out into the clearing, she saw what was coming was Duke.

Yet the creature before her wasn't Duke. This animal was enormous, larger than a grizzly. The animal looked like Duke with the tawny coat, big, floppy ears, and wrinkled head. But this dog had to be a mirage at five hundred pounds.

The oversized canine lumbered through the forest with the agility of a racehorse.

And it was speeding toward them.

Just yards away, she could see his enormous teeth, dripping with saliva as a growl roared through the air and shook the ground.

"Duke?" she cried.

Gwyon twisted her around, freeing the arm that held the dagger. Before she knew what he was doing, his dagger was hurling through the air with warp speed and sliced into the chest of the charging beast.

The animal yelped, a wail of pain and agony that broke her heart into a million pieces. She screamed. The beast slowed but didn't stop. His eyes, so close now she could see his pupils, were crazed and dilated.

Then everything happened so fast, she wasn't entirely sure if it was real or a dream.

The animal continued forward, then fell in a clump by her feet, like an earthquake. Drake or Riagan or both took advantage of the surprise and shot forward, wrenching Gwyon off her, and she was unexpectedly free.

Without bothering to look and see what was happening behind her, Wren dropped to her knees beside the big beast.

The chocolate eyes were just like Duke's. In fact, he looked exactly like Duke, just much, much larger. But his eyes—they were pleading, searching, trying to tell her something, trying to beg her for something.

Tears rolled down her cheeks as she tried to cradle his huge head in her lap. He whimpered, regarding her with familiar eyes, blinking with his heavy lids.

She knew, somewhere in the recess of her mind, that Riagan had Gwyon tied and incapacitated, but she couldn't look away from the dog. The weight of his head alone nearly crushed the bones of her legs, but she didn't care. This animal was too familiar. Too familiar.

"Duke?" she choked. "Duke, is that you?"

Drake bent down. "I will remove the dagger."

Wren bent toward Duke's face and spoke softly. "Duke, Drake is going to make it better. It might hurt, but he must take out the dagger. I'm here, Duke. I'm here and won't leave you." She was hiccupping again, crying as she saw how stoic the dog was trying to be.

She rubbed his head the way she knew her Duke liked, just between his eyes. He seemed to acknowledge what she was doing but yelped in agony as Drake pulled out the dagger.

"Duke!" She screamed as the dog's eyes shut and his chest stopped moving.

22

Hands pulled at her, but Wren shoved them away. She couldn't see anything anymore, could only feel the solid, heavy weight of the dog's head in her lap. Her shoulders heaved as grief ripped through her body.

She patted his head over and over, whispering incomprehensible words as she laid her other hand on his wound to help stop the bleeding. But something was different. She wiped her tears with the back of her hand to try and free her vision. In her lap, the dog was changing. She stopped sobbing and stared.

The animal's fur on his head was morphing into long, gray strands of hair. His body was pulling into itself, changing, altering until two of the legs became arms and the fur was gone, replaced by peachy skin.

"Duke?"

Then suddenly, Duke, the dog, vanished, and a small being, a faery, materialized in his place. His face was still wrinkled, his nose still large, but he was only two feet tall with ears that stuck out from his head like vessels. The wound on his chest was gone.

"Riagan," she screamed as the faery struggled to his feet. He wasn't smiling, but he wasn't frowning either. And he was, inexplicably, alive.

"What's going on?" she wailed, terrified and awed all at once.

Riagan crouched in front of her.

The realm lay silent around them and the trees lining the forest leaned forward, as if eager for a better view.

The faery had the same chocolate eyes as her dog, so familiar that she couldn't help but say, "Duke?"

He bowed, swinging one arm out, curling one around his waist. If he wore a hat, she suspected he would've swept it off his head.

When he straightened, he offered a crooked grin. "Hi, Wren."

"I... I DON'T...I can't believe... Am I insane?" Wren sputtered.

"You are no such thing, Miss Wren." The faery stood in front of her, rigid and proud like a palace guard.

Before she could formulate more questions to ask, commotion erupted behind her. She tore her gaze from the strange being to see Gwyon thrashing in Drake's iron grasp.

"I will take him to the hold and keep him there," Drake said. "Then we will decide what to do with this brother of ours."

"Aye," said Riagan, by her side. He never took his eyes off the faery. "I will remain here."

"I...I can't believe it," Wren muttered, finally finding words. "Duke? My Duke? How?"

The faery's face was so familiar it made her pause.

"I was sent to watch over you." His voice was exactly how she would have expected Duke's to sound—that is, if he could have talked as an animal. Deep, raspy, yet tender and full of love in a way no other voice could be.

"Watch over me?"

"Why?" Riagan leaned forward.

Duke's rich eyes turned toward Riagan. "To protect her."

"From what?" she asked, not feeling fully in charge of her own mind.

"From he who would take the Cauldron."

"Master?" Riagan asked.

"Yes. One such as she always has a protector, even before a viable threat presents itself."

"You're speaking Greek," Wren complained, trying not to whine.

"You were sent to Earth to protect her?" Riagan's eyes were focused like a pointer, his lips tight, his body tense. He seemed to need nearly as many answers as she did.

But Duke clamped his lips shut, crossed his arms, and sat down upon the ground by Wren's side, refusing to speak any further. She had to resist the urge to rub his head.

"Why would I need protection from the Master-slash-Arch Druid?" She turned to Riagan.

"I know not, but…" He stared at her as if she was a stranger in his midst and not his lover.

"Riagan, what is it?"

"There are many mysteries still to be explained—to you, but to myself as well."

Drake reappeared. "That brother of ours is locked in the hold with two of the Brotherhood on guard. The others will be here shortly."

"Their battle has ended?"

"Yes. The realm is free of enemies. Save for our brother, that is."

Wren was picking at a blade of grass, stealing glances at Duke, when she was startled by a soft humming tune coming from the Cauldron. It was a beautiful song that sounded like angels serenading her. The artifact sat a few feet away, glowing a haunting green. The Cauldron didn't look menacing, though. She felt no threat as the music entranced her. No one else seemed to notice as her entire body started to tremble, to *sing* along with the melody. It pulled her forward and she was helpless to resist.

She picked up the Cauldron.

The beauty of the song ceased immediately, but her skin didn't burn. She turned it over in her hands, studying it. Maybe this was the wrong Cauldron. Was this an imposter and the other one was either safe in its cave or gone from them forever?

As she examined the inside and outside of the artifact, she realized the world around her had gone disturbingly, encompassingly silent. She glanced around. "What?"

"By the gods of the lost island of Atlantis and all who watch over the strange happenings of these worlds." Riagan looked like he'd just woken up to find himself dressed as a peacock.

Resisting the urge to pinch her nose between her fingers, Wren took a deep breath. "What are you talking about now? Seriously, Riagan, I can't understand half the things you say. And I really hate to say this, but I don't think this is the right Cauldron. It's not hot at all."

"Redeemer?" Riagan whispered.

Her eyes flashed to Drake, ready to ask for a translation, feeling no small bit of irritation.

"Aye. Redeemer," Drake answered. "It's about time you figured it out."

"Aye," Riagan repeated. "She is a Redeemer. Och, by the gods, how did I not know?"

"Redeemer? Riagan, if you don't speak words that actually make sense, I'm leaving." Then she mumbled, "Even though I don't really know how I'd do that." She looked around, lost in this new world.

She glanced back at Riagan, curious if he would give her guidance on how, in fact, she could leave if she wanted to. The expression on his face alarmed her.

"What?" she demanded again. "Don't call me a retriever unless you care to explain what you're talking about." She gazed down at the artifact. "Makes me sound like a dog."

"Redeemer."

"Huh?"

"I called you a Redeemer. Not a retriever."

"A Redeemer? What did I redeem? This?" She grasped the Cauldron by its lip and lifted it into the air. Two pairs of green eyes widened, and their massive bodies tensed.

MAYBE THE PAIN that wove its way through Riagan's body, making him pant and his mind grow muddled was causing him to hallucinate. Was this woman, or was she not, holding the Cauldron as if it were a child's toy?

Yet, if she was truly a Redeemer, she *could* hold the Cauldron as if it were a child's toy.

These thoughts were fleeting and would not take root as the poisonous fire, no longer willing to be held at bay, consumed him. The burn started in the place where the sword had pierced his skin, so close to the place the arrow had punctured, and was sweeping its way through his body, consuming each and every fiber within its blaze.

Just as he was about to speak, to ask Drake to watch over Wren, to inform them he was dying, the poison swallowed his words. He watched the people in front of him through an oily haze. As the poison entered his brain's cells, his vision wavered. It seeped through his throat, closing his airway.

He hit the ground with such resounding force, he felt his body would shatter.

Every sense he had died in that instant. He could not hear; could not feel the ground beneath him; could not smell the sweet honeysuckle or perfumed roses that grew in abundance and were the only earthly type plants that the two realms shared. He was nothing but a searing ball of fire, in flames and being wholly and completely consumed.

Then nightmarish visions started.

First, he saw a malformed babe with a dagger pointed at his heart, prepared to be sacrificed. A look of horror and frenzy fixed on the mother's face as her screams wailed through the trees. Then he saw the black eyes of his half brother watching, watching, always watching.

Then the Arch Druid's gaze took over, his gray eyes now red, blazing like the fire that forged its way through Riagan's veins. They were no longer the eyes of his leader. They were the eyes of the Devil. He knew his own eyes were locked open and staring, though they stared at images no one else could see.

Riagan's body was telling his throat to scream against the pain, the nightmares. But the poison would not allow even that simple release.

Death would come soon.

And then…

An angel appeared before him. Her hair, dark and wild with curl, flowed down her back like thousands of dancing snakes. Her skin, pale beyond the moon's white glow, sparkled. Her eyes, bluer than the Aegean were almost too luminous and beautiful.

Then her image was replaced by the Cauldron, no longer green and luminous, but red, inflamed and turning to ash in front of him. These would be his greatest failures—the loss of the Cauldron and the loss of this woman.

The angel appeared again. He tried to blink, but the flesh of his eyelids burned against the movement, and he wondered if he would ever see again. But she was still there, familiar yet a stranger. Maybe she was a blessed dream amidst the nightmares.

As if through a haze, he watched her kneel by his side and speak to someone out of his line of vision. A hand was placed over his wound as chanting and prayer mingled to send his pain into another stratosphere. Then he felt a splash of warmth, like bath water, running over his shoulder.

His body jerked over and over as the poison worked its way toward that wound, that single entry point. He could see nothing but the white-hot pain that consumed him, like it was ripping apart his body in an effort to make it back to that one spot. It was pulling into itself, coming back from his feet and legs, his hands and arms, meeting in the exact place where the sword had sliced.

And the pain sizzled, born from the pits of Hell itself, settling in an unbearable mass at his wound.

Surely death would come soon.

Please let death come soon.

He would have cried out in agony had the poison not claimed his voice. He could not even clench his teeth against the pain. The veins clamped shut and his breath stopped. His heart ceased.

His mind lingered for a second, recognizing the end of his life.

And he felt no more pain.

But he did feel *something*. Strange, considering he was dead. But there was a feeling and it wasn't pain. No, it was as soothing as a mother's touch on a newborn babe's bald head.

Then a low, obscure pounding began in his chest, like a fly beating against his ribs. His heart had stopped so this confused him. And he could feel something warm and soothing where the sword had sliced.

It must be Wren.

She was the only one who could bring him back from the dead. The only one.

How did he know this?

The same way he now knew how he had crossed the portal.

Because he loved her.

By the gods, he loved this woman. But how? How could he feel love?

His jaw unclenched as the poison withdrew from his body. He opened his eyes and there she was, crouched before him, worry pulling her black brows together.

"Wren?" This time he knew it was no hallucination. Before him knelt his beloved. In one hand she caressed his forehead, in the other she held the Cauldron, its black mouth tipped over his wound as trickles of magical, healing water fell from its lip.

TWO OPPOSING FORCES whirled in Wren's mind and she struggled to merge them together, to figure out who she was, where she was, and ultimately who she was supposed to be. Strange things had happened that she didn't understand.

She was Wren, yet she was something more powerful, magical. Now she felt like Wren again, but different. Somehow, something new simmered within her blood, and her gut told her it was not fleeting. Rather, it was more of an awakening.

Confusion and wonder replaced anxiety and fear, though, and she knew she would soon understand.

"Riagan?" She nudged the hair back from his brow, then ran her fingers over his defined jawline.

His eyes fluttered. "Wren?"

She started to cry.

"What's wrong, lass?" Riagan asked, his voice just reaching her ears.

She chuckled through her tears. With her fingertips, she made a path over his shoulder and down his arm, ready to pinch him again. To ensure he was, indeed, alive. He winced against the pain of movement, but lifted his arm anyway and grasped a handful of her hair.

"I like your hair."

"You like my *hair*?" She glanced to her side and saw massive amounts of black curling hair flowing down to her waist. She ran her hands from her scalp to the ends, making sure it was indeed attached to her head.

"What happened to my *hair*?"

Drake chuckled, and she glanced up, having forgotten he was standing there. She was struck again by how large he was, how large Riagan was by her side, how large Duke had been before he changed shape. Everything was much grander in Riagan's land—her hair no exception.

"How did it get so long?"

She helped Riagan sit up.

"Do you mean to tell me that you've transported through a portal to the druid realm, fought a battle against an Arch Druid, saved me from death, rescued the Cauldron, and the only question you have is about your hair?" He burst out laughing. It sounded weak and breathless, but it was a laugh nonetheless.

Without thinking, she fell into his arms, the pulse of his heartbeat strong against her cheek. Her own heart's rhythm merged with his until they beat in unison. He pushed his hands deep into her hair and she melted into his touch.

Lifting her face to look at him, she couldn't help but wonder: if he didn't love her but treated her like this, would it be enough?

Maybe.

She brought her lips to his, inhaling the fresh mint of his breath. She probed his lips open with her tongue and he readily parted for her, teasing and flicking until she moaned.

She couldn't get close enough and leaned forward, pushing him backward. He fell onto his elbows and she ran a hand over his chest, surprised at the bulk of the muscles. The shirt was torn in several places, and she had to squelch the overwhelming urge to rip it off entirely and run a hand over his bare chest. Her palm brushed his hardened nipples, and she knew his body was responding in other areas as well.

The sound he made verified her assumption and she giggled, letting her breath fill his mouth. His fingers trailed down her neck and across her collarbone, igniting a path of warmth in its wake. He grazed her breast, and her body jerked. He enveloped her entire breast into his large palm, massaging. Searing delight soared through her body and she went to straddle him.

She could feel his eyes on her and met his gaze. An intensity burned there that she hadn't seen before. Or maybe it was the day's events? His lips parted, and he drew a breath in. Then with an exhale, he said, "Wren, there is something you must know."

Confused and suddenly weary, she straightened. "What is it?"

Was this when he told her this was all a fantasy? That none of this was real and it had all been a figment of her imagination? Dread began to creep into her mind.

"Wren, I…I…"

Wren searched his face, desperate for a hint of the words to come, but Riagan broke contact and glanced at Drake. "Brother. Can you and the new Duke not but leave us for a moment?" Riagan's tone was light, but there was an edge to it that sent the temperature in her lower belly several degrees higher.

"Nay, brother. We must have this Redeemer of ours return the Cauldron to its rightful place."

Before the discussion could go further, a shadow passed by the moon, causing them each to turn. But then the shadow disappeared, and though Wren strained to find it again, eager to know what new surprise this realm held, she could not. A moment later, a moan erupted near the grove of trees, capturing her attention like a fly caught in a net.

RIAGAN MOVED FAST, and he heard Wren's sharp intake of breath as his large body blocked her view of the Grove. Drake moved toward them on soundless feet and planted himself in front of Riagan. The river and the moon sat nestled against their backs.

Coming toward them were the Brothers, Gwyon supported between two of them.

"Brothers," spoke one with long, brown hair. "We must decide his fate. Should we summon a Council?"

Riagan studied their half brother with no words and no expression, never moving from his place in front of Wren.

Drake was the one who spoke. "We have never been confronted with a situation like this. A betrayal from one with the old blood."

As if summoned out of the mist, the entire Brotherhood appeared by the river's edge, ethereal and brimming with power. Many flashed expressions of shock, then comprehension over seeing Wren cradling the artifact.

Riagan and Drake exchanged a full conversation without speaking a word—their eyes and their connection making it easy to read the other's thoughts. But while they stared between each other and Gwyon, it was Wren who eased from Riagan's guard without a sound. She was heading toward Gwyon before Riagan realized she'd moved.

"Wren."

She held up her free hand as she progressed forward, the other one still clasping the Cauldron. "It's fine."

Riagan heeded her wishes but focused on his half brother like a serpent on its prey.

At her approach, Gwyon grew agitated and fought to free himself. The Cauldron's green light flared in her arms, as if sensing the traitor was near, but then settled into a dull haze.

She stopped in front of him. "I know you, do I not?"

23

Wren knew this man and was shocked she hadn't recognized him earlier. In her defense, fighting Caswallen and saving Riagan and the Cauldron had taken up much of her mental fortitude.

But she did know him—there was no doubt in it now. She'd seen him on Earth, worked with him, in fact. The clothing had changed. His beard was longer, covering his face and hiding his neck within its rough-textured darkness. He seemed to carry less weight here as his waist was thinner. But his eyes—his eyes were exactly the same—dark, only now there was less hatred than weariness behind their pointed stare.

"Dr. Martin?"

"Wait." Riagan started forward, but she held up her hand again to stay him.

"We have met before, have we not?"

Gwyon said nothing.

"You tried to kill me. Back on…Earth." She stumbled over that last word as if she still hadn't accepted how far she'd traveled from her home planet.

Her. Home. Planet.

She threw up a mental door against thinking about that now.

"What say you?" Riagan's temper flared like a lit firecracker, helping her focus her attention. "This relation of mine tried to kill you?" He grasped her arm, his embrace tight with fury, and she feared he would snap her bone. He seemed angrier at the attempt on her life than he did at the threat to the Cauldron. She couldn't help but feel a flash of joy.

"It's okay, Riagan."

Their gazes were locked for several moments, no words spoken, no words needed. Riagan released his grip and folded his arms across his torso, standing guard like the world's meanest bouncer.

"Why did you try to kill me? That was you, wasn't it? You're Dr. Martin?"

After an exasperated sigh, Gwyon said, "Of course it was me."

"Why?"

"Because of who you are."

"This Redeemer person?"

"Yes. You are a product of the union, and I didn't see it until it was almost too late."

"What union?"

"Between the fae king and the human. Your mother. Only such a union can produce a Redeemer." He couldn't look more bored if he tried.

"I don't know what you're talking about."

"I didn't know there was a child from that union. I couldn't see you past your mother. But there was a crack in the magic, and Master saw it."

"Saw what?"

"Saw you. Your existence."

"So you wanted to kill me?"

"Master told me to kill you. I was to kill your mother first, to sever the magic veil so I could find you, and then kill you."

"My mother? What does she have to do with this?" A cannonball of dread threatened to crush her heart.

"I needed the veil to die with your mother. She was a shroud of protection around you, and that shroud needed to disappear so it would leave you exposed."

"Die with my mother?" Horror gripped her around the throat. Her mother was missing. Not dead.

"I assume she is dead. I gave her a little concoction in the hospital to put her to sleep. Permanently." His words softened, quieted as he continued. "Whoever helped her escape helped a dying woman."

"That can't be." Tears the size of boulders welled in her throat, making it hard to catch a breath.

"I guess there's a chance she's still alive." He looked away from her grief.

"Brother-mine." Riagan stepped forward, tense as a famished bear. "Explain yourself."

Gwyon remained quiet, as if tired of this line of questioning.

Fae/human union? Fae? Faeries? Her mother's strange and bizarre ramblings suddenly didn't sound so strange and bizarre.

But where was her mother? She'd left the hospital. She couldn't do that if she was…

Wren couldn't allow the thoughts to continue.

"Gwyon," warned Drake. "Remain quiet at your own peril."

Behind her, Riagan whispered, "A fae/human child. That's how she became the Redeemer. Her mother—I should've known. But I was mortal and without my druid senses."

She glanced at Riagan who stared at her as if he didn't know who she was. When he met her gaze, though, and saw her distress, he was by her side an instant later, cradling her close.

Gwyon cleared his throat, heeding Drake's warning, though the bored tone remained. "You are the child of a fae and a human—a mix of the two races. Only such can produce a Redeemer. I knew of the relationship, but I knew naught that there was a child. You were hidden behind magic."

Wren didn't care about all of that. "You tried to kill my mother?"

He did not answer.

"But you are not sure if she is…gone…or not?"

He shook his head, gaze planted on the moss at his feet. "I know not. If you had succeeded in killing yourself, if you had only hit that tree a little harder, you would've made my job a lot easier. As it was, I had to take care of your mother first, in order to collapse the veil and gain access to you."

"You're a sick man," she spat, feeling green and putrid inside.

Gwyon didn't dispute her claim.

"This is ridiculous," she started, but as she spoke she knew it wasn't as ridiculous as it sounded. Many things had happened to her these past days, and she'd learned enough to know that things were not always as they seemed.

As for her mother, wouldn't she sense if her mother passed?

"So, earlier," Riagan asked softly, "when she became *different*?"

He addressed the question to Gwyon, but his lips were now clamped shut.

Drake offered an answer instead. "Her fae side came out. Redeemers often have powers."

"Yes," Riagan said. "I have not forgotten my knowledge. It just seems too much to take in."

"Yes."

"I see dead people's spirits leave their bodies, too," she offered.

The crowd studied her, weary and more than a little apprehensive.

"So *that's* the thing that's strange to you people?" She shook her head and glared at everyone she could.

"Oh, by the gods." Riagan exhaled. "I've lost all senses. That is how she crossed the portal. Of course."

Wren struggled to absorb all that was being said, to make sense of words that couldn't possibly make sense when all she wanted to do was find her mother.

"Aye," Drake replied, oblivious to her distress. "Redeemers can cross portals unassisted."

Wren bent to the ground and ran her palms over the soft moss.

I have lost my mind. There is no other explanation. When I awaken, I will find myself in a straitjacket in a psych ward with Dr. Martin pumping meds into my IV, my mother in the bed beside mine. This is all a dream.

"IT IS NO such thing, Destiny." From behind a great oak emerged a ghostly figure clad in a flowing, ankle-length robe—the same figure, Wren knew, that had been lurking in the shadows. As he came closer, everyone around her bowed in one fluid motion.

Riagan was the first to rise and speak. "King Eogabail, we welcome you to the druid realm."

"I know there has been great trouble this night, and of late." His voice was smooth and melodious.

There was a familiarity to him that held Wren's attention and she could not look away. This man was different from the rest, wearing a brown robe as intricately woven as the fibers of the trees.

He was tall, emitting a calm strength that Wren could not ignore as he came closer. She didn't sense a threat from him but couldn't move away even if she wanted to. He had her hypnotized, and she reached for his hand at the same time he reached for hers.

"Destiny." His smile was warm, emotional. "Wren, my little bird." His eyes, as pure as crystal, shone. "First of all, let me say that your mother is fine. Master's desire to have her killed went unfulfilled."

The ground beneath her quaked and quivered from the power of her relief.

"Who are you?" she managed, surprised she found her voice.

"My name is Eogabail. I am king of the fae." He paused. "And I am your father."

King? Of the fae? Father? Hers? She tried not to burst into giggles. She'd accepted Riagan's story that he was an immortal druid. She'd accepted that she had left the Earth and traveled, how she didn't know, to what they called the druid realm. She'd heard Gwyon's words about her having a fae father but hadn't time to give that too much consideration. And now she was to believe that this man before her was the king of the fae? *And* her father? She thought about the little creature who had visited her in the hospital, who had freed her from the straitjacket. That was a faery.

Her mother saw faeries.

Duke was a faery.

Here was the king of the faeries.

And he said he was her father. Fear swept up through her abdomen as the old familiar worries of psychosis threatened to erupt. "But…but…this can't be real. There is no way."

He gazed at her with eyes that were kind and loving. He raised his arm and waved his hand between them as if putting a spell on her. Fear seeped out of her body as if she were being bled. Her mind calmed, then opened as if it were the parting sea, letting in these most unusual events without question.

Joy was evident in his soft eyes. "Daughter. I have waited long to see you."

She gawked at him, relishing the surreal calm embracing her.

With smooth and gentle motion, he pulled her into his arms and something powerful washed over her. Something her gut told her was love. Love of her father.

She trembled, a sudden burst of emotion threatening to push her over the edge. Even with all of these extraordinary events, being held by her true father was overwhelming. It was like being lost and abandoned in a cold, dark, frightening forest only to be suddenly whisked away to safety on a luxurious, silky flying carpet.

A bubble of a giggle, hysterical and slightly crazed, tumbled from her lips.

He rested his hands on her shoulders and eased her out of his embrace. "Destiny, my daughter, you must return the Cauldron to its rightful place. Only you can do this. Then there will be time to talk."

"Return the Cauldron? Where do I take it?"

She waved the artifact through the air, and everyone around her jumped, arms held out, fending her off. She laughed, but then it trickled to a soft chuckle, and then to silence as their faces showed no humor. "What?"

"Daughter, for one who is not a Redeemer, touching the Cauldron after it has been stolen would mean certain death. They are right to fear."

"Oh." The Cauldron grew cold within her hand. The round pot reminded her of a cast-iron skillet her grandmother used to cook fried potatoes in. She rotated the prized possession over in her hands. There was nothing inside the Cauldron now. "Well, where do I take it?"

"Into the waters." Her father pointed to the river.

"Okay. Where?"

"The Cauldron's cave lies deep below the waterfall."

"Do I need scuba gear, or what?"

The group laughed, calmer now, though no one came close to her other than Riagan, who remained fixed by her side. "I will take you," he said.

"Aye," her father answered. "It is right."

"Redeemer." Riagan crooked his elbow and offered it to her like he was her escort to the debutante ball. "Just keep the Cauldron in *that* arm."

"Will do." She joined her hand with his arm and couldn't help but offer the bulging muscle a squeeze of admiration.

They strode forward until the water's edge rippled over her toes, cool and refreshing. They continued until the water rose over her ankles, calves, knees.

She tugged his arm. "Riagan, um, is there a path I can't see? A way to get there without going underwater?" She surveyed the area and saw nothing but the waterfall. There was no visible rock face, mountain, or solid ground across the expanse of water.

Riagan stopped at her words and turned, casting a glance at the Cauldron. "You will be fine."

"What do you mean, *I'll be fine?*" But instead of answering, Riagan swept her into his arms and planted his lips against hers. Fire seared through her body, and she wanted nothing more than to melt into his body, to merge with this powerful man and become one with him.

She parted her lips as he parted his. The jolting of her body told her that he was carrying her forward, but the feel of his mouth against hers made certain she couldn't care less about the world around them.

Careful, though, to keep the Cauldron tucked against her body, she wound her other arm around his neck, keeping his head as close to hers as she could. She flicked his tongue and he responded with a soft, deep groan.

Lost in the kiss, she didn't realize Riagan had walked deeper into the water until it touched her bottom. Her eyes flew open as he continued deeper and deeper into the water.

He continued and its coolness covered her stomach, her breasts. She did not pull away even as the water touched her shoulders, her neck, and finally her chin. As the water continued to rise, she realized he was breathing into her mouth. Breathing for her.

They submerged. At first, she panicked. Her lungs screamed. But with several deep inhales of Riagan's breath, she was able to control the human need.

She didn't know how long they continued forward but soon her hair floated around them, like strands of blackened silk. Riagan's own blond hair mixed with her curls, creating a stark contrast against the clear water. The moon's glow danced over the surface of the water, and the Cauldron glowed green in her arm.

Soon they came upon a dark opening beneath the crystal-clear water. She glanced at Riagan and he nodded, confirming what she suspected—that somewhere in this underwater cave was the artifact's home.

When they crossed through the entrance door, they entered a dark room, no larger than a home's foyer, where several pathways jutted off in different directions. She didn't realize until they passed through the opening that there was no water within this small enclosure.

Her lungs filled with air, and she started breathing on her own.

"Riagan." She gawked at the wall of water floating just outside the room. "How does the water stay out?"

"Magic." He clasped her hand and encouraged her forward. She wasn't wet, either. Nor was Riagan. Nor was the Cauldron. She shook her head. She doubted there would be anything left to question. So many odd things had already happened, but the surprises just kept on coming and coming and coming.

"The water is also enchanted and that is how we can stay submerged for so long."

"Oh."

Riagan led the way down one of the long corridors. They followed the underground tunnel until they came upon a small room. Cut into the solid rock face was an alcove with an empty circular platform nestled in the middle.

"Riagan?"

The Cauldron started to glow in her arms, its green hue nearly as luminous as Riagan's eyes.

"Once you place the Cauldron in the alcove," he said quietly, "you will be relieved of your duty. Hopefully forever."

"What do you mean?"

"Once you return the Cauldron to its rightful place, its care returns to that of the Brotherhood. You will not be needed unless it is taken again. And I will give my life to make sure that never happens."

Chills swept over her skin as she stepped forward and placed the artifact on its stand. It seemed such a harmless object—something that one might find in a flea market or a grandparent's attic. It gave no indication of the power within its bowl.

Once it was returned and she stepped back, she felt oddly unfulfilled and anticlimactic.

"Do you now fill it with anything? Water, maybe?"

"Nay. It creates its own powerful, healing waters."

"On its own?"

"All on its own."

"Like it did earlier—when I poured it over your wound, the water had just been there."

"Yes. It's a very powerful artifact, which is why it is so important to protect it. Which is also why Redeemers exist—as another line of defense."

Shrugging her shoulders, she slid over to him, eager to return to the embrace and the life-sustaining kiss. That, at least, was far from anticlimactic.

Eyes closed and arms outstretched, she waited for him to lift her. When she didn't feel the thrill of his embrace, she lifted her chin, only to find him staring down at her.

"What is it?"

His expression was a mixture of sadness and resolution.

"Riagan, what's wrong?"

He shook his head, as if responding to words she could not hear. He picked her up and closed his mouth over hers. Becoming lost in the inhalation and exhalation of his breath, she let go her questions and savored the moment.

24

Riagan did not put her down even though they were on dry land. King Eogabail was waiting by the water's edge, as were Drake, Duke, and Gwyon, who was held by rough-hewn ropes tied around his wrists, linked between two massive tree trunks. The Brotherhood stood stoically nearby, eyes alert, postures prepared, hearts hard.

"What's going on, Riagan?" Wren whispered.

Riagan had not answered her question before, and he would not answer it now for the only response to be given was awful, devastating, tragic, and he did not want to give voice to it.

He stopped just out of earshot of the others. Using the strength in his arms, he pulled her even closer into his body, crushing her against him, as if that would keep her near for always.

Fool's thought.

"I love you." He blurted the only words that he could, his heart heavier than the massive moon at his back.

"You love me?" Shock spread across her features.

"Yes. I love you. And it's a miracle, because druids of the Brotherhood are not allowed to feel love."

"Then, how do you? I'm not complaining," she rushed to say. "But…how?"

He shrugged. "I know not, nor do I care. I care only that you know I love you."

"Oh Riagan. This is all so crazy. But I love you too, and that's all that matters."

"I want to tell you why I was banished. You must know the truth because that will show you how much I've changed. Because of you."

She placed her hand on his face and offered him a brilliant smile. "I don't want to know what you did. Not right now at least."

This gentle, caring, forgiving woman. She knew nothing of their fate yet to come, and her softly spoken words only added to the breaking of his heart.

ONLY THE SUDDEN tinkling of bells erupting in the Grove could make Wren pull away from Riagan, but the sound was alluring and beautiful, and had Wren pivoting away from the man she loved. Who loved her back.

Oephille materialized, sitting on a long limb's leaf nearby. "It was no easy task to get you here, Wren." Oephille's chastising voice held notes of humor, and Wren smiled.

"I'm very sorry, little faery. I hope I wasn't too much trouble."

"Oh, you were very much trouble indeed and don't call me little. I'm about three hundred years older than you are and have five times the power."

Wren laughed as the small creature puffed out her chest. A moment later she flew forward and planted a kiss upon Wren's cheek. "Welcome to the druid realm, Wren, and thank you for a job well done. The worlds can rest peacefully again."

Wren hesitated, wondering how she should respond to the faery's comment. In the end, she just said, "You're welcome."

"Your highness?" Oephille turned to King Eogabail. "May I have the honor of escorting her return to the realm of man?"

Her father stepped forward, his hands clasped over his chest. She could never look so regal, she thought with a hint of envy as she watched him come to her side. He moved with the grace of a butterfly yet with the power of a tiger. Why couldn't she have inherited those qualities?

"I am sure you are ready to go home," Oephille continued.

"Go home?" Wren asked. "Already?" She scanned the faces around her, landing at last on Riagan. The expression on his face made her hackles rise. Something was wrong. Duke, having remained silent and unacknowledged until this point, lumbered to her side, folding his arms across his barreled chest.

"Aye," Riagan struggled to say. "You must return to the realm of man, for that is where the Redeemer dwells."

"Say what?"

Her father rested a cool hand on her shoulder, and she could feel his strength being absorbed by her skin. Why did she need her father's strength now?

"Riagan?"

"Destiny." Her father's hand applied more pressure. "You must return to Earth. You cannot remain upon this realm, for you are human and will not long live."

"Well, I can stay a little while, can't I? Like, a few years? Besides, you said I'm only half human."

"It matters not that you carry fae blood," he answered. "Redeemers dwell on Earth. Remaining on the druid realm would not provide you with the strength you need to perform your duties, should the need arise again. Further, you must return by the morn."

"Tomorrow morning?"

"Aye. Oephille can accompany you."

The truth he was trying not to state directly was dawning on her like a plague. Oephille would accompany her. What about Riagan?

He was a Protector of the Cauldron, and his job was here. On the druid realm. Apparently her job was *there*, on the realm of man.

"But I can't go anywhere," she insisted. "There is nothing for me there."

Oephille flittered forward, resting her tiny hands on Wren's cheeks. "Your mother is there."

Her father spoke next. "She awaits your return. Oephille rescued her from the hospital, much the same way she did you. She helped cleanse the medicine from her and she is healed. She is at your home now. Safe."

"Thank God," Wren breathed.

"Earth is where the Redeemer dwells, Destiny. It is there that the worlds can summon you if need be."

"Summon me? How?"

A soft humming started somewhere in the distance and grew with each passing second, collecting everyone's attention like an offering. A flash of gold shimmered as it approached, just beside the grove of trees, floating through the air of its own accord.

At first she thought it was Oephille, but she now sat upon her father's shoulder. As the object moved closer, the trees began to sway in unison, their enormous trunks moving to one side then another in perfect form. Their branches, heavily intertwined overhead, glistened in the soft light.

Soon the object was hovering in front of her, inches above her head. She looked up to find a gold diadem, with delicate wisps held together by a solid band, floating before her. Nestled in the very center of the low peak was a moonstone.

Her father stepped forward and took the diadem between his long fingers. Holding the object over her head, he said, "Destiny, the Redeemer of ancient artifacts." He settled the crown upon her brow. "This crown will travel with you back to the realm of man where you will keep it safely by your side. When there is a need for a Redeemer, the moonstone will glow. When it does so, place the diadem upon your brow, and you will be transported to wherever you are needed."

The weight of the gold was heavy but cool against her forehead. The energy from the moonstone was palpable.

"This is your destiny, my daughter. You cannot fight it. You cannot change it."

"You're all here, though." She didn't want to cry but found she was powerless to resist the onslaught of tears that hovered. "The only person on Earth is my mom, and she doesn't know who I am half the time. Please."

Her father's expression saddened. "She knows who you are. It can be difficult for her mind to stay firmly rooted in the realm of man, but she always knows who you are."

"Is she ill because of your relationship? Did that change her somehow?"

"You are very astute, my daughter. It can be difficult for a human to travel between the realms. If one does so too many times, the human brain has trouble returning to a normal, functioning state. It becomes fractured during travel, and eventually cannot heal properly."

"She traveled to your realm?"

"Many times." He gazed far off into the forest, his eyes unfocused, his mind on another time, another place. "I loved her true. She was my soulmate and I would've given almost anything to have her by my side."

"But she couldn't stay here?"

"Redeemers must remain on Earth."

Understanding dawned, and it tugged at her heartstrings. "Do you mean, had she not gotten pregnant with me, she would have been able to stay with you?"

"Even if you did not exist, she could not have lived on my realm, nor I on hers. Having you made the decision easier."

Such a tragic love story. Was another one of the same tragedies unfolding before her eyes?

"Have I ever been here? The river looks vaguely familiar, and I swear I've dreamt about it."

"Yes, child. Your mother and I brought you here when you were young."

"Why did you stop?"

"Because we became worried about how it would affect your mind."

"Oh." She thought of her mother. "How did you meet her?"

"Simple travels. That is all. I was visiting the portal near your home. She was there."

"How old was she?"

"Twenty, I believe."

His eyes closed and his lips swept upward. "We continued to meet until I realized the toll it was taking on her health."

"Her mental health."

"Yes."

"So, is she actually mentally ill?"

"According to your human medicine, yes. But beyond those rigid diagnoses lie many other explanations."

"All those times I thought she was hallucinating, was she actually talking to a faery?"

"It is likely. She became very close with many of the fae."

"Will my mind fracture like hers? Will I be visited by fae?" She glanced at Riagan. "By druids?"

She sought Riagan's reassurance, but the answer was written all over his face as if he'd scrawled it there in permanent ink. He met her stare with an expression of agony the likes of which shattered her already breaking heart.

"Riagan?"

He strode forward and pulled her into his arms. She settled against him, trying as desperately as she could to melt into his body. Leaving this realm, these people, *him* was *not* an option.

"Riagan, tell me it's not true," she whispered against his chest. Her nails dug into his skin as she tried to attach herself to his body so she could never be pulled away.

But she knew his answer by the shudder that ripped through his powerful body then tore through her own. She didn't belong on his realm, and he didn't belong on hers.

"WHY?" HER VOICE was raspy with emotion as she turned from Riagan's chest to face her father. "Why are you saying this? I can't leave. Not without…" She looked around. She couldn't be expected to just *leave*.

Riagan's arms were tight around her, as if his strength alone could remedy this impossible situation. She feared it would not be enough.

The king spoke, "The Brotherhood is charged with protection of the Murias Cauldron. There are other Brotherhoods throughout the worlds charged with protection of other artifacts whose fates must lie within a web of security and safety."

He floated back and forth. "Redeemers are a rare breed." He turned toward her, his expression serious. "A very rare breed. Only the child of a fae king or a druid male and human woman can hope to produce one such as you. And even then, it is rare, only occurring when the worlds become unsettled with the influence of evil and feel a need for a Redeemer to arise."

He took her face in his hands. "Redeemers are the only ones who, if a treasure is captured, can hope to bring it back to its rightful place. You are the only one of your kind in the worlds now. You must return to Earth. You cannot survive on this realm, and Earth is the only place from which you can be summoned."

Wren fingered the side of the diadem, its coolness mocking her. "I don't want to leave." Tears spilled over her cheeks.

Riagan was staring away from them, into the oak forest, the side of his lip twitching. Sadness covered the faces of everyone present: Oephille, her father, Drake, Duke. Even Gwyon had the graces not to smirk or laugh.

Despair settled around her heart like a vise.

Devastating despair.

Duke tugged at her sleeve. "I will come back with you, Miss Wren, and stay by your side. You won't be alone. It'll be you, me, and your mama. Just like before."

His offer brought a ripple of comfort, but his words were not enough.

"Destiny," her father started, but Riagan stepped forward and her father did not continue. Riagan lifted Wren into his arms, cradling her against him, and walked away from the group without a word. She closed her eyes and clutched his cloak in her fingers until they turned white.

He walked for a long, long time, until he finally came to a stop. They were along the side of the river but in an area that she didn't recognize. Here the trees grew up to the river's edge, the long and ropey roots disappearing underneath the surface. Across the river sat the moon, watching over them like a protective parent.

Riagan found a small opening between the closely grown trunks and sat down.

He did not let her go.

He cradled her as sobs wracked her body. Finding out she was not crazy had opened up a whole new world. And she belonged in this new world. She couldn't go back.

She belonged here with Riagan, in Riagan's world. Maybe she could bring her mother here. There must be some form of magic to allow such a thing.

"Riagan, is there no other way?"

With a deep inhale, he blew out a puff of air. "I know not, lass. This has never happened before."

"This?"

"This." He waved his hand in the air. "You. Me. The attempt on the Cauldron. None of this."

She nestled between his legs, leaning against his chest. He had such a grip on her she wondered if they just stayed locked together like this, could they *make* her go home?

"I have to leave tomorrow," she choked.

"Aye." Riagan's voice broke. "Tomorrow."

RIAGAN DID NOT want to release Wren from his arms, but when her father appeared and asked to speak with her, he had no choice. Besides, there was someone he wanted to see, and he couldn't do so with Wren by his side.

Once he arrived at the village, he found Gwyon huddled in the hut that he used to share with his mother, where he would remain under guard until his punishment was decided.

Riagan had never been inside this hut. In all the years he'd lived within the same village as his half brother, why had he never visited his small home? How poorly had he, they, treated him? Had he given Gwyon any consideration during his younger years?

Trying to halt that landslide of conjecture, he looked around. Woven tapestries covered the walls, each depicting a scene from their land. One was of the moon, nearly consuming the entire piece, but with glimpses of the countryside. Another with the river and the soft glitter of the water was captured to make it look like the water moved upon the wall. A third piece was of the Cauldron, nestled in its cave. The blackness of the treasure was as rich as oil. The faint green aura was brilliant, as if it was painted on and not created with thread. The inside of the cave was expertly depicted, an exact replica of the one just a stone's throw away.

Nestled in the bottom right corner of this piece was something unexpected, and he couldn't quite make out what it was. Riagan leaned forward to see it clearly, and froze. Woven into the bottom of the tapestry was a man, gazing upon the artifact. The image was almost too small to see but upon closer inspection, each detail became obvious. The black beard, dark hair, dark eyes. There was no mistaking who that being was, but in this depiction, the man's feet were splayed forward, straight and normal and perfect, and he wore the green robe of a Protector. He stood upright with no cane, no assistance.

Riagan touched the fabric, running his fingers over the rough surface.

"Who did these?" Riagan turned to Gwyon.

Gwyon shrugged.

"Did you?" Riagan tried to temper the surprise when Gwyon confirmed this with a curt nod. "They are magnificent."

Gwyon shrugged again and struggled to stand.

"Brother," Riagan said, and he could hear the pleading in his own voice.

Gwyon turned, leaning heavily on the cane. Suddenly Riagan was speechless. What could he say now? After all this time? He stared at his brother as regret and sadness swam through him.

Gwyon hobbled forward, the scraping of his cane never more piercing, then stopped in front of Riagan.

"I'm so sorry," Riagan managed.

Gwyon's expression did not alter from its mask of indifference, but he nodded, as if accepting the apology.

After a moment, he said, "I, too, am sorry. I should never have helped Caswallen. But in my defense, he was very persuasive."

"You were desperate. It was so cruel not to let you drink from the Cauldron's waters. To grant you immortality but not healing was unacceptable."

"Yes."

"I wish I had done something to help you."

"There was nothing you could've done. One with the gene must remain outside the Brotherhood. Our father would not strive to change that."

"But once he passed to the fae realm…" Riagan flipped through all the things he could've done but didn't.

"It is done, Riagan."

Riagan stared at the tapestry, focusing on the image of the small, healed man.

AFTER A LONG walk with her father, Wren veered off toward the forest to be alone. She was having trouble processing everything that had happened, along with everything she'd been told. Her father had offered more details of his relationship with her mother, as well as evidence of the many times he had visited Earth to watch Wren from afar. Thinking back, she often had the feeling of someone watching her, but had always chalked that up to blossoming paranoia and pending mental demise. How could she have anticipated any of this?

She had been wandering aimlessly when she spotted Riagan coming out of one of the village huts. The look on his face made her hurry toward him.

"Riagan, what's wrong?"

Without a response, he closed the space between them and grabbed her into his arms. Shoving his hand into her flowing hair, he tugged her head back, forcing her to stare up at him.

"I love you." The seriousness behind his statement made her heart at once swell and splinter.

She rested her palm on his face. "I love you too."

He scooped her into his arms and took off for one of the huts.

Words hovered on the tip of her tongue—she wanted to ask for reassurance, explanation, something to give her an idea what had happened to make him look so broody, but as soon as they entered a hut, he severed the release of those words with his mouth.

She needed his kiss to be as forceful as it was. She needed him to imprint himself on her like a tattoo. With her nails, she clawed at his back, and he bit at her skin. He yanked her garments off, as she yanked his, and when they were naked, they came together like powerful magnets.

Pushing her down on the bed, he shoved her knees apart and thrust into her. She screamed with the sudden sensation and squeezed her legs around his back, urging him closer, closer still.

He slammed into her and she took it, wanting more. More.

They were wild, desperate, clutching, raging. They took the unfairness of the situation and used it for a moment of pleasure.

Afterward, they lay shaking, breathless, and wrapped together as one. They stayed that way for a long, long time, willing that the next day would never dawn.

25

The next day Wren awoke to feel like someone was choking her. She could feel the deadly grasp of fate around her throat like a clamp, severing her airway. She tried to fight whoever was doing this to her, tried to flail her arms and legs. Someone was there, trying to help her, but the choking persisted. She was going to die. Die, and never see Riagan again.

"Wren, wake up."

She couldn't breathe. The hold around her throat was killing her. Her skin started to tingle with lack of oxygen.

"Wren."

Fingers dug into her shoulders, making her see stars.

"Wren, wake up."

Her eyes flew open to find Riagan before her. "Lass, what is it?"

She coughed and sputtered, gulping air into her lungs. There was no one there but Riagan. Who'd been choking her?

Riagan stroked her hair, wet with sweat. "You had a nightmare, my love. Shh, it's okay now."

"A nightmare? It felt so *real*. Someone was choking me. I was dying."

He said nothing as she realized the nightmare represented how she felt about leaving this realm, leaving Riagan. She would die if she had to go.

Riagan's fingers were soft and tender against her brow, but then a knock on the door made her jump in panic.

"Who is it?" Riagan's voice was gruff and impatient. Wren grabbed his cloak and pulled it around her body. She swam inside its voluminous fabric but didn't care and inhaled deeply, relishing Riagan's unique, masculine scent.

Eogabail entered the hut, his face sad, his eyes imploring. "Daughter."

At the heartache she heard in his voice, she started to cry. She stumbled across the compact room and fell into his embrace. It was at once familiar and strange, but it held the strength she needed, the strength she didn't have for herself.

"I know this is difficult."

With a shudder, she made a whimpering noise, not able to find words.

Riagan inched up behind her. "Is there no other way?"

"She cannot live upon this realm. Earth is the center from which the Redeemer must dwell. If the need arises, the gods forbid, those in need can only contact her there."

"And Duke? Duke can return? And Oephille?" Riagan managed.

Eogabail nodded.

"Were you the one who sent Duke to watch over her?"

"Yes. She must have a Protector, much the same as the Cauldron."

"Then why can't I take over Duke's role as her Protector?"

"Because you are a Protector of the Murias Cauldron. It is what you were born to do. We have no others to take your place. And, as you know, you must remain upon the druid realm. You would not long survive on the realm of man."

The thought was a Shakespearean tragedy in real time.

Riagan's fists clenched into massive balls of power. "There must be another way."

"Father," Wren started. The word sounded oddly familiar upon her lips. "Please." She choked on a sob, then broke down into tears. Riagan pulled her from her father, into his own embrace.

Eogabail stroked the back of her bowed head, nestled securely in Riagan's chest. "I will wait for you outside."

RIAGAN SETTLED WREN onto the bed and covered her with a blanket. Her face was blotchy and streaked with the tears that had lasted long after her father's departure.

Anger boiled in his blood, but it was a different anger than when he'd learned of Caswallen's betrayal. No, this anger seared itself upon him, creating a black cloud around him that he knew would never, ever disappear.

Each time he thought he had the answer, some reason or other would pop up in his mind telling him why no other way would work.

He paced around his home, his mind grasping and groping for another option. This hut he'd lived in for centuries suddenly felt alien, foreign to him, as if he didn't belong here anymore. He stepped out into the fresh air.

The realm lay silent around him. The full moon was only now losing its glow. It would never completely disappear but it would become smaller, less bright, until the next full moon. The trees were calm, beautiful in their glossy sheen.

He could see members of the Brotherhood posted at various points along the river. The Cauldron was safe now and, gods willing, it would stay that way.

Out of the corner of his eye, he saw Drake approach.

"What is it, Brother?" Riagan noted the somber expression on his twin's face.

"Brother. Gwyon's trial is soon."

"I see."

"Will you come?"

"I know not. I know not," was all he could manage and he looked away, refusing to engage his brother further.

DRAKE WATCHED THE druids of the Brotherhood of the Sacred Grove line up in their warrior regalia. Without Caswallen, Riagan, the elder of the twins by minutes, should have been the one who stepped into the leadership role until another Arch Druid was prepared. With his brother's absence, the responsibility fell to him.

Dressed in his ceremonial red robe, Drake scanned the eyes of those present: the faeries, his Brotherhood, King Eogabail, Duke, and most of the villagers as everyone was allowed to witness a trial such as this. None seemed eager for revenge, though. This half brother of theirs had cost them much, but he had also suffered.

Two guards supported Gwyon as he was brought forth from the hut, clad in an undyed robe that hung in pools over his misshapen feet. With eyes fixed on the ground, it was impossible to read his expression.

Drake cleared his throat and spoke in a loud voice, addressing both Gwyon and those gathered. "Gwyon, you are brought here, in the midst of the Sacred Grove, by this river, to stand trial for—" He stopped suddenly, unable to continue as his words became a jumbled mess in his mind. Coughing didn't help. Someone brought him a mug of water, but he spit the vile mixture out, struggling against sickness that was threatening to rise in his throat.

Gwyon observed him with his dark eyes filled with distrust and no small amount of sadness. Drake rubbed his hands over his face and stared at his half brother again. Those eyes. They were the same eyes that used to watch him and Riagan go toward their posts as Protectors. Haunting eyes. Sorrowful eyes. Yearning eyes.

How had it felt for him not to belong? Not to be given the chance to drink from the sacred waters that held the cure for his deformity? To be made immortal, but immortal in a broken body? Better would it have been to allow him to pass a normal-length life.

Suddenly Drake's eyes pricked with unshed tears. Gwyon had never been given a chance. His heart hurt, as if Gwyon were squeezing that organ in a vise. By the gods, was there no other way?

So quietly it was almost inaudible, someone said, "Drake." He refocused and there was Eogabail, his lips moving, his eyes trying to tell him something. The words didn't breach his comprehension so he stared at the fae king while everyone else stared at him, some with open mouths, others with sympathy and understanding.

Eogabail motioned him forward.

Drake moved to his side.

Eogabail spoke softly in his ear.

And like the snap of a rubber band, Drake understood. The fae king was agreeing with the sentence Drake hadn't even realized he was considering.

He returned his attention to Gwyon, who was watching him now with more than a hint of curiosity in those black depths.

A rustling behind him told him Riagan had come. He also knew Wren was beside him.

With a deep breath, Drake said, "We know the offenses so there is no need to read the betrayals."

The trees leaned forward, their long limbs reaching out over the group.

"Our Brotherhood, our realm, will never be the same. Many offenses have passed here over these moons. Now is the time to make amends for offenses made."

His gaze flipped from Riagan, now by his side, to Gwyon.

"Gwyon, you are hereby convicted of plotting to steal the revered Murias Cauldron; for aiding the one they called Master, whom we now know to be Caswallen; for betraying your ancestors and all those on your realm."

"Wait." Gwyon lifted the hand that did not hold his cane. He steeled his jaw and shifted his weight. "I know my ills, and I am ready to accept punishment for them." Tears welled in his eyes, making them resemble pieces of coal settled in a stream. "I just want to say that I am sorry for what I have done." He turned to Wren. "I am sorry I tried to hurt you and your mother. You were innocent in all of this, and I am glad I did not succeed in my endeavor."

He sighed, deflated, and leaned heavily on the cane.

After a moment, Drake lifted his arms, palms splayed toward his half brother. "As for punishment for said offenses, we hereby deem that all punishment has already been served. And from this day forward, Gwyon will enter druid training. He will drink from the Cauldron's healing waters and become the warrior he was meant to be. He will become one of the Brotherhood of the Sacred Grove."

Gwyon gasped, searching the eyes of his brothers, as if seeking and waiting for them to tell him they were joking. That he would indeed die on this day and not fulfill his life's greatest desire. He'd never dared to dream this would happen.

The gazes he met held no humor or indication the words were anything but truth.

Then Gwyon, with a deep breath that filled his chest, lifted his chin. With his full weight upon his own feet, he wobbled, but then with sheer determination, stood erect, unaided and proud.

"I will fulfill my duty as I was born to do."

"Pray that it will be so."

"What about the Council's terms that he not drink? Not train?" Riagan asked, and Eogabail stepped forward to answer.

"My sons, rules that have been made can be unmade. After seeing my daughter's heartbreak, I summoned the worlds' Councils, and an agreement was reached. Gwyon, after taking responsibility and showing regret for his actions, can take Riagan's place in the Brotherhood if he fulfills the requirements of his trainings. This does not offer an immediate solution, as Riagan must remain on the druid realm until his replacement is ready, but it is a solution I think all will agree with."

"There will be none, then, with immortal blood outside the Brotherhood," one brother stepped forward to say.

"True," answered Eogabail, his eyes sparkling like diamonds. "Perhaps Riagan and Destiny can take care of that for us."

Drake turned to Riagan. Tears glistened in their matching green eyes. "When Gwyon is taken to the Cauldron to drink," Drake whispered, "so too shall Wren. I know not if you remember from your teachings, but Redeemers can become immortals if they so wish. And, Riagan, you can also drink, and that will allow you to live on the realm of man with your love for all your days as her Protector."

Riagan's knees gave out and he fell to the ground, clasping his hands and staring at the heavens.

Wren's lovely face was frozen in shock, disbelief, and confusion. There was no need to rush to an explanation, though. Riagan would have an eternity for all that and more.

EPILOGUE

The first ray of sunshine peeked through the small slit of Wren's bedroom curtains, just enough to kiss her skin and wake her from her dreams. She rolled over and tried to fall back asleep to no avail.

Images flipped through her mind, images from the dreams that had peppered her sleep. Trees, faeries, an enormous pearl of a moon. Everything seemed so real she didn't want to open her eyes and return to reality. Dealing with her mother, her sister, her clients, and her fiancé was, simply, too much.

No, she preferred her dreams where she became someone important, someone vital to the safety of the world, and everything around her actually made sense.

It wasn't until Duke whimpered by the bedside that she knew she had to get up. Groaning, she rolled over, desperate for five more minutes before facing yet another day of drudgery. When her fingers fell upon an arm lying beside her, she froze, terror clutching at her heart. She did not remember inviting a man to her bed.

Her mind raced like an Olympic sprinter.

The man's soft, rhythmic breathing told her he was still asleep. She squinted one eyelid and peered to her side.

Long strands of white-blond hair spilled onto her pillow. A muscled torso lay exposed above the sheet. One arm was flung over his head. The other rested along her body, indicating they'd been touching, sandwiched together, in her sleep.

Ray.

She was startled to see this man who had flaunted around in her dreams so vividly. She didn't remember meeting him last night, inviting him into her home again. No, actually her last true memory of him was right after they'd slept together and he'd told her some crazy story. She remembered ordering him to leave her alone. That was months ago. Years, maybe.

Why was he here then?

She rolled out of the bed, keeping her eyes trained on him for any hint he was waking. His soft snores did not alter so she crept to her bathroom and closed the door, forgetting all about letting Duke outside. When she looked into the mirror, the image made her gasp. Staring back at her was her reflection, but somehow *altered*.

Her hair, many times longer than she remembered, hung down to her hips, tugging on her scalp. She ran her hands through the long strands to see if they were part of a wig or extensions, but the tight curls wouldn't budge.

She pushed it off her face and stared at herself again. Her features were the same, though her eyes were a little brighter, her lips a little redder. She felt taller and glanced down to see that her pajama bottoms did, indeed, fall to her ankles instead of over her feet. Maybe they'd shrunk in the dryer, though that didn't make sense as they were old and had been washed many times over.

A headache was budding behind her left eye, and just as she reached for the medicine cabinet, she heard Ray moving, then clearing his throat. He must be waking up.

She glanced back into the mirror and squared her shoulders.

So this was it—her mental break had come. She couldn't recall the events of last evening, last month, last year, and had no idea how this guy came to be in her home, in her bed. But with this realization—that the insanity she had waited nearly her whole life for was here—came liberation.

She would ask Ray to leave, and then she would spend the day writing in her journal. Maybe the observations of her own mental deterioration could help someone else. Maybe she could even write for a medical or psychiatry journal.

Wren O'Hara, writer.

Turning from the mirror, she opened the door a crack and peered out. Duke was standing there, eyes pleading to go outside. She tiptoed down the hall, careful not to look in the bedroom, and held the door open for Duke.

She glanced at the clock in the kitchen, and it read eight thirty. That gave her an hour and a half before her mother would wake up. The last thing she wanted was for her mother to see Ray. Life was upside down and topsy-turvy enough without sending her mother off the rails. She remembered all too well how her mother reacted the first time she met him.

Leaving Duke outside to take care of his needs, she closed the door quietly and walked back down the hall. As she neared the bedroom door, she slowed, peering ahead to try and catch the first glimpse of Ray before he caught one of her.

It didn't work.

As soon as he came into view, his eyes locked on hers.

He smiled. She felt nauseous.

Sunlight streamed through the window, reflecting off something that flashed in the corner of her bedroom. She blinked, then clenched her eyes shut and counted to ten, trying to ward off any visual hallucinations. She opened them again.

The strange item was still there.

The diadem from her dream.

She glanced from the crown to Ray, his chiseled chest rising and falling with his breath, his long blond hair casting a halo around his perfect face.

OCH, BUT SHE is a beauty. He hardened under the cotton sheet and willed her back to bed. *Why does she look so upset? Certainly the cries I brought forth from her last night would be cause for a smile?*

"What is it, little bird?" Her pet name rolled off his tongue. He threw back the sheets and shot her his most smoldering glance.

But she averted her gaze.

I've lost my touch. That was my best sexy look.

So he tried again. He gave a slight flip of his long hair in a come-hither move he'd seen on her television.

She turned away.

Oy! Not the best.

He glanced down to see if he was as virile as he remembered. *Hmmm, looks good.* Then what was with the lass on this morn?

He got out of bed, standing to his full, impressive, *nude*, height. Moving in front of her, he allowed her a moment to study his body. Her eyes traveled from his broad shoulders down to his stomach. When she saw his alert member, her pretty little mouth fell open and he could not resist.

She didn't protest when he brought his lips down upon her cherry mouth and kissed her deeply. She moaned in his grasp, and he pushed her onto the bed.

She seemed to change her mind and tried to rise back up, but he was faster. And more determined. Her full breasts squashed against his chest, and he could feel her hardened nipples pressing outward, begging to be kissed.

So he obliged.

She whimpered under him, then slid her petite hands into his hair, and he couldn't tell if she was pulling him toward her or pushing him away. Either way, he didn't care. This woman was his to cherish till the end of time and cherish her he would.

She wiggled underneath him. He inched his head back. She was watching him with an expression he did not understand. She seemed like she was about to cry, and her pouty bottom lip quivered.

"What is it, little bird?" He kissed that bottom lip.

Tears escaped her eyes and slid down her rosy cheeks in silvery trails. He lifted off her and gathered her into his embrace. Holding her like an infant, he rocked back and forth on the creaky bed. Eogabail said she would have moments such as this as she readjusted to the realm of man after their last visit to the druid realm, a visit that had seen Gwyon take Riagan's place in the Brotherhood.

He caressed her hair, then tilted her face back to look at him. "I love you, lass. Now tell me, what is wrong? Remember, I am your Protector."

She searched his eyes. "Wasn't it all just a dream?"

"Lass, if you believe nothing else, believe in me, your sworn Protector. I'll let naught happen to you, my beloved."

She stared at the blanket for several moments. He had to resist the urge to trace the outline of her heavy breast as he watched it rise and fall with her breath. So quietly he almost didn't hear her, she said, "My Protector?"

"Aye," he said with force. "I am your Protector, and I will never leave your side. Don't ever forget it. You are mine."

The eyes of the Aegean searched his face. After everything, did she still think she was insane? Had her travel back to the realm of man altered her mind? A pit opened in his stomach. What if she was going to turn out like her mother? The thought was too distressing to contemplate.

No matter what, though, he would protect her.

Finally, she mumbled, "I guess it wasn't a dream after all." Then she flashed a smile at him and his heart nearly burst open with happiness.

"A dream? What speak you of, lass?" He was overjoyed with this change in attitude. "I'll show you I'm no dream." He tickled her sides until she screamed, and soon he had her clothes in a heap on the floor.

When Riagan knew her fears had abated, he turned his tickles into caresses. Beginning with her shoulders and arms, he traced her body with his fingertips.

She shuddered when he flicked over her pink nipples, and he was unable to resist pulling each one between his lips. She ran her nails down his back and the pleasant pain was unbearable. He eased on top of her and stared deep into her eyes as he entered her with a powerful thrust.

She grasped his back and clung to him as if afraid he would disappear into thin air, as if she could hold him tight enough that he would remain with her forever. The little lass still didn't believe he was real, but he would spend eternity proving to her he was.

Outside the bedroom window, kissed by a new day's sun, the trees danced to their ancient rhythm.

ABOUT THE AUTHOR

Laire McKinney is the author of contemporary romance and romantic fantasy. She believes in a hard-earned happily-ever-after, with nothing more satisfying than passionate kisses and sexy love scenes. When not writing steamy romance, she can be found traipsing among the wildflowers, reading under a willow tree, or gazing at the moon while pondering the meaning of it all. She lives in Virginia with her family and beloved rescue pup, Lila.

CPSIA information can be obtained
at www.ICGtesting.com
Printed in the USA
BVHW08s0043270818
525380BV00001B/7/P